THOUGHT WARRIORS

# The Curse of Gaia

POULOMI SANYAL

**Connect with Poulomi Sanyal**

Website: https://www.poulomisanyal.com/

Twitter: https://twitter.com/sanyal_poulomi

Facebook: https://www.facebook.com/authorPoulomiSanyal/

LinkedIn: https://www.linkedin.com/in/poulomisanyal/

To follow latest updates, insightful blog-posts, book-signings, giveaways and promotions, sign-up to the author's newsletter at:

https://www.poulomisanyal.com/news

ISBN-13: 978-1-7753950-2-7

# DEDICATION

"Arise, awake, and stop not until the goal is reached."
—*Swami Vivekananda*

"There exists no separation between gods and men; one blends softly casual into the other."
—*Frank Herbert, Dune Messiah*

"Now Gaia *was* the actual earth—the rocks, the hills, the valleys … But she could also take on humanlike form. She liked to walk across the earth … in the shape of a matronly woman with a flowing green dress, curly black hair, and a serene smile on her face. The smile hid a nasty disposition."—*Rick Riordan, Percy Jackson's Greek Gods*

This book is dedicated to all those who dare to do the right thing and are daunted by naught.

# PRAISE FOR THOUGHT WARRIORS BOOK1 THE COMING OF KALKI

"… this same stylization also evokes the action-film genre, and indeed, Zoya and company would not feel out of place in a movie. Their scenes are easy to visualize, and the mix of science and myth effectively draws the reader in to the story. A cinematic … supernatural adventure."—*Kirkus Reviews*

"I'm a writer & this book intimidated me. I recommend it for everyone. It's a modern masterpiece."—*Amazon Reviewer*

"This book has a very unique blend of science and mythology. The author did an amazing job writing this complex story … This author is very talented. The story held my attention from beginning to conclusion. I'm looking forward to book 2."—*Adriana B (Amazon Reviewer)*

"It is a science fiction of a fabulous thought-provoking escapade enlightened with highest amount of imagination, thrill and breathless excitement. It is an exceptionally fascinating journey of exploring ancient secrets with modern scientific thoughts. Enriched with adequate conceptual training and background in optics in general and photonics in particular, this young promising author has made this science fiction so exciting."—*Dr. Purushottam Chakraborty, Saha Institute of Nuclear Physics*

# CHAPTER ONE

Jan Vos, the reigning President of the European Council, stood in front of the microphone wearing a black suit and navy-blue tie. Facing his sombre audience of delegates and reporters, he coughed lightly to clear his throat and began speaking in a slow and deliberate tone.

"Two weeks ago, on the 24$^{th}$ of April, the entire European Union came under the attack of a foreign power. Although investigations are ongoing, it is still unclear how we averted the catastrophe that could have engulfed our entire continent on that day. What *is* clear however, is the fact that this was a calculated, well-strategized and completely unprovoked act of war initiated against us by a hostile foreign power. Therefore, the burning question on all of our minds today is one and the same. Who could be behind this egregious act of violence? I received the report of our Security Council this morning and the deduction is unanimous." Jan paused for breath. "It is Russia," he pronounced.

A collective gasp ensued from the audience along with

the sound of low murmurs in the background.

Jan cleared his throat again and continued, "For years, we have overlooked the reckless nuclear proliferation of this nuclear-armed nation. We have failed to penalize them for flouting the guidelines of the United Nations. We have failed to unite under the banner of pacifism to curb an emerging deadly threat at our northern borders and today we are paying the price." He paused again and took a sip of water from a glass that stood next to his microphone on the podium.

"Nevertheless," he continued, "all is not lost! We might have lost the battle but we can still win the war. But for this, we must call upon our allies, the United States, the United Kingdom, Canada and the rest of the G20 powers to come to our aid and stand with us in these dark times. To the citizenry of the European Union, we promise that this audacious infringement upon our sovereignty will not go unavenged. Russia has deliberately initiated an act of war and we will respond in kind. This morning, I have personally appealed to the President of the United States to send his troops and he has—" Jan's prepared statement got interrupted as the camera now returned to the studio.

The news-lady dressed smartly in a silk floral blouse and tight black skirt, smiled mechanically and spoke in a prim, manicured voice. "That was the President of the European Union, speaking from Belgium this afternoon. Now let us hear what the President of the United States said to reporters when asked about this issue later in the day."

The camera cut to a scene on a helipad with a helicopter whirring in the background and the President of the United States (POTUS) hurrying to board his flight.

"Sir, do you think this could spark the Third World War?" asked an over-enthusiastic reporter, shoving his microphone in front of the POTUS's face. His youthful blue eyes glistening with anticipation.

"I'm not going to speculate. It's too early. We're definitely going to try and do everything to avert the scenario of an all-out war." The POTUS's voice was flat and masked all traces of emotion.

"Is Russia really behind this attack, then?" another reporter chimed in.

"The Pentagon is investigating the matter at the moment and until that investigation is complete, I am not going to speculate."

"What are your words for the people who are behind this attack, Sir?"

"Like I've said before, whoever is behind this attack is a heinous mass-murderer. They will be found and our appropriate response will be served. This needless act of war cannot and *will* not be forgiven."

"Is it true that we're sending troops to the Russian border, then?"

"Yes, we've sent a small task force and an aircraft carrier. A couple of bombers. The Pentagon will release the complete details shortly."

Wolfgang switched off the television and turned to face Wanda who was seated in one of her plush armchairs in front of her fireplace. His worried countenance appeared gaunt in the firelight.

"They still don't suspect the Aifra, eh?" Wanda asked, looking baffled.

"Nope," growled Wolfgang, tossing the remote on to the sofa and plopping down next to it.

"I'm telling you, we should tell them," cautioned Alejandro from the rattan armchair at the other end of the room.

"We've discussed zis, no?" hissed Dr. Wolfgang Müller.

"But I'm not convinced I agree with you, Wolfgang."

"When do you ever?" Wolfgang chuckled, mirthlessly.

"Gentlemen, please. There is no need to turn on each other," Wanda interjected.

"It's just friendly banter," Alejandro said with a smile. "In all seriousness though, Wolfgang, what do you suppose is the worst that could happen if we speak up? It'd blow our cover and the secret of the Hekameses. But I mean, about time, right? How long can we stay hidden?"

"As long as we possibly can!"

"Why?"

"Do you not understand?"

"Um … no," Alejandro said meekly, raising his right eyebrow.

"Do you think they're going to find out about us and then just parade us through the White House and adorn us with medals of honour or something?"

"Ooh that'd be nice! I get the gold. You can have silver." Alejandro grinned.

"When they learn about our powers, do you think they'll feel safe? Do you think they'd let us walk free?" Wolfgang continued, ignoring his friend's humorous remark.

"Yeah, I mean, I get that. But we're almost at the brink of a Third World War over here and *someone* needs to intervene with the facts, don't you think?" Alejandro asked with a very serious expression this time.

"It won't be us. Plus, they wouldn't believe us to begin with." Wolfgang sighed.

"Hmmm." Alejandro fell back into his armchair and ran both his hands through his ample hair pulling them backwards between his fingers. "So, what do we do then?"

"Like I said, we should look for Kalki," Wanda responded.

"But where? She just vanished," said Alejandro.

"I think we need Nirmala and Zoya to help us with that. After all, they were the ones who summoned her in the first place."

"Yes. And speaking of Nirmala; I have another plan for her. How much time did she say she wanted to spend with her family in India?

"Hmm. I don't know. She didn't say …" Alejandro trailed off. "I'll check with her tonight."

"By the way, I thought you gentlemen should know, Dr. Carter called me this morning." Wanda Faraday spoke, looking up from a newspaper article she seemed to be reading.

"Dr. Carter?" Alejandro asked.

"Zoya's father."

"Oh, right. How's Zoya doing?"

"She's doing fine. Her father wanted to know if she could come stay with me for part of the summer, to be closer to school. You know, for access to the libraries etc.," Wanda said with a giggle.

Alejandro laughed out loud. "Must have been Zoya's idea. Library shibrary! I think she doesn't want to miss out on the Hekameses meetings, is all."

"Perhaps," Wanda agreed. "Either way, I was planning on bringing her here, myself. Don't you agree, Wolfgang?"

"Yes. Better to have her close. Better protection that way," Wolfgang agreed.

"Any news of Albert?" Alejandro suddenly asked.

Wolfgang puckered his face, becoming thoughtful.

"No."

"None, at all?" asked Wanda.

"Very little."

"Very little? That means you *do* have some news, don't you, Wolfgang? Tell us," Alejandro urged, getting up from his armchair and rushing across the room in his friend's direction.

"Vell," said Wolfgang, slipping briefly into his German accent. "My contacts in Athens made some enquiries …"

"And?"

"Und the receptionist at the downtown Novotel seemed to recognize his picture."

"Really? Did he stay there?"

"No. She said that a couple of weeks ago, she might have seen him wait in the lobby for about half an hour and then leave."

"Was he alone?"

"He entered alone but left with two tall men who came to meet him."

"Where did they go?"

"She doesn't know. The only reason she remembers any of this is that she found the incident rather odd. They don't get a lot of portly old British tourists travelling alone at their hotel."

"That and Albert is quite a character. Rather hard to forget." Alejandro added.

"That too, perhaps. So, that's it. That's all I know."

"Could we check the security cameras of the hotel?" Wanda enquired, crossing her hands over her chest.

"They're trying. But no one remembers the exact time or day and that's making it tricky."

"Hmm. As long as his whereabouts remain unknown, it poses a huge threat to the Hekameses." Sighed Alejandro.

"It does," Wolfgang agreed. "Which reminds me, with Albert missing, Chris is manning the lab at Oxford all by himself at the moment." He turned to look at Wanda.

Wanda took off her glasses and placed them on her lap and looked directly at Dr. Müller, a knowing expression in her eyes. After a few seconds of silence, she spoke.

"Under the supervision of Dr. Lee, you mean?" she asked, softly.

"Who's *not* a Hekameses," Wolfgang added.

"I am aware. So what are you suggesting?" asked Wanda.

"Umm, what is this about?" asked Alejandro in confusion.

"I think Wanda understands my concern. In the absence of a professor to continue on with Dr. Albert Cobb's research, the University will assign someone else to the project soon …"

"And this person may not be a Hekameses," Alejandro completed. "I see. So, what do we do? We cannot let a random stranger walk-in on our secrets …"

"Precisely," said Wanda. "Alright then. I will speak to the Department Chair first thing tomorrow morning. My retirement can wait."

"Good. If you return to your former role at Oxford, we can carry on Albert's work in secrecy until he's found," Wolfgang concluded.

"Dead or alive," added Alejandro.

Wolfgang grunted and nodded in agreement, a dark expression across his face. "In the meantime, I vill be in Frankfurt tomorrow to visit my own lab and to take stock of the situation at Max Planck," he said as he hurried out of the room.

\* \* \*

Dr. Wolfgang Müller arrived at the Max Planck Institute for Brain Research in Frankfurt, Germany, at 8 AM the following morning. The lobby was moderately busy as on a regular weekday. Nothing looked out of the ordinary. Of course, there was an air of anxiety and apprehension everywhere in Europe given the recent war-like developments. But so far, this atmosphere did not seem to have permeated the research institute. Scientists after all, were not easily perturbed.

Wolfgang walked up to the front desk and smiled a half-smile, nodding in the direction of the tall, blonde-haired, lady at the reception.

"Morning, Sofia," he said.

"*Good* morning, Dr. Müller," Sofia responded, smiling affably. "Great to see you back at the institute."

"Yes. Good to see you too. How are things over here? Quiet? Busy? Normal?"

"Mmm. It's been pretty normal, I guess …" Sofia began but was cut off when a man wearing a FedEx uniform entered through the door and walked over to the reception desk carrying a medium-sized box in his arms.

"I have a delivery," he said, looking at Sofia.

"Oh, who is it for?" Sofia asked, leaning over to check the label for herself. "It doesn't have a name …"

"It was addressed to the Institute, so we brought it here," the FedEx employee explained.

"Okay, I see. Well, leave it then. Do you want to sign on it, Dr. Müller? I'm not sure I …" she trailed off, looking expectantly at Wolfgang.

"Hmm. Okay. I vill. Where do I sign?"

"Over here, Sir," said the delivery man, extending his

digital pen.

Dr. Müller signed in the designated location and was about to leave for his office when Sofia stopped him.

"Do you want to take the parcel with you, to your office? I don't know who else to give it to," she confessed.

"Good question," said Wolfgang, becoming thoughtful. "No. I don't think it's important if it isn't addressed to anyone in particular," he concluded. "Probably marketing junk. Why don't you open it, Sofia? If it is some sort of marketing trinket, you can send an internal e-mail and anyone interested can pick one up."

"Sure," Sofia said with a smile and bent behind the desk to look for a letter opener.

Dr. Müller turned and walked briskly to the main staircase and started making for his office upstairs. He had almost made it to the second floor when he heard a shrill shriek from the lobby. He quickly turned around and rushed downstairs. Once at the bottom of the steps, he scanned the lobby and noticed a small crowd gathered around Sofia's desk at the reception. He ran in that direction.

"Sofia, Sofia, breathe," came the panicked voice of a young man from behind the reception desk.

A few others were gathered in the area and were trying to lean over the desk to get a better view. There were gasps and murmurs all around.

Wolfgang pushed through the small group and made his way to the rear of the desk. There, on the floor, lay Sofia's unconscious form. A young man crouched behind her was holding her head up in his arms and sprinkling water on her eyes in an effort to revive her.

Beside Sofia was the parcel that had just arrived. It lay open on the floor, a foul stench emanating from its interior. Wolfgang peered in and immediately his stomach turned. Inside, was a bloodied head, severed from its body, putrid and decaying, the hair matted with caked blood, lidless eyes staring into the void.

"Gah," he screeched, covering his face with both his hands and pivoting quickly on his heels. "Weilhammer! You poor *fool!*"he screamed.

# CHAPTER TWO

It was a clear starry night in the small village of Mosha in southern Egypt and five-year-old Omar couldn't sleep. He sat up on his bed and gazed into the vast cloudless sky, counting the stars as he breathed deeply, filling his lungs with the warm desert air.

"Omar, my boy, you are not sleeping?" asked a shaky voice as the frail frame of a withered old man with a long beard appeared near his bed.

"Grampa, I'm scared," said the little boy looking up to see the smiling face of his grandfather, Abu next to him.

"Scared? Why? Come here," said Abu pulling the boy close and wrapping him in an embrace. "There's nothing to be scared of. Come, let me sing you a song."

"No."

"No?"

"I don't want to hear a song. I want to hear that story."

"Oh? Which story?"

"You know, that one, of the monster …"

"Why do you want to hear that story, little one? Let me

tell you a happy …"

"No!" shrieked Omar covering his face with his hands. "I want to hear that one, that one, that one," he continued, punching his grandpa softly with his tiny balled-up fists.

"Ow ow! Okay, I will tell you that one. But why do you want to hear that story so badly, my boy?"

"Because …"

"Because, what?"

"What if he's here, the monster?"

"Ha!" Abu laughed. "Is that it? Silly baby. Monsters aren't real, you know. It's just a story." Abu pulled the boy closer into his hug and gently rocked him back and forth.

"But there was that light. You know, from the pyramid. I saw it," Omar murmured.

"Oh that! Yes, everyone is talking about it. It's nothing. Just strong lightning, maybe. When I was a child, we used to have so many of those. Now with all those buildings everywhere, we don't get to see lightning like that anymore."

"Hmm. But tell me the story, pleaaaaase. I want to hear that stoooryyyy."

"Yes, of course, but first you have to lie down. Come on now, take your pillow. There we go," said Abu, tucking his grandson in, and sitting down next to the prone boy's head.

"Okay, so the story, how did it go," Abu started while stroking Omar's hair.

"A long long time ago, there was a little boy, just like me."

"Yes, just like you. Back then, the land of Egypt was very different. The river Nile flowed right next to the pyramids and there were tall grasses and palm trees along its banks. The weather was cool and it rained a lot. The birds sang in the trees and the caterpillars climbed up the legs of the children who ran through the fields."

"There was no desert?"

"No. No desert. Just trees and birds and fruits and flowers."

"So pretty. Have you seen this?"

"No, I have not, dear one. This was a long long time before I was born or before any of us were born. It was the time of the pharaohs!"

"Oh!" Gasped Omar. Although, he had heard this story before, his excitement didn't seem to dwindle with each retelling.

Abu smiled and continued. "So this boy, he lived with his family and ran through the gardens and played with the other children in the village and helped his family with farm work. Until, one day, his parents were asked to serve the mighty pharaoh."

"Did they go?"

"Yes, they had to. They had no choice. The pharaoh was like a God. Everyone *had* to obey him." Abu paused and stroked Omar's hair again.

Then he continued, softer than before. "The pharaoh was busy building things and he needed strong young men and women to work for him. So, he made the boy's parents work for him. All day, they broke rocks and dug holes and lifted heavy stones until they became so tired that they could hardly stand."

"Oh no!" said Omar in a small voice.

Abu's face became sad as he continued. "And then one day the most horrible thing happened. The poor parents had an accident while digging for rocks, the walls of the quarry fell over them and they both died."

"Gah!" the child covered his face with his hands.

"The child, now an orphan, was all alone. The pharaoh

found out and tried to take the child away and put him to work in his mines. But the village elders came up with a plan to save him. Hiding him on the back of a camel, they took him to the High Priest of the Temple of Ra and begged him to take the boy into his care.

"The High Priest saw something different in the boy. A strange power. At once he knew that this child would grow up to be someone magical. So, he agreed and adopted the child as his own. He raised the boy with a lot of care and taught him all the ancient secrets of the Gods. He dreamt of a day when he would step aside and let his adopted son take over the temple of Ra in all its might and glory. He would then watch him rise from strength to strength and become an all-powerful devotee of the Sun God, one who controlled nature itself. However, this was not to be. Seeing the growing power of the temple of Ra, the pharaoh who was not a sun-worshipper himself, became very scared. He ordered his men to capture the High Priest and his son, who was now a young man, and imprison them in his palace.

"One afternoon, the soldiers of the pharaoh came to the temple of Ra and plundered it, taking the High Priest captive as per the orders. But the son of the priest was nowhere to be seen. He had gone on a holy mission to the valley of the Nile and did not know about the raid. That night, he had a vivid dream. He saw the soldiers and their camels. His father being dragged out of the temple, beaten and bound. He woke up horrified and rushed back to the temple to find his home and the temple in a mess. Everything was ruined. All was lost. He fell to his knees and started crying. It is said that he cried for three days straight. And then at the end of the third day, the Sun God, Ra had mercy on him and sent him a gift."

"Ohhhhh! What kind of gift, Grampa?" asked Omar, clapping his hands.

"No one knows. But it is believed that it was a very very powerful gift."

"Did he open the gift?"

"Ha!" Abu laughed out loud. "No. It wasn't that kind of gift. It was a piece of magic. But no, he did not use the magic. As per the legend, the mighty Ra gave him the gift and told him never to use it unless there was no other choice. So, he took his gift and went into hiding. Into the mountains, in a far away land. And there he became a hermit."

"What is a hermit?"

"A hermit … hmmm … let's see. A hermit is a person who hides from everyone so that he can pray to God all by himself."

"Oh!"

"For many years he stayed that way. People say that it could have been for hundreds or even *thousands* of years. He became so close to God that he lived on and on for ever and ever!"

"Whoa!"

"But then, one day, there was a great storm. It tore through the sky and ripped all the trees out of the ground. The hermit came out of his cave and saw a vision. A vision of his dear Egypt burning, burning, burning to the ground."

"No!"

"So, he came back to Egypt. One last time they say. And he could not believe what he saw!"

"What did he see?"

"The whole land was a desert, barren and poor. People were fighting and killing and destroying everything. The kings and rulers had built their huge towers and monuments and markets and streets but hundreds of thousands of his people were dying of hunger. It was a horrible scene. So sad and tragic that the hermit could not bear it any longer. He left as soon as he could. Coming back to his cave he decided to use the power of the ancient magic that the mighty Ra had given him all those years ago."

"And then what happened?"

"I don't know, my boy, but many believe that he turned into a terrible creature, a monster of sorts, the monster—"

"Of Egypt," Omar completed.

"Yes, so the story goes."

"Do *you* think he has come back, Grampa?"

"Like I said, this is just a story. There are no such things as monsters. Only people. Good people. And bad people."

"What if he comes back as bad people?"

"Well, you know what they say, wherever there is great evil there is a greater good to stop it."

"Like Spider-Man?"

"Yes, exactly like Spider-Man," Abu whispered, planting a soft kiss on his grandson's forehead and watching as his eyelids grew heavy.

# CHAPTER THREE

The door opened to a small dank room without windows in the basement of a crumbling little house, and a muscular bearded man of medium height and tanned complexion emerged. Across from him on a rickety wooden chair sat an elderly, balding man with his arms folded over his chunky belly and head hanging down. His cotton, summer shirt was half unbuttoned and covered with sweat and grime. The old man squinted as the door opened, illuminating the pitch-black surroundings with a sudden sliver of light.

The intruder stood in the doorway for a few seconds staring intently at the old man. Then he spoke in a hoarse whisper with an edge of cruelty.

"Haven't eaten *again*, I see," he said. "My orders were to keep you alive. But at this rate, I can promise nuthin." He broke into a mirthless laughter.

"Oh, shut it, you thug! I was promised a rendezvous with my son. Until that happens, I have no words to waste on you!"

"Thug? How dare!" The muscular man roared. He rushed over to the old man's chair and slapped him hard across the face. "That'll teach you!" he declared.

"You don't scare me," the old man groaned, rubbing his cheek. "Where is he?"

"Who?"

"My son, you doofus!"

The stocky man went to slap him again but stopped short and glared at him instead. "Why do I bother?" he huffed, turning to hurry out. At the door he spun around briefly. "Tomorrow. We go tomorrow," he said before storming out and slamming the door behind him.

"Well, it better be tomorrow. It BETTER BE. You bring me here in a goods' truck and store me in this dingy hole like a bag of beans for heaven knows how long. I have had it with this!" Dr. Cobb screamed after his captor who was probably already out of earshot.

Hours went by and the darkness sank in, creeping into the old man's bones, gnawing on the last shreds of his happiness. He sat there, alone and tormented, too tired to get up, too anxious to fall asleep.

After what felt like an eternity, the stocky man appeared at the door again. This time he was accompanied by a taller, fairer companion who looked and walked like a CIA agent.

The stocky one, pulled out his gun and growled at the old man. "Come. Albert, is it?"

"Sir Albert Harold Cobb, Knight Commander of the—"

"Alright, alright, enough! Let's go," shouted the taller of the two as he walked up to pull Dr. Cobb out of his chair. He then shoved the old man in the back, egging him to move forward.

Dr. Cobb and his captors climbed up a narrow set of wooden stairs and into a landing area with a door on the right and another flight of stairs winding upwards to the left. The taller man opened the door and the three walked out into the open after what seemed like a millennium to Dr. Cobb.

Outside, it was still quite dark but a narrow streak of light peeked through the horizon signalling the advent of dawn. Dr. Cobb had no idea where they were. They had driven for days in the goods' truck with him huddled behind the cargo, gagged and bound. They fed him from time to time and let him use the toilet where they stopped but always in the wilderness, away from civilization. Then they had brought him to this house and stashed him inside the basement.

"Move it," the stocky man said through his teeth, sticking the muzzle of his gun firmly in the middle of Dr. Cobb's back.

Dr. Cobb tripped forward at the sudden nudge. Regaining balance, he hurried along and followed the taller man for some distance walking over a rugged ground covered with loose rocks. A few feet in front of them stood a weather-worn, black sedan but apart from that their surroundings were completely barren. For as far as Albert could see in the semi-darkness, the land in front of them was deserted and devoid of life. The only sign of life being the rundown little shack, they just left.

The stocky man pushed Dr. Cobb into the back seat of the parked sedan and got in next to him, still pointing his gun at his prisoner. The taller man took the driver's seat. They didn't bother to bind their captive this time.

*Who would ever find us in this wilderness, anyway?* thought Dr. Cobb as the car bumped along the unpaved rocky terrain.

The driver rolled down his window, letting a refreshingly cool breeze sweep over them. Breathing in the outdoor air felt like heaven, and Dr. Cobb, who hadn't slept in days began to doze off. He woke with a start at the sound of someone speaking on a two-way radio.

"Almost there, Serge. Over," said the driver.

"Pull in around the cave. Over." Came the response.

"Roger. Over and out."

The car navigated through a narrow winding road bordering a steep cliff that dropped sharply into a gully on the right. Dr. Cobb strained his neck to glance out of the window at the drop below. It seemed to be fifty feet at the very least.

"Sit straight!" Came a harsh voice from next to him.

The car made a sharp left at a bend ahead and pulled around to the front of a cave. Here, at the brow of the cliff, there was a stretch of flat land and roughly in the middle of that open space stood a helicopter, whirring its wings with a low, grating thrum.

"Move!" The tall man gave Albert a nudge, rushing him out of the vehicle. He could feel the man's gun poking him intermittently in the middle of his back.

Albert moved forward with caution; arms raised with his captors following close behind. The helicopter came into clearer focus. Its stairs were lowered and there was a middle-aged man standing right at the top of the steps. Seeing them approach, the man descended and walked towards them.

Albert gave out a small gasp. "Peter," he said in a low whisper. He felt a drop of tear spill onto his plump cheek. Albert hurried forward a couple of steps and then pausing a second, quickly whisked around and thrust both his hands upwards and outwards at his captors, as if urging them to halt.

Then something strange happened.

The two thugs behind him dropped to their knees, their heads hanging wearily over their shoulders. Then they collapsed to the ground, lolling off into a deep slumber. Albert grinned and was about to turn around when he felt someone pounce on him from behind and grabbing his arms, pin them taut behind his back.

"FATHER! STOP IT RIGHT NOW, OR I'LL SHOOT," he screamed. "I know what you're capable of. But not here, not with me, you don't," he added sticking a pistol in the old man's skull. "Now move it. We don't have time."

Albert struggled, but his son was too strong. He was pushing him in the direction of the helicopter with his arms still twisted behind his back. In the distant horizon, Albert could see the sun's first rays getting drowned out by a huge column of rain-bearing cumulonimbus clouds. They almost made it to the foot of the helicopter when a few large drops of rain leaked from the monstrous mass of cloud. Before anyone could react, the sky exploded and terrible torrential rain came tumbling down dousing every inch of earth in sight.

Albert took the opportunity to yank his arms free and turn around to face his son.

"Don't. I'll shoot, I tell ya!" Peter yelled.

"Will you now?"

"Don't test me. Get in the helicopter."

Suddenly, the earth shook. Peter, lost his balance and dropped his gun. Albert extended his hand and grabbed Peter's arm for support. The ground beneath them seemed to be giving away.

"No! Earthquake?" Peter was puzzled. But it was all happening too fast. The two men latched on to each other as the slab of rock they were standing on slid away from beneath their feet. But they did not fall. They remained suspended in mid-air, as if in an anti-gravity experiment. Panic overtook Albert.

*What on earth is happening?*

The rain abated and the storm clouds started to clear. Albert could see that they were magically suspended over a tube like opening in the ground. His heart beat frantically. And then, they started to descend slowly but surely into the belly of the earth as if via an invisible elevator. They sank deeper and deeper until they disappeared into its dark cavernous depth and the opening closed above them.

# CHAPTER FOUR

Nirmala stood outside the Munich airport in its Kiss and Ride zone, waiting for Alejandro to pick her up. She was wearing her favourite yellow floral summer dress with a light beige jacket and had her shoulder-length dark hair tied in a pony-tail that bounced happily from side to side. Dr. Müller had asked her to expect a navy-blue BMW at around five minutes past two, local time. Nirmala looked ahead at the oncoming slew of vehicles and among them, behind a taxi and an SUV was a car that matched the description. She checked the time. 2:05, exactly.

She walked up to the curb as the BMW in question pulled over. The driver opened the door.

"Oh hey, Alejandro you're just on ..."

"Get in, please," said a heavy voice from the driver's seat. Nirmala looked at him tentatively and got into the passenger seat.

"Uhmm. Dr. Müller." She cleared her throat and nodded. "I was expecting—"

"Alejandro. Yes, I know." Smiled Dr. Müller. "He was going to come, but he doesn't know anything about the project I need you for. Not yet, anyway. So, I came, myself."

"Oh, I see," Nirmala said in a low whisper, not looking entirely at ease with the situation.

"You look scared," Wolfgang observed as he swerved on to the highway.

"Do I?"

"Yes. Do you not trust me?"

"Umm, it's not that …"

Wolfgang raised an eyebrow.

"I mean … well, to be honest … I always thought you didn't like me that much." Nirmala gulped.

"Hahaha." Wolfgang roared with laughter. Nirmala shirked back in her seat at the suddenness of his reaction. "And why, may I ask, would you think that?"

"I dunno. It's just. Nothing … err … you were always cautious about having me on board, weren't you?"

"I'm a cautious man. But you have proven your abilities beyond doubt."

"Why, thank you." Nirmala finally relaxed and flicked Dr. Müller a gracious smile.

"But it's not that I didn't *like* you. In our lives caution is a must. Personal likes and dislikes have no bearing on our need to have our guard up at all times."

"I get that, now that you mention it. So, where are we going? And, oh, is this the autobahn?" Nirmala said excitedly, finally noticing where they were going.

"Indeed. It is. Have you heard of the Neuschwanstein Castle?"

"We're going to a CASTLE?"

"Not exactly. Near the castle, in the town of

Hohenschwangau, my grandparents had a little house. It's hundreds of years old. But still standing. That's where we're going. A couple of hours from here."

"I see. And what's the agenda? I mean, all I know is that this is some secret project of yours."

Wolfgang chuckled. "Well, that's all you need to know. For now."

"It's about finding Kalki, isn't it? I'm not sure I know how—"

"Don't worry, I won't ask you to do something that's beyond your capabilities."

"But you still won't tell me?"

"Of course, I will. Just, not yet. I don't like to rush things."

"Mysterious, as always," said Nirmala, flashing him a coy grin.

"Who told you I'm mysterious? It was Alejandro, wasn't it?"

"Ha! Not exactly. It's word on the street. You didn't know?"

Wolfgang roared with laughter. "Enough about me. Let's talk about you. This is your first time in Germany, ya?"

"Yep!"

"Und what is your first impression?"

Nirmala looked out of the window. The sky was a cloudless, gorgeous azure. In the distance, she could see rolling hills covered in lush vegetation. Clusters of beech and spruce and linden were sprouting fresh new leaves and the horizon was lit with riotous colours. Farther in the distance, the ominous outline of the Bavarian Alps loomed large.

"Breathtaking," she simply said, turning to smile at Dr.

Müller.

"This is just the beginning. Wait till we get to the village."

In about two hours, they exited the highway and drove into a quaint little town that looked like a set from a Disney movie.

"Wow!" said Nirmala. "This is so pretty."

"Look, over there." Wolfgang pointed to the northwestern corner of the horizon.

"Oh!" There in the distance, rose a Cinderellaesque castle, complete with its towers, gates and drawbridges. "It's magnificent. Is that—"

"The Neuschwanstein Castle." Wolfgang nodded.

They pulled around the bend of a road and drove into a little unpaved pathway bordered by a thicket of trees. A cluster of little houses could be seen about a kilometer ahead. Wolfgang didn't go in that direction. Instead, he turned right and drove around an older house, isolated from its surroundings by tall trees on all three sides and arrived at its front gate.

"Here we are," he said, parking next to the gate. "After you." He held the car door open for Nirmala.

"Does anyone live here?" Nirmala asked in a small voice, feeling slightly daunted.

"No. Only intermittently. But it's not haunted. Go in, don't be scared."

Nirmala, tentatively opened the gate and entered the small, grassy yard in front. She walked over a narrow, pebbled path and arrived at the building's modest porch. Wolfgang was right behind. He dug in his pockets for the keys and let them in.

The house had a ceiling so low that a tall man like Wolfgang could simply reach up and touch the ceiling.

The interior was sparse but neatly decorated. On Nirmala's right was a wooden staircase leading up to the low mezzanine floor and right behind the staircase was a small bedroom.

"Here, let me show you around," Dr. Müller said, turning left into the living area. "Zis is the living room. No TV. Sorry." He smiled.

"That's alright. I'm not a TV addict or anything."

"Good. Because you'll be busy."

Nirmala frowned. Not knowing what they'd planned for her was killing her, and asking Wolfgang again would be pointless.

"Okay, over here is the kitchen," Wolfgang hollered from in front of her. Nirmala hurried to join him. The kitchen was tiny, barely enough for camp life. There was a table and two chairs against the wall behind her and across from it, a door leading to the back of the house. On her left was a small stove on top of a counter fitted with a sink. To the right of the counter were a fridge and microwave. No oven.

Wolfgang turned to face her. "Downstairs you saw the small bedroom. It has a powder room. Upstairs, is another bedroom, the main bathroom, the conference room and then there is the attic. You want me to show you?" he asked.

"No, that's fine," said Nirmala, setting her backpack down on the kitchen floor. "I can see it on my own later. But what's the plan, for now?" She pulled up a chair from the kitchen table and sat down facing Wolfgang.

"Yes, that. You are hungry?"

"Starving!" Nirmala grinned.

"Good. Let's see …" Wolfgang walked over to the fridge and opening the door, inspected its contents. "We have chicken sandwich that I made zis morning, pasta from last night ... und ... und ..." Wolfgang searched around in the fridge. "Ah yes, a pot of eintopf. What would you like?"

"Eintopf?" Nirmala looked confused.

"It's a soup. German soup."

"That sounds interesting. What's in it?"

"Sausages, vegetables and what do you call it? Lentils."

"Ah, dal. We call it dal. Yeah, I'll have that. What about you?"

"No. Not me. I have to leave," said Wolfgang as he placed the pot of eintopf on the counter."

"But ... you just arrived!"

"I'll be back. In a couple of hours. I have an errand. In the meantime, make yourself at home," he said as he proceeded to microwave the soup.

"Oh, you don't need to ..." Nirmala got up. "I can warm that up myself."

"If you wish. Plates and glasses are over here, knives and forks in that drawer and there is juice in the fridge." Wolfgang pointed to where everything was in the kitchen. "Unless you want vodka of course. I have some—"

"That's quite alright, Dr. Müller, I'm not a big drinker."

"You can call me Wolfgang."

"Thanks," Nirmala hesitated. "Wolfgang." She smiled.

Wolfgang nodded and walked out in a hurry. "Call me, if you smell trouble," he shouted from the door.

"I will," Nirmala responded, poking her head outside into the living room.

*He's always in a hurry somehow.* Nirmala mused and giggled to herself.

She was famished but she also desperately wanted to get out of her travel clothes and freshen up first. Maybe take a quick shower. The journey from India was way too long and she felt sweaty and uncomfortable. Lunch could wait. She turned off the microwave, grabbed her towel, shower gel and a change of clothes and went upstairs. The bathroom there wasn't hard to find. Next to the staircase was a large landing area and the two doors right across from her were the second bedroom and the adjacent bath. She rushed inside the cramped little bathroom and closed the door. Hanging the towel and clothes on the hook behind the door she rapidly undressed and was about to hop in to the shower when she realized, there was a problem.

"What! There's no shower?" The interior of the bathroom was dimly lit by the daylight trickling in through a miniature ventilator window. But now that her eyes had adjusted to the semi-darkness, Nirmala could clearly see her surroundings. There was a sink, a toilet and a small tub all crammed into a space the size of a walk-in closet. The tub neither had a overhead shower, nor a shower curtain, having clearly been designed for traditional European baths. It did however seem to have a hand shower on the side.

"Damn." Sighed Nirmala, who'd never drawn a bath her entire life. "God, I could use a shower!" she grumbled to herself. And then, she had an idea. She had a clothes line and a rain poncho in her back pack.

"If I could attach one end of the clothes line to the towel rack over there, and the other end to the shelf above the sink … then I could hang my rain poncho … yep, that should work." She wrapped herself in her towel and headed downstairs to get the things she needed for her makeshift shower curtain.

She was at the bottom of the steps when suddenly, she

heard something at the front door. It sounded like several male voices arguing. Quickly, she hid behind the stairwell. Then, the door opened and a couple of people walked in.

"Who's there?" She thought she said, but no actual words materialized from her throat. She cowered behind the stairwell, frozen in shock.

There seemed to be several people walking around the house and a few excited male voices drifted off into the kitchen area. Nirmala knew she had to do something. But what? Ever since her association with the Hekameses, she had been no stranger to the unexpected risks of their way of life, and several times before, she herself had stepped up to the plate and reacted heroically in dangerous situations. But today, cowered behind the stairwell of a crumbling mansion in a foreign land, covered in nothing but a skimpy towel, she felt especially vulnerable and unable to react. She tried to get up. But her hand landed on a broom and knocked it over with a loud clang.

"Ooops," she mumbled, covering her lips.

"Hello," said a woman's voice. "Anyone, there? Is that you, my dear?" she continued as she advanced closer to Nirmala's hideout.

"Dr. Faraday?" Nirmala asked, peeking out.

"Ah, there you are, Nirmala. Oh my, what happened to your clothes?" asked the tiny old woman Nirmala had grown to love and admire.

Nirmala blushed and stood up, clutching onto her towel to prevent it from coming undone. "I ... I mean ... I needed a shower."

"Yes, of course. Dear me. Caught you at a bad time, didn't we?" Wanda grinned. "Run along now. Take your shower. Go on. The boys are in the kitchen. No need to worry." Wanda stood aside to allow Nirmala access to the stairs.

"The boys?"

"I will explain later. We have a meeting when Wolfgang returns."

"Alright. Actually, I also need my backpack. It's in the kitchen ..." Nirmala hesitated.

"Ha! I will have that sent up for you. You can go straight up." Wanda gave Nirmala a gentle nudge on her back egging her to go upstairs.

There was a sharp clink and Nirmala pivoted quickly to find a bright object on the floor right next to her feet. Wanda bent down and gently picked it up. Placing it in the center of her palm, she studied it carefully. Fitted to a chain of sterling silver was a locket no larger than a rose petal and luminous with an ethereal glow.

"Oh my!" she whispered; her eyes wide. "Where did you find this?"

"It was a gift. From Alejandro. He got it from the bazaar in Cairo, I believe," Nirmala explained. "But why is it glowing? I've never seen that happen before ..." she trailed off.

"It's Heka," said Wanda softly. She extended her hands and fastened the locket around Nirmala's neck. "Keep it safe," she added, cupping it with her palm and pressing it lightly against the younger woman's chest. The contact felt warm. Like a hot stone massage. This strange warmth emanated from the locket and spread to the rest of Nirmala's body before it eventually faded away.

* * *

After the shower and late lunch, which Wanda Faraday had brought upstairs, Nirmala had fallen asleep in the adjacent bedroom. She woke abruptly to a loud knock.

"My dear, come on over, Wolfgang is here," Wanda called from the door.

Nirmala rubbed her eyes and stretched. For a moment, her jet-lag kicked in and she couldn't get her bearings straight.

*Where am I? Oh, yes.*

She climbed groggily out of bed and ventured outside the room. Wanda was standing in the landing next to the stairs as a couple of young men hurried up to what seemed like the attic area above them. One more young man followed. Finally, two women of roughly the same age joined them. One of them spotted Nirmala and Wanda and smiled warmly in their direction.

"Who are these people?" Nirmala asked, clearly confused. Before Wanda could answer, Dr. Müller appeared from downstairs.

"Ah! Zere you are, Nirmala," he said. "Come on. We meet in the attic."

Nirmala cast a suspicious glance at Wanda.

"Let us head upstairs, my dear. And then, we can chat," Wanda replied.

The attic was dimly lit but fairly large in comparison to the rest of the house. The ceiling was low as expected. A few computer stations could be seen against the wall and a large cabinet stood right next to the entrance. Other than that, the space was mostly empty with yoga mats spread on the floor. The men and women, Nirmala had seen earlier, were sitting cross-legged on some of the mats.

"Sit, please," Wanda indicated, motioning to a nearby mat. Nirmala sat down facing the rest of the party and Wanda stood over her shoulder. Wolfgang was in a corner, leaning against a post. Once everyone had taken their positions, Wolfgang pulled up a chair from a computer station. Flipping it around, he sat with his arms folded over the backrest.

"Now zat we're all here," he began. All eyes turned in his direction. "First things first, I must introduce, Nirmala. She's the lady I have spoken to you about before. Finally, you get to meet her," he said enthusiastically to the group of youngsters.

"Nirmala, meet, Ahmad, Saburo, Eric, Xianbin, Masha and Patricia. Now, you must be wondering what this is all about," he continued, addressing Nirmala.

"Yes! I absolutely, am. Nice to meet all of you, by the way," she said, nodding in the direction of the newcomers.

"The time has come to disclose to you, the details of my secret project. The one I've been working on for several years now."

"Secret project?"

"Yes. You see, for the longest time I've worried that we, the Hekameses are ... very few."

"Not the Hekameses, Wolfgang. The *known* Hekameses," Wanda corrected.

"True. We haven't been able to find *all* the Hekameses. Anyway, as I was saying; we are few. Which is a problem. In case an all-out conflict was to break out between ourselves and our enemy ... the Aifra ... we wouldn't stand a chance. Despite our abilities. So, I wanted to have a contingency plan. And this is it. My contingency plan. These fine young men and women, you see here today."

"You mean, they are Hekameses?" Nirmala asked, sounding surprised.

"In training. Like you, they are not born with the special powers of the Hekameses. But with our help they can acquire them."

"And you are living proof, this can be done," said Wanda, grinning.

"Exactly," agreed Wolfgang. "And that is precisely why I brought you here. To help train them."

"And eventually, to lead them," Wanda added, whispering into Nirmala's ear.

"What? ME?" Nirmala exclaimed; her face flushed.

"You are more than capable, my dear."

"Of course, you'll not be alone," Wolfgang assured. "Wanda will be here with you once every month and more often if you need her. She's moving to Europe shortly."

"I see. Wow, this is a lot to absorb. Do the other Hekameses know?" Nirmala asked.

"No. Not yet. It was my pet project and recently, when I started seeing some success, I told Wanda. She was the one who suggested that we ask you to spearhead this initiative," Wolfgang explained, flicking a crooked smile in Wanda's direction.

"You can of course recruit others you deem fit, provided that they are willing," Wanda chimed in.

"Hmm. I certainly am honoured that you thought about me," Nirmala gushed.

"So? What's the verdict? Are you up for this?" Wolfgang enquired.

Nirmala scrunched her face. All eyes turned to her. For several minutes there was silence. The team of youngsters exchanged hushed whispers. The air in the room was taut with anticipation.

"Yes. I'm on board," she finally said with resolve. "Let's do this. When do we start?"

"I told you, she would agree," said Wanda, eyeing Wolfgang.

"Welcome to the Novo Hekameses," said Wolfgang,

extending a hand-shake. "We can start right away!"

# CHAPTER FIVE

"Whoa, whoa there horsie, cool it, cool it, good boy ..." yelled Alejandro, as he desperately tugged on his horse's rein barely able to hang on. The horse paid no attention to its rider and galloped forward in a frenzy, its mane tossing wildly in the wind.

"I'm falling, I'm falling ..." Alejandro panicked as his saddle slid along the horse's flank.

"Oh no, you don't! I gotcha," said Zoya, riding up alongside of him and seizing his horse's rein, her voluminous head of curls swirling around her face. "Easy there buddy, easy, easy, easy ..." she crooned, patting the healthy steed with one hand and tugging on its rein with the other. The horse slowed down to a graceful trot and Alejandro straightened in his seat.

"Thanks, Zoya. I think that was enough for me today," he said with a chuckle. "Can you make this guy stop?"

"Ha! 'Make this guy stop!' You sure are funny, Alejandro. He'll stop when I stop. See, here we go." Zoya laughed, slowing her horse as Alejandro's steed followed suit. "They take cues from each other."

"Neat. How did you get to know so much about horses?" He hopped off his ride and held his hand out to Zoya to help her climb down. Bending forward, he patted the dirt off his navy-blue riding denims.

"When I was a kid, we lived in Mongolia for a while. My dad served with Doctors Without Borders, over there. That's how I learned to ride."

"Interesting. Must have been before the Hekameses started tracking you."

"Oh yeah. I was super young. We moved back to the US when I turned ten."

"Makes sense," said Alejandro as they walked their rental-horses back to the stable. "My wife used to love horses too. Sadly, I never really caught on," he added with a guffaw.

"HOLD ON! You have a *wife?*"

"Had."

"You split up?"

"No. She died very young."

"I'm so sorry …"

"That's alright. It was nearly twenty years ago," Alejandro said grimly.

Zoya walked up to Alejandro's side and affectionately placed her hand on his arm. "What happened to her?"

"She was murdered."

"WHAT?"

"Right after I joined the Hekameses."

"You think it could've been them? The Aifra?" Zoya asked, lowering her voice.

"Maybe. But there are …"

The stable owner walked up to them, interrupting their conversation. "Enjoy the ride, didjya?" he asked, grabbing

Alejandro's horse by the rein and lovingly patting his neck.

"Yeah, well I'm a bit sore, but I think Zoya had fun," said Alejandro jovially while rubbing his behind with both hands.

"Aww. It's a work in progress, I say. A couple o' days more practice and you'll be ridin' like a pro," the rancher said enthusiastically before tipping his cowboy hat at the duo and walking off with the horses.

"Do you want to grab some food? I'm starving!" Alejandro asked, turning to Zoya.

"Yeah sure. Mmm … I could go for some clam chowder in a sourdough bowl right now!"

"The what?"

"Don't tell me you've never had San Francisco clam chowder before!"

"In fact, I have not."

"No way!"

"Maybe, but far less crazy than getting murdered by the Aifra," he said, lowering his voice.

"Oh yeah, I forgot. You didn't get to leave the house much, the other times you were here, eh?"

"Nope. Now with all the additional security around because of you know …"

"April 24th."

"Yep. At least we can get out of the house without worrying about them."

"Where are they, anyway … I mean the Aifra," Zoya asked in a hushed tone. "They've not been in the news at all since April 24th. That's unusual."

"It is. I'm worried too. But we can't talk about that here. So, lunch?"

"Sure. Clam chowder?"

"Why not. Do you know a place?"

"Quite a few, actually. In fact, there's one we can walk to from here."

"Lead the way, ma'am," said Alejandro, gesturing dramatically with his hand.

It had been a warm sunny morning and now as afternoon approached, a light drizzle broke out. They walked for about a kilometer and a half through beautiful eucalyptus-lined avenues and arrived at a cluster of quaint restaurants and shops.

"Ah, there it is," said Zoya, pointing to a brightly coloured shack across the street. "We can eat on the patio if you like."

"That'd be nice. Why don't you grab a seat and I'll get us the clam chowders?"

"In sourdough bowls," Zoya reminded.

"As you wish." Alejandro laughed.

Zoya found a quiet corner of the patio and got themselves a seat. It had hardly been a week since she had come back to stay at the Faraday House and already so much was happening. It was strange being in Dr. Faraday's house with the hostess herself missing in action. Resuming her Hekameses training with Alejandro had been exciting and his horse-riding lessons were an entertaining distraction. But it was impossible for Zoya to ignore the air of uncertainty and gloom that hung over everyone in these troubled times. What did the Hekameses need to do, now? There were too many unknowns, too much confusion. Zoya found herself feeling restless. She looked around to see if she could spot Alejandro and noticed that he was heading in her direction carrying a loaded tray in his hands.

"Hey, that was fast!" Zoya said when he set the tray down at their table.

"Was it?" Alejandro checked his watch. "Fifteen

minutes, I think, if you want to call that fast."

"Oh, I thought it was less. Must have gotten lost in my thoughts," Zoya mumbled.

"What were you thinking? Here, take one," he said, extending a sourdough bowl brimming with soup in her direction.

"Thanks. Can I get a napkin?"

"Sure, I brought a bunch." Alejandro passed her a couple of paper napkins and removed his own soup from the tray. The bread bowl containing steaming hot clam chowder was set on a soup plate with a couple of crackers on the side. Alejandro inspected the bowl-shaped bread by poking it with his fingers. He removed the rectangular slice from the top that served as its lid and was about to pour its scalding contents into the soup plate.

"Haha! What are you doing?" Zoya laughed.

"Trying to eat the soup."

"You don't need to pour it into the plate. You eat it directly from the bread bowl with a spoon. See, like this," Zoya demonstrated, dipping her spoon into the belly of the sourdough bowl.

"That's crazy. Then how do I eat the bread? The soup is *inside* it."

"Ha! That's the whole fun of it. When you've had some soup, the level in the bowl goes down and you eat the exposed part of the bowl. And then repeat," Zoya said with a wide grin. She dipped the lid of the bowl in her soup and took a bite. "Mmm ... it's delish. Come on, try it!"

"It's quite good," said Alejandro after trying a spoonful. "So, tell me, what were you thinking while I was away?"

"So many things. So many questions."

"Such as?"

"These horse-riding lessons for example. Why do you

think we're going to need it, you know, for our mission?"

"Mmm ... I don't know for sure, but remember, how Kalki arrived on a horse?"

"Yes, of course, how can I forget. But, so what? That was in the desert. What are the chances we need to go back to a desert?"

"We may or may not need to. But that's not the point. The significance is in the legend."

"Like, how?"

"As per the Indian legend, Kalki, the tenth avatar of Vishnu, is *supposed* to arrive on a horse. So, it's no coincidence."

"So do you think that if we were to find her again we'd have to go on—"

"Horseback, yes, that's my hunch."

"Interesting. There aren't that many places on earth where you need to go on horseback, are there?"

"Nope," said Alejandro, ripping off a large piece of his sourdough bowl and dunking it into his soup. "This is fun!" He grinned, taking a bite.

"See, I told you!"

"You see how this narrows down our options, right?"

"For eating soup?" asked Zoya, confused.

"Ha! No. For going to look for Kalki."

"Oh, okay. Yeah, I suppose. If we were to go with your reasoning."

"We have to begin looking somewhere, so why not start with this lead?"

"I see what you're saying. Makes sense, I suppose. Now we need to hone in on the places where the best way to travel is by horseback and commence our search."

"It's more complicated than that. We have limited resources and people. We can't afford a miscalculation.

We need to zero in on one or two possible locations. So, we'll need more clues."

"Hmm. Will I be going back to the lab at Oxford?

"I don't know. It may not be safe there. At least, not right now with everything that's happening in Europe … the preparations for war, Dr. Weilhammer's death, Dr. Cobb missing …"

"But Chris is there and Dr. Faraday is going soon," Zoya objected.

"You really don't like me, do you? Is it because I don't know how to eat sourbread dough?" Alejandro joked.

Zoya broke into a chuckle. "It's *sourdough bread*, Alejandro. And you are so hilarious. You *know* that it's not—"

"Yes, yes, I know, you just like to be at the center of the action."

Zoya nodded in agreement.

"I get it. I do too. But let's see what Wolfgang has planned. I'm sure he'll have projects for everyone," Alejandro assured. "Enough of worrying for one day. I think we should do something fun this afternoon. Do you want to catch a movie?"

"I'd love to! Haven't seen a movie in ages. Which one were you thinking?"

"Your choice. Ready to go? If we leave now, we can make the matinee," said Alejandro, checking the time.

"Cool. Let's go."

\* \* \*

Chris crouched on the floor of Dr. Faraday's old office at Oxford University and tightened the final screw on the new office chair he had ordered for her.

"All right, that should do it," he said, standing up to inspect his handiwork. He lifted up the assembled chair and set it behind the rosewood desk that he had wiped clean with Windex earlier. He then leaned over the desk to make sure that the computer he had set up for her this morning was all plugged in and ready to go.

*Not that she's ever going to use a computer by herself.* He mused with a grin. *But hey, I was asked to set up her office and you can't have an office without a computer.*

"Think I'm done in here," he said, looking around to make sure everything was set up and functional. "Oh almost forgot … need to get some stuff from Dr. Cobb's room …" he reminded himself as he rushed out of the room and walked over to the adjacent door.

"Err … what was the code? Ah, yes …" He punched some numbers into the number lock on Dr. Cobb's closed office door and turned the knob. As Chris let himself in, the familiar smell of aromatic pipe tobacco filled his olfactory glands, making him wistful. A plethora of emotions overtook his senses all at once. Nostalgia. Affection. Worry. Fear. Regret.

"Wherever you are old man, hope you're well," he found himself wishing, although he was acutely aware that Dr. Cobb might in fact, have abandoned them to join their nemesis, the Aifra. Chris steadied himself, trying not to get carried away in the moment and focussed instead on the task at hand. He walked over to his professor's desk, set at an odd angle with respect to the room, and removed a key from the top drawer. He then walked over to an old, wooden cabinet about waist-high that was positioned against the western wall. He bent down to open the cabinet and retrieved a box of electronics from the top shelf.

"I think we're good for now," he said to himself as he

locked the cabinet back up and straightened his back. He was about to leave when his eyes fell on an object that sat on top of the cabinet. Dusty and neglected in one corner. He set down the box of equipment and picked up the little curio. It was an ancient looking hourglass about four inches tall. But what struck Chris the most was the fact that the sand inside didn't seem to be flowing.

"That's odd. Maybe it's clogged," he mumbled, as he shook it like a rattle to help clear the clog. "Nope. That didn't work. Strange." He cupped his chin with his hands and frowned.

There was a rustling sound near the door. Chris pivoted quickly and stashed the hourglass into his jacket pocket.

"Who's there?" he inquired into the darkness.

"Dr. Cobb?" came a tentative response.

"Um, no. It's Chris. Is that … Tracy?"

A slight figure appeared in the doorway. In the darkness, Chris couldn't make out the face but the voice sounded like that of the young administrative assistant from the departmental office downstairs.

Tracy relaxed and moved into full view. "Oh, you scared me there for a second," she said, placing her hand on her chest right above her heart.

"*I* scared *you*?" Chris teased. "You're the one who sneaked up on me."

Tracy chuckled. "Sorry about that. Just here to drop off Dr. Cobb's mail. Didn't expect to find anyone here," she said extending an envelope. "Do you want to hang on to it till we … till we …"

"Find him?" Chris completed. "Yeah, sure." He accepted the envelope and examined it under the strip of light trickling in through the half-open door.

"Still no news of him, eh? Tracy asked, her hesitation apparent.

"Nope."

"What are the—"

"There's no stamp on here. Did someone hand-deliver it?" Chris interrupted.

"Umm, oh! Not sure actually. Let me see that." Tracy took the envelope from Chris's hands and scanned in under the light in the corridor. "Yeah, you're right. Weird. It was in the department mailbox. I didn't realize it wasn't stamped until now."

"Hmm."

"Do you still want it?"

"Yes," said Chris definitively.

"Alrighty then. I'm heading home. You're going to lock up after, right?" Tracy asked as she turned to leave.

"Yep. See ya tomorrow."

"Laters."

# CHAPTER SIX

Amon made his way through the crowded alleys of Cairo in the blistering mid-day heat, pushing past throngs of pedestrians, tourists and idlers to finally arrive at the humble lobby of a very old guest house, a couple of blocks from the Cairo Museum. He straightened his broad shoulders, projecting an air of confidence and smiled at the frail-looking clerk at the reception desk before walking past him straight to the double-elevators. He had never been to this guest house before but knew exactly where he was going. He alighted from the elevator at the fourth floor and stepping into the narrow, carpeted corridor, started scanning the number plates on the doors. Arriving at his destination, he knocked twice.

A minute passed and there was no answer. His heart filled with anticipation and a bead of sweat trickled down his temple. He raised his fist to knock again when there was a clicking sound and the door opened just a crack.

"Hello," said Amon, clearing his throat. "It's—"

"AMON! My good friend. So, it *is* you!" The man behind the door interrupted as he simultaneously flung the door open and extended his arms for a hug.

"Oh Sebastian, so glad to see you." Amon smiled and enfolded the short archaeologist in his huge embrace.

"Please, come in. We have much to catch up on." Sebastian stood back, gesturing for Amon to enter.

The room was relatively small with modest furnishing. There was a coffee table with two armchairs next to the window on Amon's right, and a stark four poster bed covered with a beautiful Egyptian bed-spread was lodged against the wall on his left. Sebastian led him to the coffee table where a steaming pot covered with a tea cozy could be seen on a tray along with a couple of cups and plates of ornamental china, a bowl of sugar and stirring spoons. Amon settled himself into one of the armchairs and glanced out the window. The view was of a busy alley packed with pedestrians and vendors and their colourful stores.

"I'm surprised that you forgave me," said Sebastian, jolting his attention back to the room.

"For what?" Amon was surprised.

"I mean … you know … for deserting you and Wanda in Faiyum like that. I didn't … we didn't … mean to." Sebastian hung his head.

Amon reached out and grabbed his friend's shoulder. "I know," he said softly. "Stop blaming yourself. I don't believe I would've reacted differently, if I were you."

"We did give them a bit of a chase. Fired a couple of rounds. But they were just too many," he continued agitatedly.

"Oh? How many? We heard some voices but the size of the party was impossible to tell."

"Half a dozen at least. Maybe more. We had no time to get an exact count. They were firing at us like crazy. My colleague got hit on the ankle. Somehow, we got him to the jeep and made for Cairo to seek help. By the time we were back with the cops, the site was deserted." Sebastian sighed. "We thought the worst had happened; you know?"

"Thought they took us, huh?"

Sebastian nodded. "Tortured. Interrogated. Maybe even murdered." He hid his face between his hands. "God, it was a stressful time!"

"For us too. I'm glad you were able to escape. We were worried. With us, they wouldn't have killed at first. With you on the other hand, they had no reason to spare your lives, sadly. Fleeing was the smartest thing for you to do. Fleeing and seeking help."

Sebastian smiled gratefully. "Your tea. I almost forgot. I ordered tea. Here, let me pour you some. Sugar?"

"Yes, please. One cube. Thank you."

"So, where were you since then?" Sebastian asked, sipping his tea. "You never went back to your house. We checked."

"I'm afraid that's confidential."

Sebastian raised an eyebrow.

"For security reasons, of course. I have a hideout that I can't divulge." Amon prevaricated.

"That's a good idea. Given how much they've harassed you—these terrorists."

"Yes. So, how come you're back? I thought they shut down the Faiyum site since the incident."

"They have."

"Then? You're working offsite? At the museum?"

"Umm … not exactly." Sebastian lowered his voice. "They want us to look into the incident at the Red Pyramid, you know."

"What incident?" Amon pretended to sound incredulous.

"You haven't heard? The one on 24th April. The strange ray of light—"

"Oh, that! But that was lightning. Didn't you read the papers last week? It was all there. The scientists concur. It was a momentary atmospheric ionization caused by an unusually heavy bolt of lightning. Nothing more."

"I did read about that. But … *they* have their doubts."

"Who are they? The Egyptian government? Can't be. I was speaking to my contact yesterday and he confirmed—"

Sebastian glanced around the room nervously, scratched his chin and looking Amon directly in the eye shook his head side to side in an ominous gesture. "More tea?" He then asked, in an even tone.

"Sure," Amon mumbled. "Actually, I should be leaving," he added, suddenly standing up. Once on his feet, he reached into his back pocket and pulled out a pen and post-it pad. In it he scribbled the following words:

*It wasn't the Egyptian government, was it?*

He showed Sebastian the note.

Sebastian nodded, no.

*Who was it then? Who commissioned the research?* Amon wrote on the post-it.

Sebastian shook his head again.

*You can't tell me? Can you write it?*
No, again.

"Alright then. It was great to see you Sebastian. Sorry, I couldn't stay long. Hope to stay in touch," said Amon finally, extending his hand to shake his friend's. "Will you be in Cairo long?" he added.

"Probably a month or two." Sebastian smiled. "It was good to see you too, Amon. I'll call you sometime," he added with a meaningful wink.

"Talk soon and take care," said Amon flicking him a knowing, half-grin.

Having said goodbye to Sebastian, Amon made his way out of the antiquated building and walked onto the busy Cairo streets with deliberation. His job in Egypt was done. For now. Memories tampered. Evidence destroyed. Allies sworn to secrecy. The cover-up of their April 24th adventure would have been almost perfect if not for this latest bit of information from Sebastian. What next? He pulled out his phone and dialled a number.

"Wolfgang, it's me, Amon."

"Ah, about time," answered the husky voice. "So you're finally using the encrypted phone."

"Had to this time. Germany is too far for Huma to fly." Amon guffawed.

"What do you have to report?"

"Disturbing news, I'm afraid. Someone might be onto us. I don't know who."

"Is that so? It's concerning. But I'm not all together surprised."

"What's the plan now?"

"We need to get you out of Egypt. Standby for details."

* * *

Wolfgang barely hung up the phone when Chris stormed in to his temporary office at the corner of Dr. Cobb's lab.

"Dr. Müller, look," he said breathlessly, handing him an envelope.

"What iz dis letter? It came in the mail?"

"For Dr. Cobb, yes. No stamp. No return address."

"Hmm. Let me see." Wolfgang pulled out the folded piece of paper from inside and glanced over the words typed across it as his eyes grew wide. He put the letter down, stood up abruptly and started pacing with his arms folded behind his back.

"So? What do you think?" asked Chris. "Who the hell is Peter?" He picked up the discarded letter and read it once again.

*Where is Peter?* it said in large bold font across the middle of the page. Nothing more, nothing less.

Dr. Müller paced silently for a couple of minutes and then he spoke softly as if to himself.

"Strange. Very strange."

"Yeah, that's what I thought too. Figured you'd probably have more input than I did so I rushed straight to see you. Any thoughts?"

Dr. Müller stopped pacing and walked up to his desk. He placed both hands on the table and leaned forward to look Chris in the eye.

"Peter," he said, chewing his words, "Peter was the name of a young man who disappeared more than thirty years ago. I fear it's got to be this Peter that they seek."

"Disappeared thirty years ago? Could it be … no … it is, isn't it? It's the lost son, Dr. Cobb said he was going to meet, before he deserted us."

"That's my hunch."

"How did he disappear?"

"What I know is that he was going to University in America and hardly staying in touch with his family. The intermittent phone calls came in, but with little news about his life abroad. And then one day, in his sophomore year, they stopped hearing from him altogether."

"Interesting. Just like that? No arguments or anything?"

"Not that I know of. Dr. Cobb never mentions him much, but over the years I've heard his story in bits and pieces."

"Did they try to find him?"

"Oh yes, of course. Extensively. After about a month of no communication whatsoever, Dr. Cobb contacted the University, the police, the FBI. No one could trace him. The poor man was totally wrecked. Thought him for dead, but not even a body was ever found."

"You think he joined the Aifra?"

"Ever since Dr. Cobb's sudden departure, that's what we've all been worrying about, right? But now I'm not so sure."

"Right. I mean if he's in the Aifra and his father went to join him then who's looking for him now?"

"Exactly."

"Also, look here." Chris picked up the letter and pointed to some insignia at the bottom of the page. "The letter's on a US Government notepad."

"Yes, I saw that. Worrisome, to say the least."

"Could it be that the US Government is still looking for him and has reason to believe that Dr. Cobb is hiding his whereabouts?"

"Not likely. In that case it would've been an official letter. An investigation or a summons."

"You're right. That was a silly question."

"There are no silly questions." Dr. Müller smiled. "We'll just have to wait until we have more information, I suppose."

# CHAPTER SEVEN

Chris emerged from the bathroom of his tiny London flat after his morning wash-up and shaving routine to find his new house guest already up and sitting at the kitchen table reading a newspaper.

"Morning Amon. Sleep well?" he asked with a smile.

"Yes, you?" Amon replied absentmindedly without taking his eyes off the paper.

"Yep. Slept like a baby. Want some coffee?"

"Sure … yeah. Did you read the news yet?"

"No, why?"

"Check this out." Amon tossed the paper across the kitchen table in Chris's direction.

"Hikers spot snow leopards in Siberia," Chris read.

"No, not that. The headline." Amon pointed, mildly amused.

"Oh, sorry." Chris chuckled. "Jesus! Not good. The United States has declared war! So soon? That's crazy."

"It's all very strange to me. Why on earth do they even think it's Russia?"

"No idea. But what worries me is how this complicates *everything* for us, the Hekameses."

"Yes. What do you think the Aifra are up to? They've been dangerously silent through all of this."

"Right. The war probably plays right into their hands."

"Why do you say that?"

"I mean it's a distraction, don't you think? With everyone else focusing on war with Russia, they're free to proliferate and pursue their agendas in peace."

"Good point. I didn't think about it like that. Where do you think they're hiding?"

"Well, they're certainly no longer in their Iceland base. Wolfgang sent someone to check it out."

"He did?"

"Yep, right after they killed Weilhammer. It was completely deserted. The cave opening was sealed off with boulders."

"They probably figured out Weilhammer leaked the news about the electromagnetic pulse attack in April and punished him for the betrayal."

"Exactly. I mean it must've been a pretty obvious connection to make. He was the key engineer behind April 24th, and somehow, we found out the plan and foiled it from the Red Pyramid. That's probably why they've recruited Sebastian to figure out what kind of magic we pulled that day. Stopping an EMP attack without any weapon is not something that's deemed scientifically possible."

"I agree, except for the part about Sebastian. I don't think it's the Aifra that recruited him."

"But isn't that the most logical conclusion? They certainly have the strongest motive."

"The most logical answer isn't always the correct one,

my friend."

"What *is* the correct conclusion in this case then?" Chris pulled up a chair and sat down at the kitchen table across from Amon.

"I don't know. I'm working on it. But the possibility of the Aifra being involved is negligible in my opinion."

"You think so? Why?"

"I have my reasons. I'd rather not share them 'til I'm sure."

"Did you read his thoughts?"

"No. Unfortunately, I'm still not as good at mind-reading as the rest of you."

"You can read a little though, right?"

"Sometimes. With difficulty. I can implant a false memory into the mind of another without issue. Reading thoughts, not so much."

"Hmm … if your hunch is correct though, and the Aifra didn't commission Sebastian … that'd make life more complicated."

"Definitely."

"And we don't even know what the Aifra are up to or where they moved."

"Maybe they didn't move."

"I don't get it."

"What if they were somewhere else all along? Remember how Wolfgang always says that they probably have a much larger base somewhere else?"

"I see what you mean. The hideout in Iceland may have been an offshoot. The mothership is still out there."

"Now the question is; where?"

"I dunno. But hey, maybe some coffee will clear up our brains. What do you say I make some?" Chris got up and headed towards the kitchen counter.

"Sure," said Amon distractedly, as he leaned back in his chair. "Needs to be somewhere deserted. Lax laws, preferably," he mumbled.

Chris put on a pot of coffee and reached into the kitchen closet for some cookies. He stopped himself midway and pivoted on his heels.

"Hey, Amon!"

"Yeah?"

"Could you pass me the newspaper again?"

"Here." Amon extended the paper in Chris's direction.

"Thanks. Where was it? Aha, here it is," Chris mumbled to himself as he went through the headlines. "Snow leopard in Siberia! That's it!"

"What the who now? I think you were right about that coffee, Chris. We could both use some to clear our brains," Amon joked.

"No, you don't understand."

"Clearly," said Amon throwing up his arms in mock-surprise.

The coffee was done. Chris switched off the coffee-maker and filled two mugs with its contents.

"How do you take your coffee?" he asked.

"Black. Same as the snow leopards." Amon chuckled.

"You think it's funny *now*, but wait till you hear the story," said Chris as he walked over with their coffees.

"Thank you," said Amon as he accepted his mug. "Please, do tell," he teased, taking a sip.

Chris sat down with his coffee and took a sip. "Okay," he said. "So when Zoya and I went to Iceland to search for Dr. Weilhammer, we tracked him down right to the Aifra hideout in a cave behind a waterfall. But you already knew that."

"I did."

"What you didn't know is that the cave had an unusual sentry."

"Is this a riddle or are you getting back at me for laughing at you?"

"Ha! Neither, my friend. All I'm saying is that there was a friggin' pet snow leopard guarding that cave!"

"Wait, whaat? No way!"

"Yes way! And what's more, as Zoya aptly pointed out that day, snow leopards are not native to Iceland or from anywhere nearby for that matter."

"*Interesting*. So you're saying … okay … makes sense now." Amon became thoughtful.

"You see?"

"I think I do."

"They probably brought the snow leopard from their base, wherever it is. And I'm thinking it's Siberia."

"I get your logic but Siberia isn't the only place where you can find these animals. China has some. India, Mongolia, quite a few countries, actually."

"The most logical answer isn't always the correct one, my friend."

"Ha! I see what you did there." Amon grinned. "Why do you think it's Siberia?"

"First of all, it has all the attributes you brought up. It's deserted, extremely cold. Lax law enforcement. A very secretive country."

"True. But so is Mongolia."

"Agreed, but that's where the article in today's paper becomes important."

"I haven't read it."

"It says that hikers recently spotted several snow leopards on multiple occasions during the course of their weeklong trek close to Lake Baikal. *Several.* Not an isolated sighting but *several* over *multiple* days. That rings extremely odd to me. These animals are very rare. Almost extinct. Each habitat is lucky to have at best a couple of adults. Also, they're complete loners, rarely seen in groups."

"Unless someone is breeding them." Amon breathed as realization set in.

"Not to mention training them too."

"Hmm. So the question is, what do we do now?"

\* \* \*

"Alright guys, I think we're done for today," Nirmala said to the Novo Hekameses as she helped Xianbin take off the sensors they were using for their last training exercise.

The team packed up their belongings and folded away the yoga mats. Nirmala and Wanda joined in to help. In fifteen minutes, they had said their goodbyes and were off for the day. They were holding the trainings every day but had split the trainees up into two groups. That way the whole team didn't have to be there every day and everyone could work around their schedules to find the days of the week that suited them best.

After the students had left, Nirmala went down to the kitchen to see what she could whip up for dinner, when Wanda walked in.

"My dear, I don't feel like eating at home today. Fancy going out to a restaurant tonight?"

"Sure, why not! What kind of food do you like?"

"I am particularly fond of Indian curry and have been craving it for quite some time." Wanda smiled.

"Oh, you like Indian food?"

"Of course! I'm English, grew up in England! That's

what the English eat."

"Ha! Why didn't you tell me? I could've made some for you."

"Oh no, dear girl, you have far more important things to do at the moment with the war at our doorstep and what not. I know a nice little curry place not very far from here if you don't mind the walk."

"Not at all. It'd be great to get out of the house for a change while we're still allowed to."

"Precisely. God forbid if a full-blown war were to happen, the curfews and patrols would drive everyone crazy. Such stressful times war can bring! Come, let me fetch my coat."

"Let me grab it for you. I need mine as well. It's been a bit nippy." Nirmala walked over to the coat closet near the front door and returned swiftly with their coats and purses.

"Ah, thank you, my girl," said Wanda as she got into her coat.

"My pleasure. Here, let me get the door." Nirmala pulled on her light jacket and held the door open for Wanda as they walked out into the dreamy twilight of a rustic German evening.

The scene outside was breathtaking. The distant snow-covered alps capped with the molten gold of a setting sun. Birds zooming across the horizon in elegantly choreographed aerial formations. A light cool breeze brushing against their faces, bringing colour to their cheeks. Nirmala rubbed her palms for warmth.

"You're not cold, are you?" she asked her elderly companion.

"No. I'm quite alright. How about you, my child?"

"I'm a little chilly, actually," she replied, embarrassed. "I was wondering …" she started but trailed off.

"What were you wondering? No need to hesitate, we are all friends here." Wanda smiled.

"Do you think there'll really be a war?"

"It does feel a lot like it's supposed to, before a massive war. So yes, I do think that we might be headed in that direction. But that's not exactly what you were wanting to ask, was it?"

"Umm … there's no hiding from you, is there?" Nirmala laughed.

"I *am* a Hekameses, after all. But in all honesty, I didn't try to read your thoughts this time. It was just a hunch."

"Well, it was a very good hunch," said Nirmala, as they arrived at the end of the path that led out from the house. "Which way from here?" she asked, stopping.

"We go left, towards the market. So, tell me, what was your original question?"

"Well … you talk about the upcoming war like something you have seen before. Like you've lived through great battles and know exactly how things will play out when war consumes our lives. Is it just your general intuitiveness? Or have you lived through the Second World War?"

"Ha! Excellent observation. You are very intuitive yourself, my dear. Lived though a World War, yes. Yes, I have. The Second. The First," Wanda recounted, calmly.

"The *first?* What are you saying? It can't be! You're kidding, right?"

"No, absolutely not. Do I sound like I'm kidding?" It became suddenly dark and the street lights came on almost at once, illuminating their way like medieval torches along the road to a castle.

"No. But you rarely sound like you're kidding." Nirmala giggled. "I had heard some whispers about your age but was never comfortable enough to ask anyone directly. Did I offend you?"

"Oh no, not at all. It was a fair question, by all means."

"Glad to hear. So, how old are you then?"

"I have walked this earth for over *two-hundred* years, believe it or not. It has been so long that the exact tally of years has become difficult to maintain." Wanda chuckled.

"*Two hundred!* Good God! But how?"

"How have I lived this long?"

"Not just lived this long but stayed so … fit. It's unbelievable!"

"It's Heka, my dear."

"Heka? Like the Egyptian goddess?"

"Heka is actually an ancient form of magic practiced in pre-historic Egypt and it's just as powerful as the eponymous goddess."

"I see. Is that why this group is called the Hekameses? Because they practice Heka?"

"Precisely."

"Does every Hekameses?"

"Yes. To various degrees."

"Even Zoya?"

"No, not Zoya. Not yet."

"I see. So, how does one practice Heka?"

"Aha! I thought you'd ask. That is why you and your team are here. We will get into Heka, among other things. Look," she pointed. "there it is, our curry place." Her eyes lit up like a child's, and she grinned ear to ear.

# CHAPTER EIGHT

Wolfgang paced up and down Chris's meagre living room, covering the entire distance from wall to wall in five long strides. Amon and Chris sat at the kitchen table, leaning against the wall, legs stretched, drinking beer.

"You think he forgot about us?" Amon asked after several minutes had passed.

"Nah. Wolfgang is weird like that. He becomes lost in thought when he's working on something serious."

"Well, I'm starting to get hungry. Maybe he won't notice if you and I go out and grab some dinner?"

"Ha! Sneaky." Chris laughed. "But I have a feeling he'll notice and blow his top."

"We'll bring him something. What does he eat? Currywurst?"

"Touché! You're setting yourself up for getting thrown out of the Hekameses, though."

"He'd do that? I don't think so. He needs us as much as we—"

"Okay, here's the plan," Wolfgang's deep voice interrupted.

"Am I going then?" Chris enquired, sitting up straight.

"Going where?" Amon asked.

"Chris wants to see if he can track down Aifra's main base. I believe the two of you think it might be in Siberia?"

"We do. And if he's going, I'm going with him. I have a bone to pick with those bastards!"

"And that's exactly why you shouldn't go, Amon. We need stealth not aggression. We cannot out fight them," Wolfgang objected.

"Stealth is my middle name. True story," agreed Chris. "But to be honest, given what happened the last time I went after them, I wouldn't mind some support."

Wolfgang became thoughtful. "There are other things I needed Amon's help with," he mumbled. "Yet, I can't say I'm not concerned for your safety too... alright... if the both of you feel convinced about this mission then it might be worth a shot."

"Good. Let's plan it then," said Amon standing up and clapping his hands together.

"I advise you not to be hasty," Wolfgang cautioned. "Plan it well. And we need to run it by the others."

"Sounds good to me," said Chris.

Wolfgang nodded and then he turned to Amon. "Remember our stakes. Stay under the radar and don't try anything foolishly heroic. Please. Do I have your word?"

"Of course," said Amon with a gruff pat on Wolfgang's shoulder. "When have I ever disappointed you?"

\* \* \*

Lieutenant colonel Alexander Kostas of the US Army

was on his honeymoon in Greece when the call came in.

"Hello."

"Yes Sir, I'm well, Sir. And you?"

"Thank you. Appreciate it."

"Oh, I see. Next week?"

"Alright Sir. Gotchya. I'll report in, shortly."

Alex was in the spacious honeymoon suite at their hotel in Athens, barely out of bed when the news hit him. Nearly twenty years in the military had put a real dampener on his personal life. It seems like yesterday he got down on his knee and asked the beautiful Irene to marry him. Yet, it had been over five years. How time flies in the life of a serviceman. He stood in front of the window and stared outside. A dreamy Greek dawn greeted his eyes. It soothed his heart a little.

"What is it, honey? Who called?" Irene's musical voice startled him momentarily.

He turned to face his wife who was looking up at him languidly, still in bed, leaning on her elbow. "Oh, nothing. It's just … work, babe." He smiled.

"Just work is what I'm most worried about," she said sitting up. "What did they want?"

"Hmm?" Alex was lost in thought as he looked up at her. She looked radiant. Her freshly tanned face gracefully outlined by wispy reddish-brown curls, wore an anxious expression.

"They want you back right away, don't they?"

"Not right away. They know I'm on vacation."

"When?"

"In a week."

"Did they say where they're sending you?"

"Look, honey …" He came over to sit down next to her and put his hand around her shoulder. "We knew this was going to happen when the war was announced, right?"

"Yeah … but … so soon." Irene sighed.

"I guess things are escalating fast," he explained without conviction.

*What's escalating exactly?* he wondered. Not entirely convinced that this war was well thought out. *Why attack Russia?* Somehow in Alex's head the evidence didn't add up.

"But, hey," he continued, squeezing his wife's hand affectionately, "let's not bother ourselves with that just yet. We have five days of honeymoon left. Let's make the most of it!"

"You're right," she concurred, hopping out of bed. "Carpe diem! I'm hitting the shower. The tour for Delphi leaves in an hour."

\* \* \*

They had walked through the ruins of Delphi all morning and Alex needed a smoke. Irene was standing in line for the ladies' room, so he decided to take a quick cigarette break. He waved at her and pointed in the direction of a small hillock, indicating that's where he was going to be. Irene nodded her approval.

Alex turned around and made his way a few feet up the hillock. There he found a large flat-topped rock that looked inviting. He sat down and lit a cigarette. Below him the crumbling pillars of the ancient temple of Apollo stood like Templars from a forgotten time.

"Got a smoke?" Someone asked from near his right shoulder. He turned around to find a bohemian-looking fellow standing right behind him, arms folded, smiling.

"Yeah, sure," said Alex, as he fished in his pocket for his

pack of Marlboro. "Need a light?"

"Please." The man sat down next to Alex, and lit his cigarette. Then he returned the lighter.

"Thanks."

The stranger leaned back on his arms and blew a smoke ring out of his mouth. "Here to consult the sybil before you head off to war, my friend?" he suddenly asked.

"What? How did you …?"

"Know you're headed to war?"

"Yeah."

"Not hard to tell, is it? The height, the physique, the US Army insignia on your hoodie." He winked.

"You're observant. But what sybil?"

"Aww, man! The Oracle of Delphi, that's who!"

Alex burst into laughter. "Funny!"

"I wasn't joking," said the man sitting up straight, face dead serious.

*What a nutcase!* thought Alex. "That's a myth, a legend," he said with a smile. "But if she were real, yeah sure, why not, would've asked her."

The man took a long drag of his cigarette and stayed silent for a couple of minutes. "I know what she'd say," he then declared abruptly.

"About what?" Alex quizzed, incredulous that he was still pursuing this hypothetical conversation.

"About the war. About its outcome. About the wrath of Gaia."

"The wrath of who, now?"

"Of Gaia, Mother Earth, Terra, the primordial Goddess whose seat you're here to visit!" he thundered.

"I don't get it," Alex confessed, deciding to humour his newfound companion.

"Delphi, is the seat of Gaia, is it not?"

"If you say so."

"Of course, I say so! The original deity behind the oracle of Delphi, do you know who that was?"

"Apollo?"

"Nay!" The stranger stood up and made a dramatic movement with his arms. "It was none other than Gaia, the Mother Goddess. The deity of the very earth we walk on!"

"I see. But why the wrath?"

"What a silly question. Why not? Have you not seen what mankind has done to Mother Earth? What we're continuing to do? Without mercy, without empathy, without respite?"

"Hmm. I see what you mean." Finally, the man was saying something Alex fundamentally agreed with. He did not support the practices that plundered and pillaged our environment and the creatures that inhabit this planet.

"And war ... only makes it much worse. The carnage, the destruction. The trees and forests, the people, the birds, the wildlife, the mountains, the rocks, nothing will be spared. Everything is Gaia. The Gaia hypothesis. The toxic fumes of our narcissism will burn a hole into our mother's bosom. A hole that cannot be repaired."

Alex nodded. "Hence the wrath," he murmured.

"Yes. If there's another Great War, Gaia's wrath will destroy the pest that is mankind. Once and for all."

"We don't need Gaia for that. Humanity is on track to destroy itself pretty soon, anyway." Alex laughed mirthlessly. He tossed his cigarette butt and stamped it out with his foot.

"But you don't get it."

"I don't?"

"No! Gaia's wrath is what's making us destroy each other. That's how divine forces work. They manifest through living beings."

"So, you're saying that Mother Earth is making us destroy each other for our sins?"

"Something like that. Hey, it was great chatting, but I gotta make a move here." He extended his hand and shook Alex's. He smiled, turned around and walked briskly away.

"The Gaia hypothesis," Alex whispered as he stood up. He'd have to look it up.

\* \* \*

Dr. Cobb blinked and opened his eyes. There was complete darkness.

*Have I gone blind?* He wondered.

He rubbed his eyes and squinted. Nope. Still nothing. He felt inebriated, disoriented and lost. His head buzzed.

"Is this a dream?" he whispered. A floral fragrance filled the air around him. A faint music seemed to play in the distance.

*Is this heaven?* "Am I dead?" he blurted out to his surroundings at large.

"No. You're not dead," replied a pleasing voice.

Dr. Cobb jolted and turned his head in the direction of the voice. It emanated from a shrouded figure a few feet to his right. There was an aura of bluish light around the figure that gave it an angelic appearance.

"Where … where am I?" he stammered.

"In our custody," replied the mysterious stranger.

A sinking feeling consumed him. *The Aifra—they have me!* "Where on earth—" he began.

"Lumania. Welcome to Lumania."

"Bugger!" he growled. "Where the hell's that?"

"You have what we seek," said the voice without

69

answering his question.

"No! I have nothing!" Dr. Cobb thought about Peter. He couldn't see him in the darkness. The shrouded figure started to move closer and as he advanced, Dr. Cobb's eyelids grew heavy. He wasn't sure if he was falling asleep or finally waking up. He struggled to remain conscious but failed.

# CHAPTER NINE

Zoya was standing over a shrine of some sort. Her father stood beside her wearing a navy blue down jacket, his face barely visible behind the hoodie and woollen scarf wrapped around his face. His dark eyelashes were coated with snow. Through the hood of his jacket Dr. Carter's face appeared at least twenty years younger. Beside him, a young woman knelt, cradling a bundled-up baby in her arms. She was rocking to and fro. She was sobbing.

"Mom!" Zoya yelled, but her mother did not hear her. She kept weeping and rocking as if in a trance.

"She's a still born, Celina … I … I am sorry … you *have* to accept it," Dr. Carter pleaded, placing his hand on his wife's shoulder.

"No … but no … she'll come back … they promised … at this shrine … they *promised*," she said between sobs.

"Look, there's no one here. Shrine's deserted. We have to go. Come on honey. It's getting cold." Dr. Carter put his arm around his wife and tried to lift her to her feet.

Outside, a storm howled. Flakes of flour-like dust rode in with the wind and melted into a puddle on the floor.

Celina wept on. The storm raged on. Suddenly, Zoya's throat felt constricted. She couldn't breathe. She was suffocating, flailing her limbs in desperation, sweating profusely. And then she awoke.

She threw down the comforter and sat up in her bed. She was in Wanda's house—in the little pink guest room adjacent to her library. In the past, she had learned that her strange dreams often bore a cryptic meaning or premonition, but not this one. This particular dream had bothered her frequently of late. Yet, she had no idea what it meant and didn't know who to ask. Maybe this dream was different. Not a message from the past or premonition but a fear, a fear of what lies ahead.

* * *

Wanda had left for London, leaving Nirmala in charge of the Novo Hekameses for a week, and the alone time had left her with mixed feelings about her role. Now at the end of an evening-session, on the seventh day of her solitude, Nirmala had a terrible headache. She went to the kitchen to make herself some strong coffee.

There was a knock on the front door.

"Coming," she answered as she emerged from the kitchen with her coffee. "Who is it?" she asked, expecting that one of the trainees had probably returned for something they left behind.

"It's me, Wolfgang," came the response.

"Oh, Dr. Müller … I mean Wolfgang," she stammered, opening the door. "How come you knocked? You have the keys, no?"

"I didn't want to walk in on you. I may be rough around the edges, but I'm still a gentleman." He smiled.

Nirmala cackled with laughter. "That you are, indeed," she said fondly. "So, to what do I owe this honour?"

"It has been a week since you've been on your own here. I wanted to see how things were going."

"Then your visit is perfectly timed. I was just … thinking … I mean—"

"I see," Wolfgang interrupted, sensing her hesitation. "Maybe we should chat, ya?"

"I'd like that."

"Have you seen ze garden?"

"A garden? There's a garden? I didn't know that."

"Ya, it's in the back. Out the kitchen door."

"Cool. Somehow, I thought that space belonged to the house behind us. Did you want to chat over there?"

"If you agree. The fresh air will help, I think."

"I agree. Let's go and see this garden of yours."

"Come." Wolfgang led the way through the kitchen to the open area at the back of the house. It was fairly spacious, lined with shady beech trees and intermittent hedges.

Wolfgang pointed to the southwest. "See that?" he asked.

"It looks like … an enclosed area."

"It's a small greenhouse. Let's go there."

They walked diagonally across from where they were and entered the little greenhouse that bordered the wall, separating this house from the neighbours.

"In here, we grow some herbs. Come, let me show you." Wolfgang gestured.

"What kind of herbs?"

"Medicinal. You know, for—"

"Heka."

"Yes."

"Nice. It looks like quite a selection," said Nirmala taking in all the plants around her.

"Yes, we have aloe here, some thyme and mint." Wolfgang pointed. "Several more on the other side. There's a sycamore tree outside. We also have juniper."

"Pretty much everything you need for Egyptian healing, huh?"

"Everything. Even the ostrich eggs and crocodile dung."

"The *what?*"

"Joking. Didn't Alejandro tell you that I'm a really funny guy?"

"Ha! Not really. He said that you were a 'grumpy pants'," Nirmala covered her mouth and giggled.

"He's just jealous," said Wolfgang shaking his head. "We don't just have Egyptian herbs here, there's also ginseng and Chinese medicinal plants. Some Ayurvedic ones too." Wolfgang indicated.

"Impressive collection. Who tends to these gardens?"

"Saburo. It's his pet project."

"Talking about the trainees. I was wondering when you arrived …"

"Wondering what? Let's sit down. There's a bench over there." Wolfgang gestured in its direction.

They walked over to the far end of the greenhouse where the floor was slightly inclined and a lone wooden bench stood at the top of the incline. From it, they had a 360-degree view of the arboretum.

"So, tell me. What about the students? What did you want to ask?" Wolfgang enquired as he sat down.

"It's just that … I don't know if I'm such a great teacher

for them."

"Why do you say that?"

"I don't know. I … just don't feel qualified."

"But you've had students before. Your research assistants. This should be nothing new, no?"

"Yes, but this is different. I'm new to the Hekameses, myself, and I'm not born with your abilities either … you know what I mean?"

"I do. I understand. But remember this, by not being a natural Hekameses, you're actually better suited than any of the others for this role. By being just like them, you can *connect* with them."

"I hardly know them though …"

"Aha! I see what the real problem is. Perhaps if you knew what drew me to these kids. What unique characteristic sets them apart from the average joe … would you like to know?"

"I think that'd help, yes."

Wolfgang stood up and faced Nirmala, focusing intently on her face. "Alright, who do we start with?"

"Hmmm … let's see. What about Xianbin? I find him hard to read."

"Good choice. Xianbin or Michael as they call him is quite an intriguing fellow …"

Wolfgang's voice trailed off. His frame faded away. And suddenly Nirmala found herself inside a busy shopping mall. It looked like a Walmart.

"Hello … hello … where am I? Nirmala screamed, but the words failed to materialize. She ran around the store frantically, pushing through throngs of people, but always ended up at the same place. With the same people. As if she was trapped on the set of a movie. Wolfgang was nowhere to be seen. She calmed herself and tried to focus on the scene playing out around her.

She was in the toys section of the store. Next to her, a young mother with dark flawless skin and large, innocent eyes, carried her toddler over her right hip. With her left arm she browsed through the teddy bear aisle. The toddler was leaning over and trying to gouge the eyes out of every stuffed toy she showed him. Nirmala giggled, inadvertently. There were about half a dozen other parents in that section, dragging their kids by their arms or pushing them along in strollers. Some of the kids were either trying to break free from their parents' grips or wriggling to get out of their strollers to go tinker with their favourite toys.

Over her left shoulder Nirmala could see the adjacent section that stocked what looked like more grown-up entertainment—cards, board games, Nintendos. A few young shoppers loitered in that area, occasionally stopping to check out some of the products.

Before Nirmala could fully take in the rest of the scene, there was a rattling sound and terrible screams issued from all around her. She crouched instinctively, realizing only seconds later that this reaction was completely unnecessary as a string of bullets surged through her mid-section without as much as causing a pinprick. She had no time to gather her bearings or analyze what just happened, because a masked man emerged from the shadows brandishing a raging AK47. He was shooting indiscriminately as the screams intensified and people ducked for cover.

Nirmala wanted to do something, but she wasn't a part of this scene. She was invisible, a mere apparition, a helpless witness. The man turned to face her, his eyes narrowed into slits, focussing on a spot next to her right shoulder. Nirmala turned to her right. Her eyes fell on the young mother she had seen before, her eyes wide with horror, her toddler screaming in her arms.

"Oh, no!" Nirmala panicked realizing what she was about to witness next. Powerless to act, she closed her eyes and screamed, hoping desperately for this scene to end. There was a loud thud in front of her, but the gunfire had stopped. She could hear the sound of a tussle and muted groans and grunts. She cautiously opened her eyes. The terrorist was sprawled on the floor, disarmed with a lean figure hunched over him, holding him down with his hands and knees. They were struggling. A couple of cops were rushing towards them.

"Great job. Great tackle. Stay where you are. We're coming. We got this," one of the cops growled, as he rushed forward.

Nirmala looked at the young man who seemed to have pounced on the terrorist from behind and ended this carnage. Their eyes met, but he did not see her.

"Xianbin!" Nirmala gasped.

Suddenly Nirmala's vision blurred, the scene faded away and when her eyes refocused, she was sitting on a wooden bench inside a garden, facing a grinning Dr. Müller.

"How … what just happened?" she stammered.

"It was a memory … my memory. I wanted you to see it. It was how I found Xianbin."

"So you just … I mean … transferred your memory? Like, to my brain?"

"Sort of."

"You can *do* that?"

"I'm a Hekameses!" Dr. Müller grinned.

"But Alejandro never—"

"I don't believe he has this ability. It's one of my strengths. Each one of us has—"

"A unique strength," Nirmala completed. "Yes, I've heard about that. Fascinating."

"Now tell me, what did you think? About Xianbin, that is."

"Heroic. Selfless. Willing to take a risk."

"For the sake of humanity, yes. Also, he can think on his feet. A rare skill these days."

"Very true. Lucky you were there to spot him that day."

"I wasn't."

"Oh?"

"I saw the footage on television. Recorded it and played it back multiple times. Committed the scene to memory, before I sought him out and approached him."

"I see. Is that why the vision was so clear?"

"Precisely." Wolfgang sat down on the bench next to Nirmala, and looked up at the sky. "It's getting late," he said. "Shall we continue tomorrow?"

"Good idea. I'm starving."

"Come, let's get some dinner then."

# CHAPTER TEN

Alejandro and Zoya were holed up in Dr. Faraday's elegant, well-stocked library poring over some ancient texts when Alejandro suddenly slammed his book shut and stood up in frustration.

"What's wrong?" Zoya asked.

"It's way too confusing," said Alejandro, throwing his hands up.

"What are you reading? Let me see." Zoya walked up to his desk and studied the title of the book he'd just discarded. "An interpretation of the Bha-ga-vat Gita?" she stammered. "Isn't that like the Hindu Bible? What are you looking for in there?"

"Well, the Gita is not just a Hindu scripture. It's kind of unique. Especially for us, since we're looking for the Kalki."

"Because of the Vishnu connection?"

"Right. The words in the Gita were supposedly spoken by Krishna, a previous incarnation of Vishnu …"

"So you were hoping he would've said something in there about finding his future avatar, the Kalki?"

"I suppose."

"And by the look on your face, it seems that he didn't." Zoya laughed.

"I mean, I don't know. I don't understand all of it. It's all metaphysical and symbolic stuff."

"Doesn't surprise me. Religious texts aren't *supposed* to be clearly understood, are they?" joked Zoya, still giggling.

"Apparently not." Alejandro smiled. "Hey, I have an idea. What time is it?"

"Umm … eleven thirty …"

"Not too early. Good. Let's call Dr. Sinha. He's probably awake." Alejandro whipped out his phone. Dialling the long-distance number, he then put his phone on speaker and placed it on the desk in front of them.

"Hello," the elderly Sanskrit scholar answered groggily.

"Oh, did I wake you Dr. Sinha? I'm so sorry," Alejandro apologized.

"No no, not at all. I am an early riser, and by God, it's already six! Tell me, how can I help you, Alejandro?"

"It's been a while since we spoke, but you know about our research and I think I need your help again."

"Why, of course. What would you like to know?"

"You know how we talked about the Kalki? The tenth avatar of Vishnu who's supposed to arrive in the Kali Yuga?"

"Yes, I remember."

"Okay. Now, I know you mentioned that we don't need to find the Kalki, because Kalki will find us … but hypothetically … let's say we were to go looking, where would you recommend that we start, Professor?"

"Hmm … that can be a very difficult question to answer, you see. Because God is essentially everywhere just as He is nowhere …"

*Here we go again*, thought Alejandro in amusement as Dr. Sinha drifted off into one of his trademarked rambles.

Zoya rolled her eyes and put her hand over her mouth to stifle a chuckle.

"… in the birds, the trees, the insects, in every living organism … in fact even in the—" Dr. Sinha babbled on.

"Yes, I understand," Alejandro, interrupted. "But this avatar of Vishnu, his *physical form on earth*, could we not meet him?"

"I suppose you could, if you were lucky and sufficiently pious."

"Where could we go to meet him? Assuming of course, he has already arrived on earth."

"If you ask me, I would start at one of the fabled dhams of Lord Vishnu."

"The dhams?"

"Exactly. Dhams, meaning abodes of Vishnu. It is said that there are four, each representing one of the four Yugas."

"I see … and, where are they?"

"The Char Dham or the four abodes of Vishnu were located at the four corners of ancient India, north, south, east and west such that the northern and southern dhams fell on the same longitude and the eastern and western ones were aligned with respect to their latitudes."

"Very interesting! But do they still exist? Can we

visit—"

"Why, of course! You already have. You visited Dwarka, did you not? The third of the four dhams."

"Oh, is Dwarka one of them? I didn't know that."

"Yes, the third."

"Why third? Like chronologically? Based on when they were built?"

"Yes, but more importantly, based on the Yuga in which they were established. Dwarka, as you know, being the kingdom of Lord Krishna, Vishnu's avatar in the Dwapara Yuga, was established in the third or—"

"The Dwapara Yuga," Alejandro completed. He scrunched his face and continued. "Does that mean … the first dham … is it from the Satya Yuga … and—"

"The second from the Treta Yuga, third Dwapara and fourth from Kali Yuga or modern times, yes, that is correct."

"Perfect. This is exactly the type of information I was looking for. Could you tell us where the other three dhams are?"

"Of course I can, and I *will*. The first dham, is Badrinath, dating back from the Satya Yuga and located in the north, the second is Rameswaram in the south, founded in the Treta Yuga by Lord Rama, an earlier incarnation of Lord Vishnu. In the west is Dwarka the third dham that you have already seen. The fourth and final dham is Puri in the east, and it corresponds to modern times or Kali Yuga."

"Maybe, that's where we should go looking then … Puri. What do you think?" Zoya asked softly.

"Possibly … but," Alejandro replied under his breath. "Thanks Dr. Sinha. Can I ask you one more question?" he asked a little louder.

"Certainly. Ask away!"

"Are all the remaining three dhams easily accessible? Any chance some of them could be … remote, for example?"

"I am not sure what you mean by remote, but modern India is mostly accessible, I would say. Sure, they are not in the middle of bustling metropolitan cities, but you could arrive there by public transit, if you wished to, yes."

"Hmmm … any deserts or forests to cross perhaps? No?"

"Not that I can think of …"

"Alright then, we still have enough to start with. Thanks again Dr. Sinha. We'll be in touch."

"Good day, my friend. Good day."

Alejandro hung up and turned to face Zoya who was staring into her phone. "So, what do you think? he asked.

"I think I have something here," Zoya replied without looking up.

"What is it?"

"Badrinath, the first dham, it's in the Himalayas. A rustic hill-station." Zoya paused. "It says here; 'Although the main temple site is accessible via roads and on foot, the area is home to seven other holy shrines of Lord Vishnu, known together as the Sapta Badri. The smaller temples of the Sapta Badri are located in remote villages where pilgrims have to trek for several kilometers or travel on horseback through mountainous terrain,'" she added, reading aloud from her phone.

"Bingo!" Alejandro exclaimed, slapping the desk in front of him.

"Exactly."

* * *

"Curious object," said Wanda Faraday, taking the ancient artefact from Chris's outstretched hand. "Where did you find it?"

"In Dr. Cobb's office, next door. The day before you arrived."

"Had it always been there?"

"Don't know. I never noticed. So? What do you think? Is it in hieroglyph?"

"What do *you* think?" Wanda smiled.

"I dunno. You're the hieroglyph expert!"

"Ha! I wouldn't call myself an expert. Now, where did I put my glasses?" Wanda searched her desk. "Ah, here it is. I also need ..." She fumbled in her drawer and pulled out a large magnifying glass, "this. Let's look at that hourglass again, shall we?" she muttered, training her magnifying glass on the curio.

At the bottom of the pocket-sized hourglass, etched into the metallic base, were four tiny symbols. Wanda studied them with keen attention for several minutes, and then she puckered her face and sat up.

"So? What do you think? Is it Egyptian?"

"Far from it. It isn't a hieroglyph at all. Not one I recognize that is."

"Maybe it's nothing then. Just a design."

"I would be resigned to believe the same had it not been for …" Wanda trailed off.

"Had it not been for what?"

"Well, the first symbol in particular bears a striking resemblance to another obscure ancient language. Or so it appears." Wanda stood up and walked over to a bookshelf situated next to the window at the back of the room. She stood on tiptoe to browse through a few yellowing tomes on the top shelf, and then locating what she was looking for, she pulled it out of the stack.

"Yes, here it is … I remember now. I remember what it looks like. The Harappan script from the Indian Indus Valley Civilization."

"Really? Isn't that like a five-thousand-year-old civilization?"

"It is. Just as old as the Egyptians."

"Hmm. So what does it say then?"

"I don't know." Wanda walked over to her desk and set the book down in front of her. "This language, if it is at all a language, hasn't been deciphered yet."

"That's too bad. I wonder how Dr. Cobb found such an ancient Indian artefact. Had he ever been to India?"

"I don't know. If he had, he never mentioned it. Mind you though, the similarity in the script does not necessarily mean that this object is actually from India. It could be from somewhere else entirely. Some other civilization even. The resemblance could in fact, be accidental."

"Yes, of course. I get that. Still, it's an odd thing for Dr. Cobb to have had lying on his shelf."

"I agree."

"If it really is that old though, it doesn't surprise me that it no longer works," Chis concluded.

"Doesn't work, you say? What makes you think that? Do you know what function it was designed to serve?"

"Pretty obvious. It's a clock, isn't it? Sand flows and you measure time. But look, it's clogged." Chris picked up the hourglass and shook it to demonstrate.

"Aha! I thought you'd say that, my dear. But I urge you to look more closely. Here, you can use this." Wanda handed him her magnifying glass, and sat down behind her desk.

"What do you want me to see?"

"Look into the glass, young man. Look at the sand."

Chris gave her a puzzled look before placing the hourglass in the palm of his hand and examining the sand inside. "Oh!" he exclaimed. Setting the hourglass down on the desk. "The sand around the constriction … it's … it's suspended. How?"

Wanda shrugged. "Could be any of several possibilities. Some obscure ancient magic."

"Or science," whispered Chris. "Some sort of electrostatic levitation."

"Or acoustic even," Wanda added.

"That would be a feat, though. To sustain a standing wave of sound inside a less than ideal medium for God knows how long …"

"There are many things we don't yet understand."

"Truly."

"What do you plan on doing with the object?

"I'd like to run some tests."

"Alright, but keep it safe."

"Of course."

# CHAPTER ELEVEN

A young man in a dark brown hooded jacket waved as a four-seater Cessna 182 Skylane landed about a hundred feet in front of him in the picturesque mountain resort of Arshan in southern Siberia. He ran towards the plane as two passengers appeared to disembark. It was a chilly afternoon, just before sunset with the magnificent snowy peaks of the Sayan mountains decorating the horizon.

The man approached the passengers and lowered his hood. "Welcome, welcome. So glad to meet you. I am Nikolai," he said, smiling and extending his hand.

"Ah, Nikolai. Lovely to meet you too. I'm Chris and this is Amon—"

"Your wildlife photographer. Yes, we've been expecting you," Nikolai interrupted, leaning forward to shake Amon's hand. "Come, let's get you inside. You must be cold."

"Brr … I'm freezing," agreed Amon, rubbing his hands together.

"I'm sure. Winter is coming. It's a horrible time to visit these parts of the world. Shall we go?" Nikolai gestured with his hands, indicating the way.

"Yes, please. It's been a long day." Chris smiled as he followed their host. "Our permits took way too long to come in. We applied in the summer."

"I heard. The war is holding everything up, sadly." He sighed. "But the ceasefire was a sign of hope."

"For now," Amon grunted. "We'll see if it lasts. Negotiations aren't looking good."

"We're keeping our fingers crossed over here," said Nikolai. "We don't need this to escalate … for ourselves and for the wildlife. Funding is already drying out. Imagine, what'd happen if the war got worse."

"I agree," said Chris. "We're lucky to have gotten our permits at all, this time."

"Almost there. We're going to that red building." Nikolai pointed. "It's the only inn that's open, with the drop in tourism."

"Do you get a whole lot of tourists here on most years?" Amon asked, scanning his surroundings. The streets of the small town were all but deserted with a bare modicum of houses that seemed to be occupied.

"Not year-round. But in the summer, we get a handful. Enough to keep the local businesses alive. The spas draw most of the business but the spill over to the other hotels and inns is decent."

"Is your team here at the inn?" Chris asked.

"No. They're going to meet us in Tuva tomorrow. But I'll be staying here tonight. Ah, I see the innkeeper at the door. Must be waiting for us." Nikolai jogged up to the front of the inn and spoke to the man at the door.

"Come on in. Make yourself at home," he then said holding the door open. "Vasily doesn't speak English," he added, patting the innkeeper on his shoulder.

Chris entered first, followed by Amon. The inn was designed like a log cabin with a roaring fireplace inside. There was a bar and a restaurant around the fire and a tiny reception desk right next to the door. The desk and restaurant were completely empty at the moment. A lone employee could be seen behind the bar, but he disappeared quickly into what looked like the kitchen area in the back.

"Cozy little place," said Chris smiling.

"It is, isn't it?" agreed Nikolai. He picked up two envelopes from the reception desk and handed one to Chris. "Here's your key. Your room is just up the stairs. Vasily is getting dinner ready. Are you hungry?"

"Starving," said Amon.

"I'm sure. Shall we eat in an hour then?"

"Sounds good to me," said Chris. Amon nodded in agreement.

"Perfect. I'll meet you here in an hour."

\* \* \*

Chris and Amon arrived at the inn's restaurant in about an hour just as planned and found Nikolai seated at a table for four, sipping a drink. The table had been set with plates and cutlery and a bread basket at it's center, that filled the room with the delicious aroma of freshly baked bread.

"Mmm … the bread smells great," said Amon as he took a seat across from their host.

"Have you been waiting long?" asked Chris, settling himself next to his friend.

"No, not long. About fifteen minutes. Would you like a drink?"

"That would be great," said Amon with a huge grin. "I need something strong. What do they have?" He searched for a menu.

"Vasily doesn't have any menus, I'm afraid," said Nikolai pre-emptively. "He usually serves chef's special meals. Traditional Siberian fare with house wines, vodka and other choices of liquor." He waved at the waiter. "Do you want to try the wine?"

"No. Not tonight. I need something stronger. Do they have whiskey?" Amon asked.

Nikolai spoke to the waiter in Russian and nodded in Amon's direction. "Whiskey for you. Straight?"

"Please."

"And for Chris?"

"I'll try the house wine, thanks."

The waiter took their orders and left for the kitchen. Nikolai took a sip of his drink and rubbed his eyes. "I'm tired," he said, smiling.

"Did you arrive today?" Chris asked.

"Yes, this afternoon. It's a long trip from the wildlife reserve. You'll see tomorrow."

"When do you want to leave tomorrow?"

"No hurry. You've had a long trip from Moscow. We can leave by noon. Is that okay?"

"That should be fine," said Chris.

The waiter returned with their drinks and a big plate of appetizers.

"Wow, that's a lot of food," said Amon, his eyes gleaming.

"A Siberian sampler plate for the table. It's a signature item at this inn."

"Sweet," said Chris as the scent from the assorted delicacies made his stomach grumble. "So what's what? You have to tell us. We're not that familiar with Siberian cuisine."

"Ah, of course. Let's see what we have here ... some smoked Baikal omul, a local fish, steamed pelmeni dumplings with meat filling, fish rolls or what we call, gruzinchiki and I believe this is a sampling of traditionally cooked venison."

"What are we waiting for then ... cheers!" said Amon, raising his glass and proceeding to fill his plate with some appetizers.

For a few minutes, the ravenous company ate in silence. The waiter brought in the main course. The dining area immediately filled with the smoky aroma of freshly roasted game meat, marinated with fresh taiga herbs, garlic and fern, garnished with a homemade cowberry sauce and served with a side of broiled potatoes.

Finally, Nikolai looked up from his plate and dabbing his lips with his napkin, smiled a satisfied smile.

"Boy, was I hungry," he said.

"Weren't we all," Chris agreed.

"We'd be lucky to eat this good starting tomorrow," Amon chimed in, rubbing his belly.

"And luckier still if we don't get eaten," Chris joked. "Speaking of which, have there been any more sightings since we last spoke?" he asked Nikolai.

"Unfortunately, no. Big cat sightings are so extremely rare that I'm surprised we saw that many to begin with."

"I agree, and that's why we're here. Snow leopards are already near-extinct, and so many of them in one place … I still can't wrap my head around it," Chris mused.

"We are … all of us over here … we're very excited about your technology. If we can track these animals … using their brain waves … I mean … it'd be such a great tool!" Nikolai said with visible excitement.

"I'm glad you feel that way. If you think we can help, we'd be honoured to contribute to your efforts to conserve these gorgeous creatures."

"Oh absolutely. I think you can do wonders. It's non-invasive you say, your procedure?"

"Yes, completely safe, non-invasive. We've had great results in the lab with rhesus monkeys."

"Even better. The last thing we need, is to experiment on them with harmful technology. Irkutsk University would never approve that."

"I'm no scientist," Amon chimed in, "but I know that an injured tiger is the worst kind."

"You bet!" agreed Nikolai. "Although, injured or not, several months in the Sayan, tracking these beasts could be extremely dangerous. You are equipped for the journey, I hope?"

"Yes, yes. I think we should be okay. We have our tranquilizer guns and everything we need. My friend Amon here, is a man of the wilderness, a lifelong tour guide." Chris turned his head and smiled at his companion.

"Good. I'm glad you came prepared. We were surprised that your team was so small. You must be very brave," said Nikolai admiringly.

"Ha! Thanks, for the compliment. It's less about bravery and more about the success of our mission, I suppose," Chris explained with humility.

"Yes, exactly. A big cat would never venture near a large group of people," Amon added.

"There is truth in that. Anyway, I'm sure you must be tired. I don't want to hold you up. Should we call it a night?" asked Nikolai.

"Probably a good idea," said Chris. Amon nodded in agreement.

They summoned the waiter and settled their bill, made some chit chat and then went up to their rooms to rest.

# CHAPTER TWELVE

It was almost midnight, but the Indira Gandhi International Airport in New Delhi was busier than usual. Pieces of luggage of various sizes and shapes were strewn all over the floor with their tired owners huddled around them—some seated on top of suitcases, some curled up on the floor, and yet others fast asleep and almost falling off the chairs in the waiting area. Throngs of passengers gathered around the TV monitors displaying flight arrival and departure information. Delayed. Cancelled. Delayed. Cancelled. The bright red announcements dotted the screens everywhere, painting a grim picture.

Zoya reached into a brown paper bag and pulled out a samosa she'd just bought. "Do you think we're wasting our time?" she asked, biting into her samosa.

"Say, what?" asked Alejandro startled. He was reclining in the seat next to her and the sudden question surprised him. He sat up and rubbed his face with his hands. "For sure," he said. "I mean, look at this mess. If we'd taken the train, we'd be halfway there by now."

"Dr. Müller warned us this might happen. The fog is horrible this time of the year. Taking the train would've been super hard though … we don't speak local languages. But that wasn't what I was asking, really."

"No?"

"Nope. I meant about … you know … our mission. The war, the Aifra and our involvement in all of this. I mean, do we really need to play a part?"

"Ah! You want to know the answer to life, the universe and everything? Let me think … let me think … I believe that answer is 42." Alejandro pretended to count on his fingers. "Yep. It's 42. Any more questions?" He deadpanned.

"Cut it out, Alejandro. I think you're a funny guy, I do, I swear. But I'm serious, this time," she protested, smacking him playfully on the knee.

"I see. Well then." Alejandro sat up straight and looked at her with a serious expression. "Do we have any more of those salted crackers?" he asked. "I can't think on an empty stomach."

"Think so, yeah." Zoya searched inside the bag of snacks they'd bought at the airport. "Here you go."

"Back to your question," said Alejandro plopping a couple of the bite-sized crackers into his mouth. "Are we wasting our time? Well … do you want the practical answer or the philosophical one?"

"I'm thinking, practical one, but let's hear the philosophical one first."

"As you wish. Look, my theory is this," he stopped to finish chewing, "nothing in life ever seems to go as planned, does it?"

"Guess not."

"We think we know the things we want from life, what our goals are, how we're going to reach them, et cetera, et cetera, et cetera. We always like to believe that we're in the driver's seat here. That things will happen based on our actions. Action and reaction, action and reaction and so on. But it's never like that."

"I agree. But what's your point then? Be fatalistic?"

"No. I don't want to go into a discussion about fate. I have my own issues with fatalism. What I meant is, instead of thinking that *we* are driving our lives, why not let our lives drive *us*? You see what I mean? It's different from fatalism. It's going with the flow. Go where life takes you."

"Like a self-driving car?"

"Hey! Look at you making jokes!"

"I must be spending too much time with you. Your sense of humour is rubbing off." Zoya giggled.

"Nah, I think you're a natural." Alejandro winked. "Jokes aside, I'd never trust one of those automatic cars. No way, man! But you see my point, right?"

"Yeah, I suppose. But it still doesn't answer my question. What if going with the flow is still a waste of time?"

"Okay, then let me ask you this: what if you did everything according to your own plan? You went to college, studied hard, graduated, you got a job, you got married. Just as you had imagined since you were a child. And then, one day, something tragic happens, that changes everything. You lose your career, you lose your limbs or you lose the love of your life." Alejandro paused. "Everything you did, leading up to that moment, suddenly feels like a waste of time then, doesn't it?" he added, lowering his voice to a hoarse whisper. He leaned forward with his elbows on his knees and hung his head between his hands.

Zoya became silent. "Is that what happened to you?" she asked gently after a couple of minutes. She turned to him, a softness in her eyes.

"Yes, kind of. I thought I knew what I was doing. I was young and arrogant and in full control."

"Arrogant? I could never see you as arrogant. Confident, for sure. A little rash; most definitely! But arrogant? Nope."

"Ha! Well, maybe. But I was certainly a little overconfident. Had my career and life all planned out. Got my degree and my job and the girl of my dreams. What could go wrong, right?"

"Right. Is that when you found out you were a child of Heka?"

"About a year after I got married, Wolfgang hunted me down. Boy, was I shocked!"

"How did you react?"

"Didn't want to have anything to do with them, of course. I mean, what the heck? 'You can't just barge into my life and interrupt everything?' I remember saying to him."

"Haha! Sounds almost exactly like my reaction."

"I know. That's why Wanda wanted me to watch over you, I suppose. She saw similarities."

"I bet. I can be rash too, they say," said Zoya, flicking him a coy grin.

"We know." Alejandro smiled.

"So what changed your mind, then?"

"Changed my mind?"

"You know, about joining the Hekameses?"

"Oh that! Well, I didn't really have any choice."

"How come?"

"The moment Wolfgang left for Germany, the threats began."

"Threats?" Zoya gasped. "Like from Aifra?"

"Yep. Letters. Like the ones you received and Chris intercepted."

"That's uncanny. How do they know? Ohhhh ... could it be ... you think ..." Zoya fell silent.

"A traitor in our midst? I've thought about that," Alejandro confessed.

"Dr. Cobb, you think?" Zoya inquired sheepishly.

"It may not be that simple," Alejandro mused.

"Care to explain?"

"I'd rather not. All I have are theories and I don't want to bias your judgement."

"Hmm. Alright then. Tell me what happened after that. Wait, let me guess, you asked the Hekameses about the letters and they told you to join them?"

"Something like that. It was also, Maria."

"Maria?"

"My wife. She encouraged me to join. She thought it is was my destiny."

"And was it? Is it?"

"Like I said, I'm not a fatalist. But what I've learned is that, if you plan your life a certain way and things blow up, in the end you tend to blame yourself. On the other hand, if you go with the flow, like flotsam … riding the waves, then whatever happens, you face it instead of blaming yourself for ending up in that spot to begin with."

"Hmm. You have a point."

"If you're not the driver but the passenger then you're no longer responsible for guiding the ship. You can sit back and enjoy the ride."

"Yep, you were right. That got very philosophical very quickly." Zoya laughed.

"But tell me, after you joined the Hekameses, didn't you get upset when they couldn't protect, your wi … Maria?"

Alejandro shook his head. "No, her death … her murder … it changed my life forever. The only person I blamed then was *myself. I was the one who was supposed to protect her.* She was *my* responsibility. You don't see? Who were the Hekameses? I'd hardly known them then. I didn't expect them to take on what was essentially *my* responsibility."

"So, in your own words, you weren't flotsam yet."

"You catch on quick!"

"Ha! Did you want to avenge her death?"

"Always."

"Still?"

"Of course."

"I get it now. You chose this path to avenge what happened to you …"

"Initially, yes. At first, I clung on to the Hekameses even more, knowing that they were probably the only ones who could help me get to the bottom of what happened. But then—"

"You became flotsam."

"Exactly. I let my life choose my next course of action. Didn't it start the same way for you too? With the disappearance of your friend? Your roommate?"

"I guess it did, yeah." She became pensive. "But now … I've found her. Now what?"

"That is where you have to make a decision. Do you want to be the driver or the passenger?"

"If that was a straightforward question, I'd say passenger. I hate driving." Zoya laughed. "But first, tell me what's your practical answer. Do you think we're wasting our time chasing the Aifra and all of the world's problems?"

"It depends on what you mean by wasting time."

"I mean, what if this isn't our problem to solve?"

"Ah! Well, whether or not we solve this problem, now that we're marked, the Aifra will never leave us or our loved ones alone. Even if we don't want anything to do with them."

"Yeah, Chris told me. I wonder why that is …"

"That's what we're trying to find out! At least that's one of the things."

"True that. Hey, you think I should tell my parents about us?"

"About the Hekameses?"

"Yeah. My mom is really intuitive. I think she already senses something."

"Oh, yeah? Maybe she's a Hekameses as well." Alejandro grinned. "To answer your question, no. My recommendation is, no. And I think everyone else would agree. It'd put them and all of us at further risk."

"You're right. We don't want that. I just hate keeping secrets from my mom."

"One day, maybe, you don't have to. Remember ... flotsam? Just go with the flow." Alejandro reached over and squeezed Zoya's shoulder. "If we're gonna stay here all night, I need some coffee," he said, standing up and stretching his legs. "Want some?"

"Yes, please." Zoya smiled.

# CHAPTER THIRTEEN

It was a chilly evening in late November, a week after the ceasefire with Russia, when a grey, weather-worn, mud-caked jeep ground to a halt at a military checkpoint on the Ukrainian side of the Russia-Ukraine border. A tall, gruff man in a hooded jacket emerged lugging a travel backpack on his broad shoulders. His eyes were narrowed into slits and his well trimmed French-cut beard was speckled with snow.

The checkpoint was scantily staffed because the border situation had relaxed a little since the ceasefire. The two uniformed men manning it, were busy sharing anecdotes from their various misadventures, when the tall stranger approached their post.

"Passport," said the shorter guard on the left, extending his hand.

The stranger obliged.

"You are German?" the guard asked, raising an eyebrow. "What business you have here?"

"I'm with the press," the German replied.

"You have papers?"

"Of course." The traveller unzipped the outer pocket of his backpack and removed a Manila folder. "Here." He presented his papers to the guard.

The guard scrutinized the documents for a couple of minutes, alternating between relaxing and tensing his facial muscles.

"You write a *book*?" he finally asked, an incredulous look in his eyes.

"Yes, Sir. And the lieutenant is aware of my visit as you can see from the correspondence over here," the German confirmed, indicating the correspondence in question.

"Wait here." The guard disappeared to the back of the checkpoint and appeared to make a call. He returned in about five minutes with a rubber stamp the size of his fist, and proceeded to emboss the documents in front of him. Once stamped, he returned the passport and Manila folder to their owner. Then he whispered something to his companion and exited the kiosk. He mounted a motorcycle parked out front but he did not ride away.

The other guard came out of the kiosk shortly, carrying a hand-held metal detector.

"I need to check your luggage," he said.

"Sure." The traveller volunteered his backpack. The guard ran the metal detector over it and conducted a cursory check inside all the pockets. "Any thing else? In the car?" he asked when he was done.

"Nope. That's all I have."

"Okay." He gave his companion on the motorcycle a thumbs-up. "Get in your car and follow him," he said, gruffly. "He will take you to the camp."

"Thank you," said the German, bowing slightly.

The jeep followed the motorcycle along a bumpy unpaved path through the eerie darkness of war-battered country. Along the path were low hedges alternating with barren patches of drying foliage. The motorcycle turned a corner and came to a halt. The jeep pulled up behind it. In front was an enclosed military encampment with a handful of soldiers in US military uniform, lounging near the entrance.

The guard walked up to the jeep and spoke to the driver.

"We are here. Battalion 11. Park your car and follow me."

The German did as he was told. Inside were tents of various sizes and shapes. A campfire roared behind a rocky ledge where half a dozen drunken young men were singing, "Bye Bye Miss American Pie", with raucous tuneless enthusiasm.

Soon they arrived at a clearing with a cluster of semi-permanent, portable military sheds ranging in design from cubic single-storied buildings to gigantic semicircular structures, large enough to serve as airplane hangers.

The guard walked over to a small cubical shed made of military-grade metal and walked up a couple steps to the front. He rapped on the door and went in before anyone could respond and gestured for the German to follow. A young military official walked up to them and nodded at the guard and then he turned to the German.

"Mr. Schmidt?" he asked, scanning the visitor up and down with his eyes.

"Yes. Otto Schmidt," replied Otto, extending his hand for a handshake.

The soldier nodded curtly and shook Otto's hand. "Come. The lieutenant is waiting."

Schmidt followed the young man into an office towards the back of the building. The soldier knocked.

"Come, in," said a deep voice. They entered the fairly small, but well organized office of the battalion commander and he motioned for them to take a seat.

"I'll be outside, Sir, if you need me," said the soldier escorting Otto as he bowed and took off. Otto walked over to the lieutenant colonel's desk and took a seat.

"Welcome, Mr. Schmidt, is it?" said the officer with a smile.

"Otto Schmidt. Nice to meet you Lieutenant Colonel Kostas." They shook hands.

"Same," replied Colonel Kostas. "Call me Alex."

"Sure. You have read my letter of intent, Alex?"

"I have. And I'm intrigued by your proposition."

"How so?"

"We don't get a lot of war biographers following us around on every mission, you see. So, I'm a little surprised. You're a journalist. We get journalists. But..." Alex furrowed his forehead and leaned forward. "My question is, why write a book?"

"Not sure I understand your question. People write books about wars all the time, don't they?"

"Sure. Great wars, game changing wars with historic leaders and ... ohhh," Alex's eyes lit up. "You're not thinking that this could end up becoming a much larger war, are you?"

Otto shrugged. "Perhaps. But what do I know? I'm a mere journalist. It's not my place to understand the politics of war. It's yours."

"Isn't mine either, honestly. Figuring out politics is not our job. We execute strategy. We follow orders. In fact, I think some journalists understand world politics a great deal better than even the politicians."

"You seem very skeptical about the book I proposed to write, yet you did not object to my being here. Why?" asked Otto, crossing his arms and becoming serious.

"Maybe I share you fear."

"Do you, indeed? I'd like to hear more about that."

"And that's why you're here. But not today. In small doses," said Alex, as he stood up. "For now, let me get someone to show you to your accommodations."

\* \* \*

Chris and Amon finished setting up their tent behind a rocky crag at the foothills of the Sayan mountains and lumbered back with most of their luggage from the research truck. Nikolai and a couple of other researchers from the reserve had driven them up to this spot earlier in the day and now they helped with stocking their tent with supplies.

"I think this is the last of the rations," said Nikolai, plunking a fully-loaded rucksack inside the tent next to some equipment.

"Thanks, man. I appreciate the help." Chris beamed.

"Hey, no trouble. Starting tomorrow, you're on your own. I don't envy you one bit."

"How encouraging!" Amon quipped, a sarcastic grin dancing on his lips.

"Ha! I'm sure you'll be alright. You guys look totally up for the task. If you need us though, we can drive up in half a day."

Chris wasn't paying attention to this conversation. Kneeling next to his equipment kit, he was busy inspecting its contents.

"Sensors, check. Battery, check. Cables, check," he mumbled.

"What's with the check, check, check? You have a check in there or something?" Amon guffawed as he walked over.

"Ha! I wish. Making sure we have everything," Chris replied, chuckling.

"Ohhh! Is that it? The gear?" Nikolai asked. He was bent over the pieces of equipment Chris had removed from his bag.

"Yep. This is it. This is how the magic happens."

Nikolai picked up a handheld device the size of a smart phone and inspected it eagerly. "What does this do?"

"Oh! That's the detector I was talking about earlier. It's loaded with software that can recognize snow leopard brain patterns and let you know if there's one nearby ... like within a certain radius."

"Brilliant! And what radius is that ... ten, fifteen kilometers?"

"More. They run fast, these guys. So we've optimized the sensors for a maximum range of about thirty kilometers with a plus or minus five percent error."

"Nice. So it gives a signal? When it spots one?"

"Yeah, the light over here flashes red and an alarm goes off." Chris pointed out the light at the center of the box.

"Have you been able to test them, though?"

"Yep. We tested them at a couple of zoos. Can't say it's full proof, but what research ever is, right?"

"Right." Nikolai was sitting cross-legged on the tent floor, scanning the scattered equipment with the eagerness of a toddler at Legoland. "But … I have a question."

"Sure."

"How do you know it's picking up the right brainwaves? What if it's another animal or a human even?"

"Great point," said Chris. "We've accounted for that, of course. The AI was trained to match the waveforms to an existing database of signals captured from other snow leopards. When a mismatch occurs, that waveform is filtered out. It's pretty accurate, actually."

"Okay, I didn't understand any of that," said Amon, throwing up his arms in exasperation. "So, it can find the puma or not?"

Chris and Nikolai chortled. "Leopard not puma," Nikolai clarified.

"Yes, it can," said Chris. "Here let me show you." He switched the device on. The blue power light flared up. The anticipation in the room became palpable. They waited a couple of minutes, but no sound emerged.

"Nope. None, in the neighbourhood right now, I'm afraid," Chris said finally, putting the gadget down.

"I don't know if I should be happy or sad," Amon confessed.

"Ha! I'm a bit of both," said Nikolai, as he picked up a sort of headset made of a wire mesh and embedded with what looked like antennas and sensors. "What is this headgear over here? It looks like … something out of a science-fiction movie."

"Ah that! That's the crown jewel," Chris gloated.

"He means literally. Because you wear it like a helmet," Amon deadpanned.

"Quite right," Chris continued. "It helps us hone in on the animal once it's within the thirty-kilometer radius."

"Does it give you the exact coordinates?" Nikolai asked.

"Almost."

"Wow! Can I try it?"

"Of course!" Chris helped Nikolai get into the helmet and strapped it with a leather belt under his chin.

"Cool. Let me turn it on," said Chris as he pushed a tiny button behind the ear area. The helmet made a clicking sound and switched on.

"What am I supposed to see?" asked Nikolai.

"Nothing. It announces the locations of the animals and where exactly they are. But it won't work now. There aren't any nearby, remember?"

"Oh, right. I forgot. Fun toy, though. Would've been cool to see it in action." Nikolai removed the headset and stood up, dusting his pants. "Are you hungry?" he asked.

"You bet," said Chris.

"Good. I'll warm up some stew inside the van and be right back."

"Stew would be nice," said Amon, rubbing his belly after Nikolai had left. "By the way, Chris …"

"Yeah?"

"I thought that helmet only worked for you."

"It does. But we couldn't tell him that."

"Right. He doesn't know about your abilities."

"Yeah, and we'd better keep it that way."

"I agree. What happens when you use the helmet, Chris? You really hear a sound?"

"No. I see a vision … of the creatures in the vicinity. Just like when I'm on a telephone tower. Wolfgang and I tried to replicate that situation with the helmet … with the strategically placed RF antennas et cetera."

"Well, I hope it works," said Amon.

"Me too."

Before Chris could say anything more, Nikolai appeared at the tent entrance carrying two steaming bowls of soup. His two colleagues were with him, each carrying similar bowls.

"Wow, that smells really good! What is it, guys?" Chris asked.

"Siberian borscht. My girlfriend made it," said Nikolai, turning his head to smile at the tall lady next to him.

"Probably our last hot meal for a little while," said Amon.

They gathered around in a circle and dug into their meals making loud slurping sounds as they savoured the tasty mouthfuls.

"Are you leaving right after lunch?" Chris asked between sips.

"That's the plan," said Nikolai. "We want to make it back before it gets dark. These roads are dangerous."

"I agree. Drive safe."

"Thanks. You have the two-way radios. Don't hesitate to call us if you sense trouble."

"Or if there's a sighting."

"Of course. My advice is, if you want to go deeper into the mountains, then do so in increments. It's a lot of uncharted territory out there. We don't want you to get lost."

"We'll be cautious. We have the maps," said Chris.

"And a compass," Amon added. His mind floated wistfully to his falcon, Wassem—his trusted guide—who he had left behind in Egypt with his housekeeper, Abu.

"Yes, you'll need that," Nikolai agreed. "Alright then, all the best! We should probably head back," he added, standing up. They shook each other's hands.

From outside their tent, Chris and Amon watched the party board their van and drive off down a narrow mountainous trail until they became a mere speck against the dimming horizon.

When the van could no longer be seen, Amon let out a deep sigh.

"Now it all begins," he said.

# CHAPTER FOURTEEN

Zoya and Alejandro descended onto the tarmac of the Jolly Grant Airport in Rishikesh beset on all directions by panoramic views of the Himalayan foothills. Zoya let out a mild gasp. The fresh mountain air and the cool serenity of the surroundings was a welcome relief from the stuffy, overcrowded confinement of the Delhi airport where they were holed up for the last couple of days.

The moderate-sized terminal wasn't terribly busy that day. In about half an hour they had collected their luggage and made their way out of the airport. Once outside, Alejandro scanned the crowds expectantly, hoping to spot a placard with their names written on it.

"I don't see anyone," he said.

"Did Wolfgang say the driver would have a sign?" Zoya asked.

"I couldn't reach him this morning, but that's what he'd said before. Wait here with our bags, will you? I'll check the taxi stand."

"Sure."

Alejandro dropped his backpack next to Zoya and dashed off towards his right. Zoya was tired. Her whole body ached from the lack of sleep and travel-fatigue. She set her backpack down next to Alejandro's and collapsed on top of it.

There were about half a dozen travellers waiting in line at the taxi stand. Another ten to fifteen folks were near the airport entrance, either arriving or departing passengers, or their kin. A couple of security guards were at the door. Other than that, Zoya could see some locals. Some of them were hawking stuff, snacks, maps and a variety of touristic paraphernalia. Others were touting their tour packages or rides from the airport. Seated on a discarded packing crate, close to the taxi-terminal, was a bearded man in a saffron robe with long braided hair tied on top of his head in a conical top-knot. He had his back turned to Zoya and didn't seem to be in a hurry to be going anywhere.

Alejandro returned in under ten minutes looking exhausted.

"Nope. Can't find him anywhere," he said, breathlessly.

"Did you try calling Dr. Müller?"

"Still can't reach him. Which is unusual ..." Alejandro cupped his chin and frowned.

"You think something's wrong?" Zoya asked, worried.

"Nah! It's probably nothing."

"Our delay probably threw everyone off."

"Right."

"So? What do we do now?"

"We could stick with the plan and head to Badrinath on our own. There's a bunch of guys offering chauffeured transport over there." Alejandro pointed. "Or …"

"Wait for Dr. Müller?"

"Yeah. I mean, not here of course. The city's center isn't far. We could take a cab there and check in at a hotel until we get news from Wolfgang."

Zoya opened her mouth to respond but before she could say anything, she heard a voice—loud and clear in her head—just like the first time she met Chris.

"THIS WAY," the voice said. It was emanating from the man in the saffron robe with his back still turned towards them.

"I …" said Zoya when she heard it again. This time echoing inside her head like a church choir.

"THIS WAY!" the strange voice thundered.

"What is it?" Alejandro asked, noticing Zoya's puzzled expression.

Zoya motioned for Alejandro to lower his head, and then she whispered into his ear. "You see that guy over there. Dressed like a monk or something?"

"Yeah. He's a sadhu," said Alejandro, recollecting his trip to Dwarka. "What about him?"

"I think he's trying to tell us something …"

"Are you sure?"

"Positive."

"Let's go ask him then." They picked up their bags and walked up to the man in question as quickly as they could.

"Hello … er … Babaji," said Alejandro, tentatively. "Were you saying something?"

The man didn't respond. Didn't even look at them, for that matter. He kept staring into the distance—his gaze focussed on nothing in particular.

"Maybe he doesn't understand English," said Zoya, softly.

"Maybe."

"Need car? For travel?" a greasy-looking man asked from behind.

"No, we're alright," Alejandro turned to say. He then nudged Zoya lightly in the arm and motioned for them to leave. They had barely turned around when the saffron clad sadhu interrupted them.

"You should stay here, tonight," he said, bluntly.

"I'm sorry?" said Alejandro, startled.

"Going to Badrinath?"

"Ummm … yes. Yes, we were."

"Stay. Don't go," he reminded.

Zoya and Alejandro exchanged a quick glance.

"You can stay in the town," the saintly man added.

"Do you know a place?" Alejandro asked, meekly.

"Come." The sadhu stood up and started walking.

Alejandro glanced at Zoya through the corner of his eye. She was nodding her assent. The sadhu raised his hand and waved at an open wooden cart drawn by a cyclist.

"Riksha!" he hollered.

The cart started to make its way towards them. It halted in front of the sadhu and the driver spoke to him in a local language. He then disembarked and attempted to pull Alejandro's backpack off his shoulders.

"Hey!" exclaimed Alejandro, clearly alarmed.

"It's okay. Give him," the sadhu assured. "He'll load the cart."

After the driver loaded their luggage onto the cart, Zoya and Alejandro hopped on, followed by the surprisingly limber sadhu.

Normally, in a situation like this, Alejandro's hand would slip instinctively to the pistol in his pocket. But today, neither did he have his trusty Browning Hi Power in his pocket—having had to check it in with his backpack—nor did he seem at all uncomfortable with the situation. Something in Zoya's demeanour had made him feel at ease. Beside him, Zoya smiled a knowing smile.

*This heightened intuition is one of the key advantages of being a Hekameses,* she thought.

The journey on the open cart, or the rickshaw, as the sadhu called it, was pleasant and somewhat lulling. Before long, Zoya found herself nodding off. She woke up with a jolt at the sound of loud conversations nearby. The rikshaw had come to a halt and the sadhu was standing near it speaking animatedly with two younger gentlemen in similar attire. They were at the gate of a campus that looked like a rest-house of some sort. The sadhu returned to the cart and motioned for Alejandro and Zoya to get off. One of the younger men from the rest-house walked up to the cart-driver and stuffed a couple of coins into his pouch. He also gave him a small bag of what looked like grain. Maybe rice. The driver put his hands together and bowed reverentially. He then drove down the way they had arrived.

"This is an ashram," said the sadhu who was waiting for them at the door to the complex. "You can stay here, tonight."

"Thank you," said Alejandro smiling. "How do we book a room?"

The sadhu surprised everyone by breaking into a hearty, belly-jiggling laughter. He was of medium build with a protruding rotund belly, and dark brown complexion, Zoya noticed. He wore a saffron garment around his waist and another one like a shawl over his shoulders. From his neck hung a necklace of dark-brown beads.

"Rudraksha," the sadhu said, lifting the necklace. He had stopped laughing.

"Oh, sorry, I didn't mean to stare." Zoya blushed.

"No problem. Everyone is curious. These are rudraksha beads. Like the rosary. Now back to your question." He looked at Alejandro. "You can follow him. He will give you a room." He pointed at one of the younger men who was still standing there.

"Great. And … eh … where do we pay?"

"It's free. Just do service," said the sadhu as he walked away.

Alejandro wanted to ask him for a clarification but the younger man stopped him.

"Let him go," he said. "It is seva. Come."

"Seva?"

"Yes. Help for prayer. Serve food. Clean." His English was choppy, but Alejandro got the gist.

"We need to do some community service in exchange for our stay, am I right?" Zoya asked.

The man stared back at her blankly, clearly not understanding.

Alejandro nodded his head in her direction and they kept walking. There were low buildings on either side of the muddy pathway on which they were walking. Each building had in front of it, a long, open veranda supported by pillars and accessible from street level in three directions. Beyond the verandas were doors to the rooms which looked like the lodgings. There was the sweet wispy aroma of something familiar in the air.

Zoya nudged Alejandro. "Pot?" she asked, grinning cheekily.

"I think so." Alejandro sniffed. "Looks like they know how to party." He winked.

"No kidding."

The third building they passed seemed to be their destination. Their escort jauntily climbed on to the veranda and brought them to their room.

"Room," he said with a flair of his hands. The door to the room was wide open without any mechanism to lock it from the outside. Inside, there were two bedrolls in the corner, a jug of water, a charcoal stove and an empty pot on top of it. There seemed to be no heating inside. Neither were there any windows.

"Toilet," said their companion pointing to a hut in the distance. He then bowed and walked away.

"This is going to be interesting," said Zoya, as she dumped her luggage in a corner.

Alejandro was busy inspecting one of the bed-rolls. There was a rug for the floor, a sheet and a woolly blanket. No pillow.

"Yep," he replied in-between the inspection. "And cold."

"Well, there's a stove," Zoya assured.

"Do you know how to light a charcoal stove?"

"Umm … can't be that hard. Like a charcoal grill, I'd imagine. I did some camping."

"I don't think that's what the stove is for, though. The smoke in here … no windows … it isn't the best idea."

"True that. They gave us a pot. So it's probably for cooking."

"Maybe on the veranda."

"Right. I'm hungry," she groaned.

"Me too. Hey, back there … what was the deal with the sadhu? What did you sense?"

"Don't know what his deal is. But he's a telepath."

"Interesting. He seems to have brought us among his kin."

"You think they're all telepaths here?" Zoya looked stunned.

"No. I mean, I don't know. But they're all sadhus."

"Oh, that. Yep. Sure looks like it."

Alejandro who was sitting on his haunches next to the bedding, stood up and stretched. "Whaddya say we go look for some food?"

"Not a bad idea, but what about our stuff?"

"I have a padlock on my backpack where I store my gun. We can lock the door and leave them here."

"Cool. Let's go then!"

"But first left me call Wolfgang." Alejandro dialled the number. "Hmm, weird."

"Voicemail?"

"Switched off."

"I wonder what's up," said Zoya, thoughtfully.

"Me too. But let's worry about that after dinner, shall we?"

They locked up and walked outside. It was nearly dusk, with the twilight reaching its tentacles into every nook and cranny in sight. The day had been sunny, and the setting sun left behind traces of a balmy mellowness characteristic of the tropical winters in these parts of the world. Rishikesh was a hill station, so the nights, they had heard, would tell a different story. Without a heater or a fireplace, they would probably have to sleep in their sweaters.

The rest-house or ashram, as their host had called it, seemed to be occupied albeit not completely full. They walked around a bit through the muddy walkways and saw signs of life inside many-an-open-door along the way. At the center of the complex was a temple with bells ringing inside and a strong scent of incense in the vicinity.

As they approached, the bells stopped ringing, and a handful of people emerged from the temple. Without noticing Zoya or Alejandro, the group made its way towards the far end of the complex. On her left and right, Zoya noticed a few others heading in the same direction. Some of them engaged in spirited conversations along the way, others walked alone in meditative silence. Zoya tugged on the sleeve of Alejandro's sweater.

"Do you think we should follow them?" she asked.

"Probably a good idea."

They had barely made it past the temple when the purpose of this mass migration became abundantly clear to them. The crowd seemed to be flocking towards a tarpaulin-covered, pavilion from which a waft of spicy aromas emerged.

"Looks like there's food in there." Alejandro pointed, enthusiastically.

"Sure looks like it," Zoya concurred.

They hurried the last few steps to the enclosed area and let themselves in. Inside, there was a cemented platform on which a couple of dozen of the guests sat cross legged waiting for what looked like their dinner. A couple of massive charcoal stoves were burning in front with huge tumblers full of steaming food perched on top of each. At the stove closest to Zoya, a man was ladling large spoonsful of a tumbler's contents into a smaller bucket with handles on both sides. A young boy of about fifteen was going around distributing plates made of leaves and terracotta cups to the seated guests. Another man with a food bucket was serving large helpings of its steaming contents to the guests seated at the back. He seemed to be moving from row to row with practiced dexterity.

"Ummm … should we just join them?" Zoya asked, meekly.

"Why not. That's what everyone else is doing."

The two found a vacant area around the middle of the pavilion and sat down to join the dinner. Although they were sitting on a bare cement floor, it did not feel cold. The glowing fires of the several stoves around them, warmed the area up quite well.

Soon the boy handed Zoya and Alejandro their plates and cups, nodded and moved on to the next row. Another man passed by and filled their cups with water. Zoya stole a glance to her right and noticed the man next to Alejandro rinsing his plate off with this water.

"What kind of leaves do you think these are?" asked Zoya, lifting her bio-degradable, leafy plate up for inspection. "They're so perfect. Just like paper plates ... except ... from leaves."

"Leaves of the sal tree," said a rough voice from Zoya's left, before Alejandro could answer.

Zoya gave a little start at this unexpected comment and turned her head towards the speaker. He was a tall elderly man with a head full of shaggy grey hair and an equally unkempt greying beard. He was dressed in white—a knee-length kurta and baggy pyjamas, that showed signs of heavy wear and tear.

"I'm sorry?" Zoya asked, clearly not used to being spoken to by strangers.

"The plates are made of sal leaves. You asked. I answered," said the man.

"Oh, I see."

"You are a tourist?" the stranger continued.

"Sort of. Yeah."

"From America?"

"How did you know?"

"From your accent."

"Oh, of course." Zoya looked abashed. But just at that moment, as if to save her from further embarrassment, a man and a woman arrived with the food. The man served them a fragrant buttery rice and the woman topped up their plates with two kinds of savoury vegetables. One of them was a leafy green fried in a concoction of spices and the other, a mushy dumpling dunked in a rich creamy gravy. Zoya didn't see any cutlery anywhere and the stranger who had just spoken to her seemed unfazed by this predicament. He rinsed his hands with the water in the terracotta cup and dug promptly into his meal, making loud slurping sounds as he licked his fingers.

Noticing this, Zoya did the same. They had set out on this journey, expecting vegetarian meals along the way, given that they were visiting some Hindu religious pilgrimages where vegetarianism was mandated by law. But never had Zoya expected these meals to be this delicious. They ate in silence, enjoying the sensuous delights of using one's God-given appendages for this purpose. After a few minutes, a sweet-dish was served—a rotund lump of buttery goodness studded with cashews and pistachios.

"Laddu," the server said, before depositing the dessert on Zoya's plate.

They finished their plates and followed the crowd to the massive trash cans along the side of the building. Disposing their plates and cups, they rinsed their hands with water from a bucket positioned next to the garbage bins.

Through all of this, Zoya had completely forgotten about the man who had spoken to her briefly before the meal. Now as she wiped her hands with a paper towel from her jacket pocket, she suddenly noticed the stranger standing next to her.

"Your husband?" the man abruptly asked, pointing at Alejandro. Zoya started at the question.

Noticing Zoya's discomfort, Alejandro jumped in to save the day.

"No, Sir. She's my niece. Is there anything I can help you with?"

"No, you cannot help me. But maybe I can help you. It's not easy being stranded, when you are a tourist," he said, grimly.

"Stranded? Who said we were stranded?"

"Two foreigners. Tourists. Staying at an ashram like this. And you say you're not stranded?" He pulled out a joint from the pocket of his kurta and lit it.

Zoya started to feel uneasy. She tugged on Alejandro's arm egging him to move out of here. But Alejandro's curiosity was piqued. He had to find out what this guy knew about them, if anything at all.

"Do you come here often?" he asked, hoping to figure out the stranger's motives through questioning.

The shabby old man blew out a puff off acrid marijuana vapour through his nostrils and broke out laughing.

"Come here, you say? Come here … my God." He continued to laugh. "I *live* here."

"At this ashram?"

"Why, of course!"

"Then you must know that Babaji who brought us here. He was wearing saffron robes and a rudraksha—"

"Bangali baba. Yes, he's a mysterious one. Your life was narrowly saved."

Zoya and Alejandro exchanged a quick glance. "Why do you say that?" Alejandro asked, without making any effort to hide his surprise.

"You'll learn in your own time."

By now they had started walking down the narrow unpaved pathways of the ashram, following the stranger almost inadvertently, and Zoya noticed for the first time that their guide was barefooted.

"Aren't you cold?" she blurted out, looking awestruck.

"Cold? What is cold? It's nothing but a state of mind."

"True." Alejandro nodded, now looking more relaxed in the company of this man. "So, since you know this Babaji, would you mind telling us where we can find him?"

"I will show you," he replied curtly and continued walking. After about fifty steps, he stopped in front of a guest house and tossed the vestiges of his joint into the mud.

Then he turned to Alejandro and said in a sleepy voice, "My room is over here. But do you see that little hut, up on the slope over there?" He pointed due north.

"I do, yes."

"Bangali baba stays there. Namaaste." He joined his hands together and bowed slightly before turning promptly towards his quarters.

"Weirdo," Zoya mumbled when he had left.

"Oh, you'll find a lot of those around here … from what I've read on travel guides." Alejandro chuckled. "So? Are you up for a little trek to that hut to look for our baba?"

"Sure, I don't mind. Too jet lagged to sleep now, anyway."

"Maybe some of that pot would've helped, huh?" Alejandro teased.

"You bet." Zoya giggled. "Hey, by the way, why did you tell that guy I was your niece?"

"Oh, that? They get funny in these parts of the world about a man and a woman travelling together unless they're related. I didn't want any trouble."

"Makes sense. The dude was seriously creeping me out."

"Yeah, I sensed it. But I don't think you should worry. He seemed harmless."

"How do you know? Gut feeling?"

"Ha! Hekameses feeling!"

"Good one! At least he knew where to find our Babaji … what did he say his name was?"

"Bangali baba."

"Funny name. Never heard that one before."

"It's probably not his real name."

"You think it's like a nickname?"

"Kind of. I mean, you know what Bangali means, right?"

"Ummm, no …"

"Ah okay. Well, it's what they call people from Bangladesh or from a province in Eastern India, the province of Bengal. The English term is Bengali. It's a reference to a culture."

"Ohhhh! I see. So cool that you know this stuff."

"I'm an anthropologist, remember." Alejandro winked.

They were at the foot of the grassy incline that led up to the hut when Zoya strained her neck and cupped her hands over her eyes to get a better view. "It looks completely dark inside," she concluded.

"It does, doesn't it? Maybe our Babaji has gone to bed."

"He wasn't even at dinner."

"Right. But nope. Looks like there's a padlock on the door." Alejandro hurried up the mound and tugged on the lock for verification. "Yep. No one's home."

"That's too bad. I wanted to ask him about that message … at the airport …"

"Don't worry, we'll look for him in the morning. Hang on, my phone's ringing. Must be Wolfgang."

"Hello. Finally!" said Alejandro, relived to hear his friend's voice.

"Where were you?"

"Ah okay, well as long as you're alright."

"We're in Rishikesh. Yeah, the driver didn't show up …"

"Oh, he did? Half an hour? Yeah we had left."

"Long story."

"What? What time?"

"Are you serious?"

"That's incredible. We were really lucky!"

"Sure, I can do that."

"Tomorrow morning? That would work."

"Okay. Keep us posted."

"What is it? What did he say?" Zoya asked, when he had hung up. There was a sense of urgency in her voice.

"You know how that weirdo told us that we had a lucky save today?" asked Alejandro, plopping down on a step leading up to bababji's hut.

"Yeah, and?" Zoya sat down next to him.

"Apparently there was an avalanche today. On the exact same road that would've taken us to Badrinath."

"Oh? Is that why the driver didn't show up?"

"No. That's the strange part. The driver fell asleep, apparently. By the time he arrived, our flight had already landed and we weren't at the airport."

"So if we had waited for him …"

"Then he would've driven us to Badrinath. And …" Alejandro closed his eyes and calculated with his fingers.

"No! You're kidding?"

"You'd think, eh? But if Wolfgang gave us the timings right then it seems likely we would've been in that area when the avalanche hit."

"Crazy!"

"Really is."

"So what's the plan now?"

"Wolfgang asked me to send me our GPS location. He'll send the driver tomorrow and we can leave when the road is cleared."

"I hope we can see the Babaji before that."

"Me too."

# CHAPTER FIFTEEN

It had been five days since Chris and Amon set up camp at the foot of the Sayan mountains, when a terrible blizzard broke out—the first of the season. They lugged some heavy boulders from the surrounding area and created a barrier around the front of their tent, hoping to shelter it from the heavy winds. The rear of the tent was well guarded by the steep rock face they had set their base against.

Chris secured the tent firmly with additional harnesses before going inside and zipping up the entrance. Inside, Amon was preparing dinner.

With a pocket knife, he expertly sliced up some onion and spread it evenly on a slice of bread. Then he added the salted omul, some mustard and a slice of pickle.

"Pickle for you?" he asked.

"Sure, why not."

"This is the last of the bread," he said, as he stuffed a pickle inside Chris's sandwich. "But we still have couscous," he added. "Plenty actually."

"Good. It'll come in handy when we can light a fire again."

"Tomorrow. I think, tomorrow," said Amon, biting into his sandwich.

"Hmm. Maybe." Chris sat down to eat.

"I don't know if we'll ever find those suckers at this rate," Amon grumbled between bites. "It's been six days and not a single sighting."

"Five."

"Right. I'm losing track of time."

"I don't blame ya."

"I say it's time. Let's move into the mountains when the blizzard clears. No?"

"I guess … we have to, at some point …"

"Then? What are we waiting for? Nikolai's gang didn't find any leopard around here for months either, remember?"

"True."

"I'm starting to wonder if this was a bad idea from the start."

"The whole mission? Or camping out here?"

"The whole mission. How do we even know, the Aifra base is out here? All we have is a hunch."

"That's how we've done these things all our lives, no? Based on a hunch. Isn't that how you and Wanda went to Faiyum to search for the script of Ra?"

Amon nodded. "And look what we found! I suppose you have a point."

"Besides, have you *seen* the blizzard outside? What better location for a terrorist hideout than a treacherous one like *this*?"

"It has its pitfalls too, though."

"Pun intended?"

"Ha! Perhaps." Amon laughed out loud. "Oh, did we even check the sensor today?"

"Not since noon, actually. I switched it off. We won't be able to charge it again 'til the sun comes up. So we better use it sparingly." Chris got up and walked up to his toolkit. He pulled out the sensor and stared at it thoughtfully for a few seconds. "Wanna try it now?" he finally asked.

"You look like you received a divine revelation." Amon laughed.

"Maybe," said Chris, with a coy grin. "Let's give it a shot." He switched on the sensor and the blue power light came on. Balancing the sensor on his flattened palm he stared at it intently as if trying to move it with his mind.

"Are you trying Alejandro's trick over there?" Amon joked. "Where he manipulates electronics with his mind?"

"You know I can't do that. It's Alejandro's thing, really." He sighed. "How would I benefit from tricking you like that, anyway?"

"I dunno, just for a laugh maybe?" Amon shrugged.

"Here, you try. Maybe you have the magic touch," Chris joked, as he tossed the sensor across the room.

Amon caught it deftly and placed it on the ground in front of him. In an instant a siren went off and the red blinker on the sensor flickered to life.

"Oh my God!" Chris yelled, running over to his friend's side. "Can you do it too?"

"Do what?" Amon looked puzzled.

"Turn on sensors with your mind." Chris sputtered, saying all the words at once in his excitement.

"Umm … no … this is the real thing. It's here the snow cat … we found it!" Amon stood up and hopped up and down a couple of times. "Quick, grab your headset."

Chris hurried to the other side of the room and returned with his headset. He sat down on the tent floor and quickly got in gear.

"So? Do you see it? Or them? How many?" Amon was gushing like a child at a toy store.

Chris closed his eyes and focused. "Barely. Just a glimpse. Oops … it's gone. Back again … nope it's gone." For a minute Chris sat there with his eyes closed trying to find the animal again, while the siren went berserk in the background. And then there was silence. The siren stopped and the red indicator turned dark.

Chris removed the headset and sighed. "It went out of range," he said.

"Where was it?"

"Due west from here. Up the Sayan."

"How far do you think?"

"Between fifteen to thirty kilometers."

"Are you sure?"

"Well, the range of this sensor is around thirty kilometers … and … my visions have a range of about ten… in crowded locations … and fifteen around here …"

"So when we stopped seeing it, it was more than fifteen kilometers away but less than thirty, because the siren was still on."

"Exactly. Then it moved beyond the thirty-kilometer range. Or maybe not, because the blizzard reduces the sensor's range." As they were speaking, the siren went off again. In a few seconds it stopped.

"It's going in and out of range," Amon noted.

"Correct." Chris switched off the sensor.

"So? What do we do?"

"I wanted to ride out the storm ... but ... then it might be too late ..."

"I say let's make a move. We can make a good five kilometers before bedtime. And then we set up camp and track again. If it makes sense we travel again in the morning."

"Okay, I agree. There's a cave on the other side of this cliff. We'll leave some of our stuff over there. Can't carry them all."

"Good idea. Let's go!"

\* \* \*

In the morning after their arrival in Rishikesh, Alejandro woke early to find that Zoya was still asleep. He decided not to wake her and instead, went for a walk around campus by himself. His first thought was to check-in on Bangali Babaji to see if he had returned. He made his way up the dew-laden pathway and reached the lonely hut on a hillock, shortly before day break. A wet translucent fog still hung heavily in the atmosphere. He peered through this mist to detect signs of life within the dwelling, but it appeared as abandoned as before. When he got closer, his spirit sank as he saw the padlock from last evening dangling solemnly from the door knockers. By the time he traced his way back to the center of the campus, some of its residents were up and about. He noticed an elderly lady in a white saree sitting in one of the building verandahs, boiling a pot of water on a charcoal stove. Next to her was a packet of tea leaves.

Alejandro thought longingly of his morning cup of coffee. He didn't think he could find any until they left the ashram. His mind immediately went to Wolfgang.

*When did he say the driver would arrive again?* he thought, as he pulled out his phone to check for messages.

Surely enough, there was a text message waiting for him.

"Driver will call after ten," it said. "Be ready."

Alejandro checked the time. Six o'clock. He turned around to get back to their room.

"Ah, there you are," said Zoya, as he entered. "I was worried there, for a second."

"*Good* morning!" Alejandro greeted, cheerfully. "Just went to check on Babaji."

"Is he back?"

"Nah. No sign yet. Do you want to go see if there's breakfast?"

Zoya rubbed her eyes. "Sure. I could use some coffee."

"Me too. But from what I've read, tea is the more popular drink around here. Not likely we'll find coffee 'til we're in a more touristy area."

"Aww, that's too bad. Tea would work too if we can find some. Wanna go check?"

"Sure."

They rolled up their sleeping bags, locked the door like last time and headed towards the temple. To their delight, breakfast was indeed being served in the pavilion behind the shrine. They helped themselves to hearty portions of puri and halwa and scalding cups of masala tea. On their way back, they noticed some residents sweeping the temple courtyard and the building verandahs in the vicinity. Alejandro remembered how they were informed upon their arrival that service in lieu of payment would be expected from the guests of this ashram, and he tapped Zoya lightly on the shoulder.

"Hey, do you see those brooms in the corner?" he asked.

"Yeah."

"I think it's there for us to help with the chores."

"You're probably right." Zoya nodded.

They picked up a broom each and went straight to work. Alejandro was focussing on getting a bunch of dry leaves off a staircase when he saw someone familiar. On the verandah in front of him, sat the elderly man from last night, quietly smoking his joint and stirring a pot of tea. He was wearing the exact same attire as the evening before, but looked significantly more disheveled, if that was even possible.

"Want some tea, traveller?" he asked, in his rough accent.

"No, we just had some, thank you," said Alejandro, putting the broom down and looking up. "By the way," he continued. "do you happen to know when the Bangali Babaji will return?"

"Return? What do you mean? He lives here. Like me."

"Oh really? Well, he wasn't here last night." Alejandro paused. "Or this morning," he added.

"Strange. Very strange," said the man, as he closed his eyes and took a drag on his joint.

"So, this … has never happened before?"

"During the day, yes, he's out somewhere or the other. During the night, no."

"Should we be worried? Or call the police, maybe?"

The haggardly man waved off this suggestion dismissively and concentrated on his joint, eyes still closed.

Realizing that he wasn't going to get much more out of him, Alejandro abandoned the conversation and went to look for Zoya instead. He found her seated on the temple steps. They returned their brooms to where they had found them and made towards their room. On their way back Alejandro relayed to Zoya what he had just learned from their new acquaintance. With their saviour Babaji nowhere in sight, all they could do now was wait for their driver to take them to Badrinath. If they left before noon, they could still make it to their hotel before dinner and finally start their search for Kalki, putting this entire unexpected detour behind them.

# CHAPTER SIXTEEN

C hris and Amon hauled the last pieces of their luggage into a cave behind the cliff. It was a tiny little space, a mere crevice in the gigantic rock face, and they almost had to crawl in through the entrance. But it served their purpose. They needed a safe storage for those hefty boxes of reserves they couldn't carry across the rocky terrain ahead.

Past the low opening, the cave ceiling opened up slightly so that they could stand up to their full heights. It was here that they stood, taking stock of their supplies.

"I have everything I need in my backpack over here," said Chris. "It should be good for three to four days, hoping that we can get back before that."

"Three days should be enough if we take that circular route, I showed you on the map. Here, this one," Amon pulled out a map from his backpack and held it up in front of them. "We go northwest … up this way … right around this leg of the Sayan and back by the Mongolian border," he said, tracing the path with his index finger as he spoke.

"Right. Makes sense. That's where we got those signals. If we want to spot one, this area over here is our best bet." Chris's finger circled an area on the map to the northwest of their current location. "Are you packed?"

"Yes. I packed what I need." Amon fumbled through his backpack for a last-minute inspection. "Oh! Did you take your two-way radio? I only see one here …"

"Ummm … no," Chris hesitated. "I want to keep the weight to a minimum … just the essentials … I already have too much equipment … and climbing gear … it's a steep climb."

"WHAT?" Amon yelled. "Don't be crazy. The radios are our only connection to civilization. What if we need help?"

"We're gonna stick together. We have one between us. We should be okay," Chris assured.

Amon was having none of that. He walked over to Chris's side, grabbed him by the top of his arms and shook him. "Where is it? The other one?" he hollered. "I'm packing it for you."

"Amon, no seriously, calm down. I'd much rather have the other one here … safely hidden in case we lose or damage the first one."

"But what if one of us dies? Gets dragged by the tiger? And the one who remains has no way to seek help? Have you thought about that?"

"It's not a tiger, Amon. It's a snow leopard."

"To hell with the semantics! What's the difference?"

"There *is* a difference. A huge difference, actually. I'll tell you if you calm down," Chris urged placing his hands on his friend's shoulder and looking him straight in the eye.

"Okay, tell me. I'm listening." Amon sat down on the cave floor; knees folded upwards.

"Well, the thing is, these snow leopards, they aren't like other big cats, especially tigers—the most aggressive and powerful. The Bengal tigers, in particular. Anyway, snow leopards don't normally attack humans. Unless we provoke them. Fires will chase them away, and I have plenty of lighter fluid. We should be okay."

"What if one of us falls into a canyon?" Amon asked gruffly, intent on arguing his point.

"We won't. I brought climbing ropes. We'll be harnessed to each other."

"Hmph," Amon grunted. "Have it your way then," he finally said, standing up. "But on one condition."

"What's that?"

"If we only take one radio, *you* need to carry it. Here, put this in your bag," he said, shoving his hand-held into Chris's palm.

"But ... I ..." Chris tried to protest.

"No. I don't want to hear anything. I'll trade you for some food supplies ... to adjust the weight. That way, if I get stranded by myself, I won't die of hunger." Amon grinned.

"I dunno ... I don't feel so good about this."

"You don't trust my endurance?"

"Of course, I do. But this is strange country for you—the mountains and the snow. I'm a climber, it's different for me."

"It's not really that different, Chris. I have been a tour guide all my life … like my father before me and his father before him. Generations. This is in our blood for generations. The rugged wilderness. No sign of life. No water to drink. Here you have snow. There you have sand." Amon walked towards the cave opening, bent his head, and peered out as he spoke. The storm raged on beyond the cave and showed no signs of abatement. "It's the same. Tiny, treacherous particles in blinding blizzards and whirling sand storms. Snow is white but sand is yellow. One melts. The other doesn't. But in the end, it's all the same. The differences … they are … how do you say it?"

"Superficial."

"Yes."

"That's deep."

Amon shrugged. "This is a desert too, in a way. A frozen desert."

"Speaking of frozen desserts, I could have one right now." Chris chuckled, trying to lighten the mood.

Amon turned around and smiled at him. "But this will be our first time doing this together," he said.

"I know. We've known each other for how long now? Fifteen? Sixteen years? Yet, here we are on our first joint adventure at long last."

"Hmm." Amon became thoughtful. "That's not exactly true."

"Oh?"

"Come, let's sit down. There's something I want to tell you before we leave." Amon walked over to the back of the cave and perched himself on a box of supplies.

"What's up, Amon? Now you're scaring me," said Chris, as he took a seat next to his travel-companion.

"No, no. Nothing to worry about." Amon waved off Chris's concerns. "Just a story I thought you should know. In case … you know … we don't make it back."

"Oh we're definitely making it back. Trust me." Chris grinned, patting Amon playfully on the shoulder. "But please tell me your story. Now I'm curious."

"Alright then. Remember when Wanda first found out you were one of us? How old were you? Fifteen?"

"Fourteen actually. Yeah, you bet I remember that. Wanda loves to tell that story over and over again," Chris reminisced fondly. "I had bumped into her on a sidewalk, and apparently, that's when she knew …"

"Yes, exactly. I've heard it too. So when this happened … shortly afterwards actually, you went on vacation to Cairo. With your family. Am I right?"

"Yep. That Christmas. Me, my brother, Rob and our parents. They were still together then—one happy American family. Those were the good times!"

"I remember them, yes. When Wanda and Wolfgang found out where you were headed, they contacted me, of course. To keep an eye on you."

"Oh right! You were in Cairo the whole time, weren't you? Why didn't I ever make this connection? It would've been a very Wolfgang thing to do—assign someone to watch over a possible Hekameses."

"Very true. Wolfgang called to give me your coordinates. I booked myself a room next to your family, at your hotel."

"No way!"

"Oh, yes! It was fun though. Following you around. Doing touristy things. I could sense it too back then. I could sense that Wanda was right. You *are* one of us."

"I'm glad that you did. Glad to have met you, my friend," Chris said, his voice heavy with emotion.

Amon put his arm around Chris's shoulder. "And you know what else?" he asked.

"Tell me …"

"Your family went on that Nile cruise, remember?"

"Oh yeah! That was fun. Rob was a real ass, as usual. But mostly it was fun. So awe-inspiring. Being there. Amongst the spirits of the God-Kings of yore. At that age those things really move you, don't they?"

"Certainly. And that was not the only thing that moved you on that trip. When we were about to take off, you were leaning over the deck-railing, with your binoculars focused, completely absorbed in whatever you had seen, but just then the gangway moved, and the boat suddenly tilted to the side. You nearly toppled over. Then someone grabbed the collar of your jacket and jerked you backwards. You fell on your back, but on dry ground. On the deck of the boat instead of in the river. You thought it was your brother. But it wasn't."

"It was *you*!" exclaimed Chris, as realization set in. He felt the corners of his eyes moisten.

Amon nodded. "You lost your binoculars, though. It splashed into the water right in front of my eyes."

"I remember. All these years … and you never said anything? How come?" Chris wiped his eyes with his wrists.

"Wolfgang didn't want you to interact too much with everyone early on. And by the time he did, I had forgotten all about this."

"That's *so* Wolfgang. Secrets, secrets and some more secrets."

"He's just trying to protect us. Done a great job of it so far, don't you think?"

"That he has," Chris mused. "I think we should head out now. The storm seems to have cleared a bit."

"You're right," said Amon, standing up. "One more thing. Promise me something before we go."

"Of course, anything."

Amon looked directly into Chris's eyes and held his gaze with a steady determination as he spoke. "If something happens to me up there. Swear to me that you'll save yourself and return to safety. Do you promise?"

"No can do, Sir. But I *will* promise you one thing. Nothing—I repeat *nothing*—is going to happen to you up there. Not if I can help it."

* * *

Alejandro and Zoya had set out for Badrinath at around ten in the morning, earlier than they had expected. Wolfgang's arrangements had worked impeccably, as always. The driver, the hotel, the route they were going to take, meal-breaks, everything was carefully planned out and executed as per his instructions.

The road to their destination was incredibly scenic and the misty fog that hung low over the landscape, interrupted only by the towering snow-capped peaks of the Himalayas, had a calming effect. Throughout the drive, they found themselves alternating between nodding off and gazing wide-eyed at the mesmerizing natural vistas on display.

The driver, Hemnath was a friendly bloke who diligently pointed out the important peaks and river-crossings along the way. He asked them if they needed a break. Stopped at tea stalls for refreshments and suggested a suitable venue for lunch.

The winding mountainous highway often veered treacherously close to the edge of steep, bottomless gorges or dense coniferous forests, making for an absolutely exhilarating experience.

The driver played some Indian songs in the car that reminded them of Arabic tunes that often drift out of the sheesha bars around the United States. Zoya dozed through most of the morning, relaxed by the combined effect of music and scenery.

With lunch they had their first coffees of the day. It really helped wake Zoya up. She also appeared a shade more inquisitive, once her appetite was sated.

"So what's the plan when we get there, Uncle Alejandro?" she asked, teasingly.

"*Uncle?* Oh right! I remember. That's what I'd said back there at that ashram." He laughed.

"Yep. And from now on you're officially my Uncle Alejandro." Zoya giggled.

"Fine. I'm okay with that."

"Good. So that's settled. Now tell me, what do we do in Badrinath? What did you have in mind?"

"Hmm." Alejandro checked his watch. "It's one o'clock. Hemnath said we have at least seven more hours from here. So when we get there ... I'm thinking ... dinner?"

"Funny. No, I meant in terms of our search." Zoya lowered her voice. "You know ... for Kalki. Where to start?"

"Ah that! Well, the temple of Badrinath would be a great place to begin, in my opinion. Legend points to the temple as the abode of Vishnu's twin avatar from the Satya Yuga. It should be a likely place to spot His latest avatar, what do you think?"

Zoya nodded. "I suppose. But twin avatar? How do you mean?"

"The avatar of Vishnu who's the resident deity of Badrinath is Nara-Narayana, and it's not one deity but *two* ... Nara and Narayana ... twin brothers with Nara being the human and Narayana his divine sibling and constant companion. It's a metaphor born of Hinduism really, which is a religion that believes man and God are not separate but complementary to one another."

"Deep. So are we going to the temple tomorrow, then?"

"Yeah. First thing in the morning, before it opens to the public."

"Oh boy! Why so early?" asked Zoya with a grimace.

"Because there are huge lineups to get in and offer prayers. But Wolfgang worked with the owner of the hotel we're staying at, to get us an after hours' exclusive access." Alejandro grinned. "We don't even have to disguise ourselves as ISKON devotees like Nirmala and I had done at the temple in Dwarka."

"God! I remember that story. You guys nearly got killed! It had nothing to do with the disguise of course, but I'm becoming superstitious lately. It's best we steer clear of those costumes. By the way, speaking of Nirmala, where *is* she, anyway?"

"All I know is that Wolfgang has her working on some pet-project of his. Don't ask me what that project is. I have no idea."

"*You* have no idea? About *Nirmala?* I find that really hard to buy!" Zoya covered her mouth and chuckled mischievously.

"Hey! What's that supposed to mean?"

"Aww c'mon. You *know* what that means. So what's going on between you two, anyway?"

"Don't be silly. There's nothing. We're just—"

"Look at you! You're blushing. Did you know that? I've never seen you blush before. This is *so* cute!" Zoya teased.

"Alright, alright stop it." Alejandro smiled. "Now, back to your question, I seriously don't know what Wolfgang put her up to, and I haven't spoken to her in a while. So your guess is as good as mine regarding her whereabouts."

"This is your perfect opportunity to speak to her then. You're in her country … does she know?"

"Yeah, I mentioned it, but briefly when we were planning the trip."

"Why briefly?"

"She seemed to be really busy … I dunno … she was panting like after a run."

147

"Maybe Dr. Müller has enrolled her into the military or something," said Zoya, without making any effort to hide the sarcasm in her voice.

"Ha! With Wolfgang, I wouldn't be surprised!"

"E-mail her then. It could help with our search too, you know. She used to study the ruins at Dwarka. After all, *she* was the one who first thought about the Meerabai connection …"

"You have a point. I'll think about it," said Alejandro, becoming thoughtful. But in his mind a resolution had already taken shape. Once they got to the hotel and had access to the Internet, he would write to her and explain all about their mission—the Char Dhams, the search for Kalki—and ask for her inputs. Yes, he definitely longed to talk to her.

# CHAPTER SEVENTEEN

The storm thickened as Chris and Amon made their way up the narrow mountain pass at the eastern extremity of the Sayan mountains. Visibility was down to a minimum, and the blowing snow frosted their eyelids like icing on a cake. They were bundled up from head to toe with only their eyes exposed to the brutality of the elements. Chris led the way with the sensor beeping inside a pouch that hung from his harness. His head gear helped them hone in on the snow leopards a little bit better, with each step they took towards their destination.

Amon took the rear of their procession, harnessed securely to Chris with climbing ropes and carabiners. The sun hadn't set yet, but the sky was heavily overcast and an eerie translucent darkness loomed around them.

"How much further?" Amon shouted to his friend through the storm.

"We're within ten kilometers of the leap by my estimate," Chris hollered back.

"Leap? We have to leap? When? Where? How?" Amon sounded shocked.

"No, no. It's just a term for a pack of leopards. A pack is called a leap."

"Okay. How many in the pack?"

"Four, I think. Could be five. A couple are moving in and out of range …"

"That's four too many, no?"

"Absolutely. Leopards normally don't hang out together."

"You think we nailed it? Could it be? Is this the den?"

"Of the Aifra?"

"Yeah."

"Looks like it."

"What to do? Should we turn back? Get reinforcements?" Amon stopped to pant.

"Are you alright there, buddy?" Chris hurried down a few steps to catch up with Amon.

"Yeah, I'll be fine. Breathing trouble."

"It's the low oxygen. The higher we go the worse it'll get."

"And the snow isn't helping." Amon hunched forward and plopped down on a boulder at the edge of the pass.

"Be careful. The gorge is stee—" Chris was cut short by a crumbling sound as the boulder skid backwards under Amon's weight.

He held out his hand to grab his friend, but it was too late. The edge of the pass had broken off and the boulder was tumbling down the treacherous ravine, dragging Amon with it. Chris reacted quickly. He grabbed the safety rope between them and wound it around a jutting rock formation behind him. While applying tension to the rope thus, he simultaneously dug deep into the ground with the heels of his spiked boots to prevent himself from sliding.

"HOLD ON TIGHT. I'M PULLING YOU UP!" he screamed.

"SKIDDING," Amon hollered back.

"I gotchya. Just hang in there." Chris applied tension to the safety rope and pulled it towards him. "Try anchoring your feet to the rock face and climbing up as I pull," he instructed.

Amon was dangling about fifteen feet from the edge of the pass and grappling for support, but Chris could tell that he was hauling himself up along the cliff somehow.

"Almost there. Keep pulling," said Amon. His voice was closer now.

Chris's feet were skidding slowly but he knew it wouldn't be much longer before Amon could reach the ledge. He allowed himself to slide forward slightly so that he could bend over the edge and watch his friend approach. Amon was about five feet below when Chris felt a massive tug on the safety rope between them. He fell with a thump and was sliding rapidly towards the deep ravine when he struck a jagged piece of rock with his mid-section making him groan with pain. The rock arrested his fall but the impact with its serrated surface caused the rope between them to snap in an instant.

"Noooo!" screamed Chris, still latching on to the jagged rock. He heard the tumbling sound of breaking rock below him and then a thud of something heavy hitting a surface below.

Then there was silence.

"AMON!" Chris yelled, from his prone position. "ARE YOU DOWN THERE? ARE YOU ALRIGHT?" There was no response. Chris felt the weight of the universe descend upon him. He struggled to his feet. His body ached. "AMON!" he howled again, leaning over the edge, his voice raspy, heavy with emotion. He felt the corners of his eyes moisten despite the blizzard all around. He bent over the edge and strained his eyes to spot any sign of movement below him but the storm was too heavy and visibility was extremely low. He thought about the walkie-talkie. He needed help. Immediate help. He rushed back to his backpack and rummaged inside it in panic, strewing the area with scattered pieces of his belongings as he searched. Pulling out the handheld he hastily switched it on.

"Darn it! No signal." He shoved it back into his bag along with his leopard-tracking equipment and the other items he'd removed. Then he focussed on his climbing gear. He was an expert top rope climber. Now, he just needed an anchor.

It took Chris about fifteen minutes to hammer the bolts into the rock wall and set up the anchor solidly enough to support the weight of two people on the way back up. From the thud he heard earlier when Amon fell and a visual inspection of the ravine, Chris with his keen mountaineering intuition estimated a roughly twenty-foot drop to a level surface below. The bottom of the ravine was possibly further down, but it was impossible to tell for sure from where he was currently standing.

Chris leaned over the edge and tossed down an additional harness tied to a climbing rope that he intended to use to haul Amon up later. Then he attached his own harness and lowered himself into the ravine. For Chris, it wasn't a particularly difficult descent, but the stormy weather certainly added an extra level of challenge.

In about twenty minutes, Chris's feet landed on flat surface. It was a ledge about six feet wide and thirty feet long. Below it, as Chris had suspected, the ravine continued downwards until it disappeared into a misty darkness of unknown depth. He stabilized himself on the snow-covered strip of rock and looked around. There was a patch of snow in front him that bore the imprint of a heavy object. He rushed over to that area. Surely something heavy had crashed into that spot and carved a shallow pit into the snow. There were signs of flailing limbs. And … footsteps. Definitely footsteps. Heavy-booted footsteps. Chris's heart fluttered with excitement.

*He survived the fall!* he thought. "Amon! Amon! Where are you, big guy?" he called out, cupping his mouth with his hands.

But Amon was no where in sight. Chris stayed close to the rock wall and hurried along it, scanning the entire ledge surface. Nothing stirred except for the relentless pounding of the blizzard. The wind howled, and darkness descended around him like the Grim Reaper.

"Shit," said Chris, as he sat down on a flat rock. Suddenly, his eyes fell on an opening in the cliff wall in front of him. "A cave …" he whispered. His heart skipped a beat as he approached the entrance. "He's gotta be in there," he said. "Amon! Amon! I'm here. Are you …" Chris looked around, but the interior was completely vacant. It was too dark to check for footprints on the floor, but if anyone was in there before, they couldn't possibly have hidden themselves in that tiny space.

Chris rammed his fists into the cave wall and cursed loudly. Winking back tears, he crouched down on the floor, his head between his hands, unable to think.

\* \* \*

On the third morning of their arrival at Badrinath, Alejandro and Zoya returned from a morning walk around the ancient town feeling frustrated and demotivated. Since they had arrived at this hill-station pilgrimage a couple of days ago, they had seen everything several times over—the temples, the hot springs, the ashrams, the dharamshalas. They had interviewed countless locals, store-owners, tour-guides and priests, yet they were exactly where they had started, with respect to their search for the latest incarnation of Vishnu. The good news was that, people here seemed generally aware of the legend of Kalki and his prophesied arrival during the Kali Yuga. The bad news— they had no idea about his whereabouts.

"I don't know what else we could try," said Alejandro, as they entered their hotel lobby.

"Me neither." Zoya shook her head. "But I could use some coffee. Let's ask the front desk if the restaurant's open for breakfast yet."

"Good idea," said Alejandro as he walked up to the reception. The clerk wasn't at his desk, but seeing Alejandro approach, a plump elderly lady stepped out from the management office and greeted him with a smile.

"Good morning, Sir! How are you?" asked the amicable lady, who Alejandro recognized as the owner's wife they had met on the night of their arrival.

"Doing fine, and you?" replied Alejandro, feigning a grin but without any genuine cheer in his tone.

"I'm alright. But you look a little down. Has there been a problem? Are you not enjoying your stay?" Unlike the receptionist who usually sat at this desk, the owner seemed to speak English quite comfortably.

"No, no … it's not that. We … actually … never mind. Could you tell us if the restaurant's serving breakfast yet?"

"Yes, absolutely. It's six thirty. We open early. This is a religious town, you see. Even the tourists wake up early around here."

"I'm not surprised. They're mostly pilgrims, I suppose. We saw a bunch of them bathing in the hot springs bright and early, getting ready for prayer."

"Yes, exactly. I don't want to sound inquisitive, but *you* don't look like pilgrims at all. What brings you here to this unlikely destination? Tourism?"

"Yes, you can say that …" Alejandro trailed off.

"Well actually, maybe we should tell you," said Zoya, flicking Alejandro a sideways glance.

"Yeah, maybe you can help," Alejandro agreed. "But it might be a long conversation, and we don't want to take you away from your work."

"I'd love to help if I can. My guests are my priority. Why don't you head into the restaurant and grab breakfast and I'll join you as soon as Hari is back at the desk?"

"That'd work, miss … er," Alejandro fumbled for words, realizing he hadn't asked the lady her name.

"Kamala. My name is Kamala. I'll be with you in just a few minutes. Hari should be back any minute now," she assured.

"Thanks," said Alejandro with a smile.

They had hardly placed their breakfast orders at the restaurant when Kamala arrived as promised. She took a seat next to Zoya and ordered a cup of coffee and biscuits.

The restaurant was pretty empty at this hour, with only a couple of other tables occupied. It was a spartan establishment with naked white-washed walls, a rough wooden floor and cheap wooden tables with benches for the guests. During peak hours, it tended to get rather noisy, but right now, the setting was perfect for a peaceful conversation.

The waiter brought their coffee almost instantaneously and Alejandro took a large sip from his cup before speaking.

"This is good coffee," he said to their host across the table.

"Thank you. My husband is particularly picky about coffee. He doesn't like any compromise in that area. He's from southern India. Coffee is very popular over there." Kamala laughed.

"Oh, I see. And yourself? Are you from the south as well?"

"No, not at all. I'm absolutely a local girl. My family has lived in this area for generations. I lived in Delhi for a few years. When I was in university. But our roots are certainly here in Uttarakhand."

"That's prefect!" Zoya's eyes lit up. "Then you'd know all *about* this area and its history."

"Absolutely. I can tell you everything you need to know. Are you here for journalism? Or filmmaking, perhaps?"

"Filmmaking! I wish!" Alejandro guffawed. "No, nothing that fancy. You see, I'm an anthropologist and Zoya here is my niece."

"Nice to meet you Zoya and …"

"Alejandro."

"Lovely to meet you Alejandro."

"Same." Alejandro smiled. "As I was saying, Zoya and I are here to explore an Indian myth. It's a project of mine and I managed to get Zoya all excited about it so she wanted to tag along."

"Oh, if you're researching Indian myth then Badrinath is certainly an excellent place to start. This area is a hotbed of ancient Indian secrets."

"So we've heard," agreed Alejandro. "The particular myth that intrigues me is the one concerning, Kalki, the tenth avatar or Vishnu, you must have heard about her?"

"Her? You mean *him*, right? Kalki avatar is believed to arrive in the form of a man."

Alejandro and Zoya exchanged a knowing look.

"Umm, okay. I mean you're absolutely sure that Kalki will be a man? How can you be so sure?"

"That's what the legend says."

"But Vishnu has arrived in the form of a woman before, hasn't he?" asked Zoya.

"He has, as Mohini. He has had avatars who were human-animal hybrids as well. So, who knows? But a majority of the people I know tend to think, Kalki will be a man." Kamala shrugged.

"I see. I guess we'll find out if we ever meet him." Alejandro chuckled.

"That'd be very fortunate, if you did," said Kamala.

"For sure. Speaking of meeting Kalki, by the way, that is primarily what my research is about. I'm trying to see if we can find him or her or traces left behind by him or her. You know what I mean?"

"Ohhhh! What a grand mission. Basically, you are looking for God!"

"You can say that. And that's why we're here in Badrinath. We thought it'd be a great place to start."

"Of course. It's the abode of another avatar of Vishnu—"

"Nara Narayan. Yes, we know."

"Looks like you've done your research! So tell me, how can I help with this search?"

"Well, so far, everywhere we've looked, we've learned the things we already knew about Vishnu and his avatars and none of that information sheds any light upon where one might go to find the Kalki if, he was already here on earth and hiding out here somewhere."

"Hmm … hiding out, huh? I like that term. Hiding out. Hiding out. Let me think." Kamala scrunched her face and bit into a biscuit. "If I were you …" she started, still munching on her biscuit. "I would probably start looking where a *previous* incarnation of Vishnu supposedly left his footprints … or where his story was originally written, you know, Lord Krishna's story, the Mahabharata, it was written here, near Badrinath!"

Alejandro's jaws dropped to the floor and Zoya almost choked on the roti she had rolled up into a wrap. "Say what now?" Alejandro asked, incredulously.

"The Mahabharata—this is where it was written. A few kilometers to the north of here, actually. You didn't know?"

"Nope. I don't believe we did," Zoya confessed. "But please tell us more. North of here, where exactly?"

"Well, there's a village called the Mana village, the last Indian village."

"The last? How do you mean?" asked Alejandro.

"It's a border village, at the border of Tibet."

"I see. And the Mahabharata was written there, you say?"

"Yes. Near that village, there is a cave called the Vyasa Gufa, where the sage Veda Vyasa is believed to have composed the epic poem that tells the story of Lord Krishna, the eighth avatar of Vishnu."

"Very interesting. But what were you saying earlier about Krishna's footprints? Can we find those there too?" Alejandro asked, sitting up straight, his curiosity piqued.

"Not in that cave, per say, but nearby." Kamala leaned forward across the table and lowered her voice conspiratorially. "It is said that there is another cave, not far from there, slightly remote and it's known as the Muchukand Gufa. It's in there that the original footprints of Lord Krishna are believed to have been preserved for *centuries.*"

"Alejandro, we have to go there. What do you think?" Zoya asked.

"Definitely. As soon as possible. Do you think you can give us the directions, Kamala?"

"Actually, I can come with you. There's a sadhu who lives in a cave not far from the Muchukand Gufa and he'll probably know a lot more than me about all of this. You should meet him, but he doesn't speak English. I can ask your questions for you."

"That'd be fantastic!" Beamed Zoya. "When did you want to leave?"

"Hmm … let's see … I need to balance our accounts for this month but I should be done by lunchtime. How about we leave at around one?"

"Works for us," said Zoya.

"Good. I will meet you at the lobby at one o'clock then. Let me get back to my office and wrap up quick. Enjoy the rest of the morning!" Kamala smiled and got up to leave.

"We will, thanks!" said Zoya.

The intervening period passed idly. They checked the weather forecast for the afternoon. Snowfall was expected. Zoya's camping instinct kicked in and she packed a few supplies, sleeping bags and a change of clothes for eventualities. Alejandro went out for an information gathering stroll and returned with some local insights about the Vyasa Gufa and Mana village. He learned that the area was in fact, a notable pilgrimage, owing to its legendary connection to the fabled epic, the Mahabharata. Apart from the couple of caves Kamala had mentioned, there seemed to be several other attractions of mythological importance in the vicinity including a rocky connection over the river Saraswati, believed to have been constructed as a bridge, thousands of years ago by Bhima, a primary character of this epic. Alejandro took detailed notes of his findings and marked out key locations and pathways on a map he had secured from the hotel lobby. He packed his trusty pistol, first-aid kit, flashlight and some other provisions as he deemed fit, before going to the restaurant for lunch.

"Do you think we're actually going to run into Kalki up there?" Zoya asked over lunch.

"No, not likely. Unless we camp out for days. I don't think Kalki just hangs out there in plain sight."

"I agree. What's the plan then? What do we look for while we're there?"

"I'd start with looking for clues of something … anything supernatural that someone might have seen or heard perhaps. An incident from recent times, not from the days of the Mahabharata, of course. If Kalki has ever been here, *someone* would definitely have witnessed something unusual or miraculous."

"You're right. Good idea. Let's go. It's almost one. Kamala told us to wait in the lobby."

Alejandro gulped down whatever was left of his coffee, and they head out to the lobby together to start their trip.

Kamala was waiting for them as promised. She had brought along their family car and driver.

"The drive won't be long," she explained. "Once we get to the last village, that is, Mana village, there is a bit of trekking on foot to be done. I want to take you to see the sadhu first. He doesn't meet any visitor after dark. Unless, of course, you'd rather start with the Vyasa Gufa."

"No, no. We also prefer to speak with the sadhu first. There isn't much we'd understand visiting the Vyasa cave on our own. I'd rather chat with someone with knowledge about the region and its history," Alejandro concurred.

The drive up to the Mana village was indeed quite short, so they still had several hours of daylight left to try and cover all the spots of interest before they closed for that evening.

"You see that path over there?" Kamala asked, pointing to a narrow mountainous alley ending in a flight of stairs.

"Yep," Zoya and Alejandro replied together.

"That'd take us to the Vyasa Gufa. We're not going there at the moment. If you'll follow me, we'll take this trail on the left. It's a little steep, along the edge of the river Saraswati, so be careful. As far as I can remember, there is a cave about three kilometers up that track where the sadhu baba I told you about, has lived for years." Kamala turned around and made her way towards the trail.

Alejandro and Zoya followed close behind. Walking in a single file they navigated their way slowly up the rocky tract. Although there were quite a few tourists around where they got out of their car, this part of the village was far less crowded. As they advanced further up the mountain, the vegetation thickened but human sightings became few and far between.

"Do you come here often?" Alejandro asked, when Kamala had stopped to catch her breath. She was clearly not very athletic and was having a hard time keeping pace with the other two.

"Often? No. The last time was maybe five or six years ago. I was here with another sadhu who was looking for this Babaji."

"Oh, that sounds like quite a while," Zoya said. "Are you sure he still lives here?"

"Most probably. The Himalayan sadhus are quite sedentary. Sometimes they spend all their lives in remote caves, meditating. It is their way of life."

"What about food and supplies? Where do they get those?" Alejandro asked.

"The disciples. They bring offerings when they come to seek their blessings."

"Oh no, we didn't bring anything. Should we have?" Zoya asked, embarrassed.

"Don't worry about it. Sadhus don't mind. He'll see that you're foreigners and forgive you." Kamala smiled.

"I might have some pot. Would that help?" Alejandro grinned.

Kamala looked lost. "You know, like … what do you call it … ganja," Alejandro explained.

"Oh that!" Kamala laughed out loud. "You seem to know a fair bit about the sadhus around here."

"That's the one bit I understand. I mean, if you spend your entire life trying to connect with the supernatural, what better way to zone out, right? The mind-altering substances certainly help."

"That's one way to think about it. Although, if you look at it from the angle of Hinduism, the ganja serves a different purpose."

"Really? What do you mean?"

Kamala stopped again and leaned on her knees to catch her breath. "Well, a fundamental concept of Hinduism is to shut out your external sense organs and look inside … like inside your soul for answers. Because our sense organs only perceive the material world and are misleading. You know what I mean, right?"

"Most definitely. I know exactly what you mean. So basically, you're saying that pot ... I mean ganja ... helps cut off the external world and that's why the sadhus rely on it."

"Exactly. We're almost there. You see that saffron flag? That should be the entrance to his gufa."

The cave or gufa in question arrived soon and Kamala asked them to wait outside while she went in to seek an audience.

"He's ready and willing to allow a darshan. Follow me," she said softly, emerging from the cave in a couple of minutes.

Alejandro entered first, followed by Zoya. The cave was the size of a walk-in closet. There were blankets on the floor to the right, possibly the sadhu's bed. The lighting was poor and came primarily from a kerosene lamp in one corner. There was a strong smell of flowers and incense mingled with the unmistakably acrid scent of marijuana vapour. In the center of the room, sat a bearded man with a bushy mane of matted hair and eyes closed, his pot belly hanging out, a garland of rudraksha beads balanced over his rounded tummy.

"Bangali baba!" Zoya gasped.

"Shhh," said Kamala, raising a finger to her lips. "Not so loud. He's meditating."

"Sorry. I was just saying. I think we know him. We met him in Rishikesh."

"You did? That's strange. But he hasn't left this dwelling in years."

"I'm fairly certain that it was him," Zoya whispered. "We definitely saw him a few days ago. Do you mind if I ask him?"

"Let me ask him for you. Like I said, he doesn't speak English."

"No, I believe he does," Alejandro interjected. "He spoke to us just recently in Rishikesh like Zoya was saying."

"You must be mistaken."

"I assure you, we're not," Alejandro objected.

"Alright then. If you say so. Ask him a question. Go ahead. Kneel before him, join your hands together and address him as 'Babaji' before you speak to him," said Kamala, nudging Zoya forward.

Zoya walked up to the sadhu and put her hands together and knelt before him as instructed. The sage's eyes flew open.

"Babaji," she began, "it's us, again. We met at the airport. You took us to your ashram. Remember?"

The sadhu looked confused. He said nothing for a while and stared intently at Zoya.

"Kya bol rahin hain bachchi?" he then asked, addressing Kamala.

"Koi nahin, galti ho gayee hain Babaji," Kamala responded.

"He doesn't understand you," she then conveyed to Zoya. "You must be mistaking him for someone else. It's alright. Just ask me your questions and I will get your answers for you."

"Umm ... Alejandro, did you want to ..." Zoya hesitated.

"Yeah, sure," said Alejandro walking up to them. "Madam Kamala, could you please ask him if he has seen the Kalki, I mean the Kalki avatar?"

"Okay, sure," said Kamala, before posing the question to the sadhu in Hindi.

The sadhu erupted into a belly-jiggling laughter. He continued laughing for a couple of minutes.

"He even laughs like the Bangali Babaji," Zoya whispered into Alejandro's ear. Alejandro nodded in agreement.

The sadhu stopped laughing and looked at each one of them separately with a piercing inquisition in his gaze. He then offered his response in Hindi.

"He says that the one who has seen God is a siddha purusha or enlightened one and he need not continue to live as a mortal. He can take his leave from this world of desires and merge with the Brahman or godhead."

"Ouch," said Alejandro almost inaudibly. "I framed the question wrong. Okay, could you tell him that … that we're looking for a saint … someone with legendary supernatural abilities and … we have good reason to believe that he might be around here somewhere … or at least he could have been sighted around here … does he know if such a saint existed … in recent times or at least in the last century?"

Kamala nodded and asked her question. This time the sadhu didn't laugh and responded quickly.

"Yes, there was but not here in India, he says," Kamala explained.

"Oh, really? Where then?"

"Up north. A long time ago there was a saint who could bring a dead man back to life." Kamala found out from the sage.

Alejandro's eyes went wide, and Zoya gave out a small gasp. "Could Babaji tell us who this was and where he lived?"

Kamala translated the question to the sage and received a brief response from him.

"The frozen saint of Baikal," she said, turning to Alejandro.

"Baikal? That's like … in Russia!" Alejandro exclaimed.

"In Siberia," Zoya added. "Whyyy does this name sound familiar …" she mumbled.

"And where is this saint now?" Alejandro asked.

"He disappeared about fifty years ago, after the Second World War. Hold on, Babaji is saying something else." Kamala paused to listen. "He said, that according to legend, several escapees from the Russian gulags had discovered him in a frozen state near Lake Baikal. They thawed him and he bestowed their dying with new life."

"Fascinating. Has our Babaji met this sage?"

"He's saying, no. But there's still a shrine in his name in Siberia. It's on the shore of Lake Baikal, close to the Mongolian border and some people still go there to pray for the terminally ill."

"Oh!" said Zoya. "I've been there!"

"You *have*?" Alejandro looked at her, amazed. "*When*?" he asked.

"I don't know. I don't remember. But …"

"But what?"

167

"I can feel it, you know? I can *feel* that I've been there," Zoya struggled to explain.

"I think we should leave now," Kamala interrupted. "Babaji just told me that it's time for his prayer."

"Sure thing. We were done anyway. This was really helpful," sad Alejandro. "Thank you, Babaji, namaste," he added, joining his hands and bowing a little in the sage's direction.

"Namaste." Zoya joined in, putting her hands together.

"I'm so sorry, but do you mind if I take a few more minutes?" Kamala asked tentatively when they were about to leave. "I left in a hurry today and forgot to bring any offerings so I was thinking, maybe I'll cook a hot meal for Babaji's dinner. As a service, that is."

"Oh yes, absolutely. No problem at all. It's wonderful of you, in fact," said Alejandro. "We'll wait outside for you."

"Thank you. I promise I'll be really fast. Fifteen, maybe twenty minutes at most."

"No worries. Take your time. Come Zoya, let's wait outside," said Alejandro as he tugged on Zoya's arm.

Sunset was still a couple of hours away so they had ample time to get back and visit the Vyasa Gufa before it closed for the day. Alejandro leaned on the cave wall right outside the entrance and let out a sigh.

"That was an interesting discovery in there," Zoya said, appearing next to him.

"Sure was."

"Could be worth a visit, this shrine in Siberia, don't you think?"

"Perhaps. We'll have to sleep on it and discuss with Wolfgang or Wa—"

Alejandro was cut short by Kamala's sudden appearance at the cave entrance.

"Ah, there you are," she said, looking flustered. "I have a small problem."

"Why, what happened?" asked Alejandro.

"It seems that Babaji has completely run out of grains and other supplies. He's been living on just apples and dates and puffed rice for weeks now. I have nothing here to cook him a hot meal."

"Oh no! How did that happen?"

"It seems that he hasn't had any visitors, pilgrims, disciples or travelling sadhus up here in over a month …"

"Travelling sadhus?"

"Yes. There are some sadhus from other holy sites in India who visit these caves temporarily. They stay in the Himalayas, meditate and leave. They bring offerings for the local sages. But the winter isn't a popular time for them to come here. This month they didn't come to Badrinath much at all."

"That's too bad. So what do we do now? We should get him some—"

"Supplies, yes. That's what I was thinking as well. But there is no need for us all to go. In fact, we don't even need to go all the way down to the village to get the grains. I know a grocer who lives down the track behind this cave. It's a ten-minute trek at best to his house. I can buy some supplies directly from there. I should be back in an hour max. Do you mind waiting here?"

"Yeah, we can wait. Sure you'll be okay on your own?" Alejandro asked.

"Of course. It's just a quick trip. I'll be back soon." Kamala smiled, as she turned around to leave.

Sounds of bells and chants emerged from the cave as Zoya and Alejandro watched Kamala lumber away to the back of the cave and ultimately disappear from view.

"Oh shit!" Alejandro said, after a couple of minutes.

"What's wrong?" Zoya asked.

"I forgot to ask for her number."

"Don't worry, I doubt that we'll need it."

"You're right," said Alejandro, as he perched himself on a slab of rock and lit a cigarette.

"Hey! I thought you're just a *social* smoker!" Zoya objected.

"I am. But I'm bored." Alejandro chuckled.

An hour had passed and Alejandro was on his fourth cigarette, when the sky went really dark and snow descended upon them in large fluffy flakes.

"This doesn't look good," said Zoya, gazing up at the sky. "Should we go look for her?"

"Probably a good idea," Alejandro agreed.

They followed the trail Kamala had taken and made their way to the rear of the cave. There, a rickety pathway dropped steeply towards the river valley, but the grocer's residence couldn't be spotted from where they stood.

"Wow, that looks treacherous. I hope she didn't fall or something," Zoya said.

"Yeah, it's pretty steep, eh? Let's go, we need to find her."

They started down the path, treading cautiously, clinging on to the rock wall beside them, but before they could advance more than a hundred meters, there was a loud explosion. Zoya almost toppled over. Alejandro reacted quickly and grabbed her arm, arresting her fall. A cloud of dust rose up in front of them, dramatically reducing their visibility. There were sounds of voices from far below, chaotic and confused, appearing to originate from the village area.

When the dust cloud cleared from their field of view, Alejandro squinted to see ahead. There was nothing unusual until where the path bent sharply around the rock face.

"Wait here," he said. "I'll check around that bend to see what's going on."

He jogged back in a few minutes looking disappointed.

"Something exploded further ahead. I don't know what, but further down, this path is completely blocked up with boulders that broke off from the mountain," he said.

"Another avalanche, you think?"

"I dunno." Alejandro shrugged. "Could be a man-made explosion."

"But why would they explode things up here?"

"I'm not sure it was a regular thing. I could hear sirens below. Police cars maybe."

"That's not good!"

"No, it isn't. Let's go back up and see if Babaji would let us stay in his cave tonight." The snow started pounding really hard as he spoke.

"I don't want to go back there. It's getting slippery and I can hardly see ahead of me. I have a better idea. See that

171

fork over there?" Zoya pointed to a branching in the road right behind them, less than twenty feet away from where they were standing.

"Yeah."

"I went up to check out what it was and it's like a tunnel that ends in another cave. It's pretty sheltered. We can stay there 'til the storm clears."

"Good find. Let's go."

They hurried the few steps up the mountain and entered the tunnel. It was less of a tunnel and more like a discontinuity in the rock wall, a couple of feet wide. At the end of it, as Zoya had promised, there was indeed a small cave. It was completely dark inside. Alejandro pulled out a flashlight from his backpack and lit it.

"Looks like someone's been here before," he noted, looking around.

"You're right. They even made a fire over here." Zoya was leaning over a mound that looked like a crudely constructed clay stove with burnt charcoal inside. "And, hey! They left a pot," she said, lifting an empty aluminium saucepan from the floor next to the stove.

"Perfect. We better get comfy then. The forecast said it'll snow all night."

"We'll be fine. I brought sleeping bags and some food."

"Smart cookie. I brought some stuff too. But first, let me call the hotel and see if they have heard from Kamala or have her number."

"Good idea," said Zoya.

"I don't have much signal in here. I'll go outside and make the call. Be right back."

Alejandro returned rather quickly.

"No luck?" Zoya asked.

"I reached the front desk, but the guy hadn't heard from her. He said he didn't know if she had a cell phone either. They usually call her on her home phone, but he didn't want to give me that number."

"That's too bad. She probably isn't home, anyway. Did you leave a message?"

"Yeah I gave him my name and number and told him to ask Kamala to call us as soon as possible."

"Good. There isn't much more we can do at this point."

"Right."

"I'm hungry. Do you want to see if we can start that stove? You have a lighter."

"Yeah we can try. But what are you gonna cook? All I have are some fruits and cookies."

"I packed a bunch of chapatis at lunch. If we can heat them up over the stove, I have some hotel-sized butter and jam to go with it." Zoya grinned.

"Nice! Looks like you thought this through." Alejandro laughed. "Now let's light the … wait my phone's ringing."

"Must be Kamala!" Zoya said, enthusiastically.

"Hello … hello … who … wait I can't hear you … the signal's on and off. Hang on, hang on …" Alejandro rushed outside to take the call.

This time Alejandro took quite a while. As she waited, Zoya unpacked their sleeping bags and rolled them out on the floor. She also removed the food items and placed them on top of her sleeping bag. Then she crouched by the stove to see if it had enough charcoal. Alejandro walked in as she was inspecting the stove. He was wearing an uncharacteristically glum expression.

"So, was it her? Is she back in the hotel?" Zoya asked, anxiety apparent in her voice.

"No," Alejandro responded, furrowing his brows. "It wasn't her. It was Chris."

"Chris? Really? Isn't he in Siberia or something? Is everything alright?" She blurted all the questions out at once, as she walked over to stand beside him.

Alejandro sat down on his sleeping bag, knees folded upwards, hanging his head between his hands. "He's in trouble," he mumbled.

"What's wrong? What did he say?"

"A few days ago, he and Amon had spotted some snow leopards in the Sayan mountains. They were following the trail when an accident happened."

"Whaaat?"

"Yeah, Amon fell over a cliff. He's missing. Gone. Disappeared."

Zoya was shocked. She stared incredulously at Alejandro, unable to utter a word.

Alejandro looked up at her and continued. "There was a terrible storm and Chris had no reception on his walkie-talkie. Phones of course, don't work up there. He spent the night inside a cave, crying. Then he made his way across the mountain to the nearest village he could find on a map. That's where he's right now, this border village near Mongolia. He arrived this morning and passed out. He was burning with fever. An innkeeper has picked him up and his family is taking care of him."

"Oh my God. This is bad ... what did Dr. Müller say?"

"He doesn't know, yet. Chris tried all afternoon, but Wolfgang's phone is out of range. That's when he called me."

"Out of range? In London?"

"We don't know that he's in London. He could be in Germany ..."

"Right. But still ... it's Germany! We should call Wanda."

"I will, in the morning. She's sleeping and Chris is safe at the moment. Now we need a plan of action."

"And rescue mission."

"Yes. We might have to cut this trip short ..."

"You're right. We should go. We're the closest."

"No, not you. Just me. I'll have to put you on a flight to London."

"Don't be crazy. You'll need all the help you can get. I'm coming. Did Chris tell you the name of the village? I might know it. I grew up in Mongolia, remember?"

"He said he couldn't pronounce it. But he sent me a text. Here, look ..." Alejandro showed her the text message.

"I can swear I know this place."

"You've been there?"

"I dunno. It feels like I have, although I have no recollection of when. I know I can take you there, though."

"Interesting. I'm still not sure you can come. Wanda would definitely object to it."

"Then we don't have to tell her."

Alejandro gave her a stern look. "Let's discuss this in the morning, okay? Now let me see if I can get that stove lit."

# CHAPTER EIGHTEEN

Alejandro woke up to the sound of gunshots. It was dark and dank and he couldn't remember where he was. He reached under his pillow for his phone, but there was no pillow, just a sleeping bag. He sat up quickly and allowed his eyes to adjust to the darkness. He remembered having dinner with Zoya and going to sleep in the cave near Mana village. He turned to his left where Zoya had made her bed. She was gone! There was nothing there. Not even her backpack! He stood up hastily and reached into his pocket for his phone. The battery had drained overnight. Next to his bed was a folded piece of paper with a message—from Zoya.

*I'm sorry Uncle Alejandro, but I had to go. I had to find Chris. It's my intuition, again. Please don't be mad. Will call as soon as I can. Be safe,* the letter read.

"Crap!" Alejandro exclaimed. He stuffed her note along with his phone into the pocket of his jeans and checked his watch—half past five in the morning.

Another gun shot. It seemed to have come from the village below.

Alejandro reached into his backpack, grabbed his revolver and dashed outside. There were footsteps in the snow leading away from the cave—possibly Zoya's. He followed them to the mouth of the passage. It had stopped snowing, so the prints on the ground were still fresh. But that didn't mean Zoya hadn't left a while ago. With nothing to do last evening, they had fallen asleep by seven. He wondered if he should go back, up the mountain path and pay a visit to the sadhu. But he decided against this idea. Even if the Babaji knew anything, they wouldn't be able to communicate without knowing each other's language. Since the gunshots seemed to originate from the valley down the hill, Alejandro made up his mind and walked cautiously in that direction, his gun raised.

Further downhill, there were more footsteps and not just Zoya's. There were signs of heavy booted feet walking up the mountain and then another track in the reverse direction. Someone else had come up here—someone with large feet, larger than his own. Walking slowly, he carefully rounded the bend in the road. Beyond the bend, the barricade formed by fallen boulders had been partially cleared. He navigated between the boulders and kept walking forward, swinging his gun right and left as he advanced.

He had made it down about a kilometer or so when a crashing sound behind him made him swerve on his heels in alarm. A man had jumped from the ledge above his head and landed about a hundred feet behind him. He brandished a gun.

"Don't move!" growled the burly man, looking menacing and bear-like behind his heavy winter-jacket.

Alejandro turned around and started to sprint, picking up speed as he fled. There was little chance for his potential assailant to hit a moving target in this semi-darkness. He could hear the thug behind him in close pursuit, but he didn't look back and ran as fast as his legs would carry, slipping and sliding along the path as he went. He knew he was losing elevation fast when his ears popped. His pursuer yelled something, a foreign word or a name, he couldn't tell.

He kept running. He was about to take a turn when he realized what, or rather who, the goon was yelling at. He had an accomplice. A shorter wiry man stood about half a kilometer downhill from Alejandro. Upon hearing his partner scream, he started to make his way up towards Alejandro.

Alejandro was cornered. He felt the blood draining from his face.

He instinctively raised his hands in surrender. On his right was a vertical rock face. On his left a steep decent into a thirty-foot gorge below. The floor of the gorge was lined with tall deciduous trees. A trickle of a river meandered between them. The ground in between the trees was covered with head-smashing, brain-splattering boulders. Alejandro saw a trigger being pulled in his direction. Crossing his fingers and making a judgement call, he dived into the gorge to his left.

As the ground slid away from beneath his feet, Alejandro heard a gun shot. He swore audibly and reached frantically for a tree branch just centimeters away. He had eyed that sturdy bough before he dived and aimed his jump in its direction. He barely managed to grip the branch with his extended right arm as another leafy branchlet smashed into his face, scratching him everywhere. He swerved just in time to save his eyes.

"Did you get him?" someone yelled.

"No, Boss. I'll try again."

Another shot was fired. It hit his branch, splintering a section close to where Alejandro held it. He swung his legs up in an attempt to straddle the trunk. But the trunk was too thick. He managed to hook his left foot into a branch attachment, his right leg hanging free.

"I'm climbing down," the first voice announced.

"Aight! I'll take the track down the hill and join you from the other side," his companion responded.

Through the corner of his eye, Alejandro saw a figure struggling down the rocky wall of the gorge. The branch he was hanging from made an ominously crunching sound and snapped.

"Argghh!" Alejandro found himself hanging upside down, his left ankle horribly twisted. He tried to raise his upper body and bend double just like the sit-ups he did every morning. Except, this time, he was up-side down. This complicated things. He was able to reach a lower, flimsy branch but it wasn't enough to hold his weight. The branch snapped and his foot slid from the jolt. Before he knew it, he was tumbling down to the rock-studded gorge bottom.

Alejandro must have blanked out from the impact because he didn't remember hitting the ground. Now he lay on a rocky surface, his head and face dunked in muddy snow and slush. He had fallen on his side. He couldn't feel his right leg or much of the right side of his body. Luckily his head had not hit the rocks. Or had it? Was he dead? He tried to move his right leg.

"Ow! Ow! Ow! Nope, definitely not dead."

There was a fair bit of mud along the shore of the narrow stream and now it was covered with pockets of melting snow. His head was snuggled into such a patch in between a couple of the darned boulders that had crushed his leg.

His mind was fuzzy but he thought he heard voices. Someone was rushing towards him. There was a loud thumping noise.

*Helicopter blades? No, multiple helicopter blades,* he thought. Someone was shouting. Words. Incoherent words and among them a name. *His* name.

"Come on Alejandro, grab it! You can do it! We'll pull you up," someone shouted. A familiar female voice.

*Nirmala? No, I'm dreaming.*

He hoped against hope and tried to look up. His eyes were covered with mud. He rubbed his left wrist over them. There was a helicopter above his head and from it a rope ladder hung. The ladder was close to him but try as he might, he couldn't grab hold of it. Anything that bent his body enough to put pressure on his right leg made him wince with agony.

"I'll go get him," said a man's voice from the helicopter.

A lean young, Chinese man began to descend down the ladder. He has carrying a coil of rope around his shoulder. In the distance Alejandro saw a tiny speck that was advancing with roaring velocity. It was a man on a motorbike. Behind him, the thug who had climbed down the rock wall was standing still, looking flummoxed. Someone fired. It was from the helicopter this time. Alejandro's pursuer had taken a hit on the leg and collapsed. The Asian man dropped down next to Alejandro, but the motorcycle was at bay. The rider was the larger of the thugs who had given him chase, earlier.

"Xianbin, watch out! Motorcycle at twelve o clock," said a familiar woman's voice.

Xianbin pointed his fist at the motorcycle, a wristlet sparkling right below his balled-up fingers. The motorcycle's engine sputtered and stopped, toppling its rider over to one side in a manner Alejandro immediately recognized as one of his own tricks.

Soon a cable was being attached to Alejandro's waist and he was being hauled up into the belly of the helicopter and laid down on a stretcher.

Once inside the transport, his eyes focused on a lovely face. The pear-shaped, dark and intelligent visage of his friend.

"Nirmala?" he managed to mumble, still incredulous at this miraculous turn of events.

"Yep. It's me. Don't worry, we've got this under control. This is a military air-ambulance."

"What? How?"

"I'll explain later. Now, tell me, how are you feeling?"

"Think I broke my right leg. Or maybe even a rib." Alejandro groaned.

"Not good. Not good. Nurse." Nirmala waved at someone. A lady in a white nurse's uniform appeared next to Alejandro's head. "I believe my friend here is injured. Could you please take a look?"

"Yes," she said, as she checked his pulse. She then moved over to his side and gently bent his left knee. Then the right. Alejandro screamed bloody murder.

"Sorry, sorry. Very sorry," said the nurse. "I will give you painkiller." She went to the rear of the helicopter and re-appeared carrying a loaded syringe.

"We need to find Zoya," said Alejandro through gritted teeth, as the needle pierced his skin.

"You don't know where she is?" Nirmala asked, looking shocked.

"No. She left while I was sleeping. Wrote a note."

"Dang. Left for where? Did she say?"

Using his uninjured left hand, Alejandro fished her letter out of his pocket.

"Here. Read it."

"*Uncle* Alejandro?" Nirmala giggled, in spite of herself.

"Inside joke." Alejandro smiled, immediately realizing that it hurt to do so.

"So where is Chris?"

"In Siberia somewhere."

"What the …"

"But she'd have to go to the hotel first, to book any flight."

"You're right. Where's your hotel? Let's go there. She couldn't have made it far."

Alejandro gave her a card from the front desk with the hotel's name, address and phone number. Nirmala handed it to the pilot and briefed him in Hindi. The pain injection was starting to kick in and Alejandro felt relaxed and sleepy. He had questions, so many questions, but first they had to find Zoya.

"We're going to land on the hill behind the hotel and I'll walk over to look for her." Nirmala let him know. "The other helicopter hasn't spotted her around town, but they have rounded up the Aifra goons," she added.

"Aifra? They were Aifra?" was all Alejandro managed to mutter.

"Yes, we think so. Okay, we're landing. Haresh come with me. Xianbin stay with Alejandro," Nirmala instructed.

*Haresh … Haresh … where have I heard that name before?* thought Alejandro.

The Chinese fellow who had rescued him just moments ago, came over to sit beside Alejandro. He had an endearing smile. Alejandro nodded at him.

"You must think I'm ungrateful," Alejandro said.

"How come?" Xianbin looked puzzled.

"What you did back there was heroic. You saved my life and I didn't even thank you."

Xianbin dismissed the apology with a wave of his hand. "Don't be silly. You were in terrible shape. That's not a time for formalities."

"You are too kind. I'm Alejandro, by the way."

"I know. I'm Xianbin, but you can call me Mike."

"Nice to meet you, Mike. So, how do you know Nirmala?"

"I'm her student."

"I see, you're a marine archaeologist and oh, now that I think about it, so is Haresh. I remember meeting him when I was in Dwarka."

"Ummm … you're right about Haresh, but me, I'm no archaeologist. I'm a pharmacist."

"Oh! I don't get it … I thought you were Nirmala's student."

"I am. I'm a Novo Hekameses."

"The what?" Alejandro tried to sit up, surprised. "Ow, ow, nope, can't sit."

"Please don't try to sit until they get you in a cast. You might damage that leg even more," said Mike as he eased Alejandro back into a lying position. "You haven't heard about the Novo Hekameses? Oh look, Nirmala is coming back." He got distracted.

The helicopter door opened and Haresh and Nirmala got in. Zoya wasn't with them.

"So?" Alejandro asked, looking at Nirmala.

"She isn't there. The guy at the front desk said she checked out early in the morning. She paid for her room and said that she had to suddenly leave for Delhi due to an emergency."

"Did he tell you anything else? Like when she left? If a car came to pick her up?"

"He did, actually. He said she was asking about the bus that plied to Rishikesh every day. She wanted to know where the bus stop was. The receptionist said that he walked her to the bus stop. There was a bus at six. She must have taken it."

"Let's go to Rishikesh then. We'll wait for her at the airport."

"Not with you injured like this. We need to get you to a hospital. We're going to Delhi. The other helicopter will hand the Aifra over to the police and go after Zoya."

Nirmala announced, authoritatively. "Here, take this," she then said, handing him a pill. It will help you sleep through the flight."

# CHAPTER NINETEEN

A gentle, dreamy twilight was seeping into a spacious bedroom with huge Victorian windows, when Alejandro woke up, his right leg in a cast. He had a choppy recollection of the hours that passed since his accident. He remembered landing in Delhi and being carried out of the helicopter in a stretcher. Someone had given him soup—tomato soup in a cup. There had been a doctor and a nurse in the room where they took him, but it was not a hospital. It appeared to be a large mansion reminiscent of colonial times. He remembered feeling safe and drowsy. After that, he didn't remember much more.

He yawned and stretched his arms. He was lying on a intricately carved, wooden bed. A lady in a nurse's costume sat in a corner in an antique armchair, dozing with her head against a window-seat. A faint aura of crimson highlighted her kindly face like a halo.

"Ahem, excuse me. Where am I?" Alejandro asked, clearing his throat.

The woman started and sat up. She looked puzzled. "Wait," she said raising her hand and left the room.

She returned momentarily accompanied by Nirmala.

"Ah, you're up already?" she asked with a smile. "We were just having tea. Want to join?"

Alejandro's stomach growled. He realized he hadn't eaten anything all day. Except that soup. But soup didn't count. "Yeah, I'd love to. I'm famished," he said.

"Come. I'll bring the crutches. Or do you need a wheelchair?"

"No, crutches will be fine. I think."

Nirmala grabbed a pair of crutches that were reclining against the wall behind his bed. Alejandro crawled out of bed carefully and leaned on the props. He felt much better than this morning.

"So what did I break? Just the leg? No ribs?" Alejandro felt the right side of his chest. It was tender but not terribly painful.

"Just the leg. There were some other bruises. But nothing else broken. You were lucky."

"You bet!"

Nirmala threw his arm over her shoulder and grabbed his waist to give him support. "Here, lean on me," she said.

They walked slowly out of the spacious bedroom and into a corridor lined with wooden panels. "This is a fancy place! So where are we, exactly?" Alejandro asked, looking around.

There were expensive paintings hanging on the walls next to them.

"At the private residence of Raghav Pandey, Marshal of the Indian Airforce. The top air force official in the country."

"You didn't tell me you were so well connected," said Alejandro, raising an eyebrow.

"Ha! It's not me. It's our gang leader."

"Gang leader?"

"You know, Wolf-gang." Nirmala chuckled.

"He's Wolfgang's contact?"

"Remember, he had a mystery contact in Delhi? The one who always made arrangements for us, when we got into trouble in India?"

"Yeah, the guy who never showed his face."

"That's him. Marshal Pandey. He had to stay hidden because of his high-profile position."

"So how did you blow his cover?"

"Ha! The war has created an unprecedented situation. He realizes that we need him now more than ever before. So when I came here on a recruiting mission a couple of weeks ago, he told Wolfgang that he wanted to help me actively."

"A recruiting mission? You lost me."

"Yes, for the Novo Hekameses. It's a new wing of the Hekameses comprised of volunteers like me, who weren't born naturally into the powers but would like to be trained. Wolfgang wanted me to take charge of this team. So here I am, building a youth army!" Nirmala chuckled.

"Ohhh! So *that's* the secret project he put you on, eh?"

"Exactly. I knew I wanted to ask Haresh to join. I think he has the right spirit. Marshal Pandey is helping me identify others. It helps to have a Hekameses— "

"Wait, he's a Hekameses?"

"Yes. One of those, tracked using the Faiyum papyrus. When he was originally asked to join, he only wanted to help from the shadows. Without any active involvement."

"Makes sense. He has an illustrious career. I wouldn't have wanted to jeopardize it either, if I were him."

As Alejandro was finishing this sentence, they arrived at the end of the corridor that connected the bedrooms to the living area. Looking around, they found themselves standing at the far end of an enormous dining hall that spanned the entire width of this nineteenth century building. At the center of the room was a polished rosewood table for ten, standing on sturdy ornamental legs, richly inlaid with engravings. Haresh and Mike were already there, sipping beverages and conversing with a grey-haired, moustachioed Indian man seated at the head of the table. Behind them, a server in a white, buttoned up, neatly pressed and starched uniform waited on the guests carrying a silver tray steeped with pastries, puffs and other goodies.

"Fancy," said Alejandro under his breath.

But before Nirmala could respond, their Indian host noticed them and shouted out from the dinner table. "Ah, there you are. Feeling better Mr. Garcia?"

"Oh, please call me Alejandro," Alejandro insisted, walking up to shake his hand. "Yes, definitely a lot better. You must be Air Marshal Panday."

"Raghav Panday. Nice to meet you," the host responded, firmly shaking Alejandro's hand.

"Trust me, the pleasure is all mine."

"Please, take a seat. You must be hungry." Raghav gestured the waiter over to Alejandro's side.

"Would you like some tea or coffee, Sir?" the waiter asked, as he extended his plate of snacks.

Alejandro helped himself to a pastry and some samosas. "Coffee would be great," he said.

"With milk and sugar?"

"No need. Black is fine."

The waiter quickly disappeared out of the dining room to fulfil the order. Alejandro turned to smile at Raghav.

"You have no idea, Sir, how grateful I am to you today for saving my life. It was quite a miracle. How did you manage to find out where I was?"

"Ah that!" Raghav Pandey relaxed into his chair and folded his arms across his chest. "Ever since you and Nirmala ran into trouble with the Aifra here in India, Wolfgang alerted me to their newfound interest in this region. Especially surrounding sites of religious significance. Specifically, the ones connected to the legend of Krishna or rather Lord Vishnu and his various manifestations. Naturally, we increased remote surveillance of the temples and pilgrimages that we considered to be particularly vulnerable to attack."

"Badrinath must have been one of those at risk, eh? It figures."

"Correct. It's a very famous and ancient pilgrimage associated with Vishnu. We had our eyes on it. All the more so because Wolfgang told me you'd be travelling that way."

"So you had your helicopters there the whole time?"

"No. I couldn't justify doing that, without reliable intel pointing to an impending attack. But I had informers and as soon as there was a tip, it was last night I believe, that an attack was happening and the Aifra might be behind it, I called Nirmala, because she had recently made contact with you."

"I tried calling you right away," Nirmala chimed in. "But it went to voicemail."

"Probably didn't have signal," said Alejandro.

"We thought so too but we weren't sure. But when I couldn't get through after several attempts, I thought your phone might be off or out of power. So I tried Zoya, and the same thing happened. That's when I called Air Marshal Pandey in complete panic."

"We were about to send a search party," Raghav said, "when an idea popped into my head. I decided to have my surveillance team track your phones. If they were turned on, but simply beyond coverage, then we could probably pinpoint their locations. Turned out, the plan worked. That's how we located the spot where our helicopters found you this morning."

"Wait, when was this?" asked Alejandro.

"Late last night," said Nirmala.

"Do you remember the time?"

"No … not exactly. Do *you* remember?" Nirmala asked, looking at the Marshal.

Marshal Pandey was busy looking for something on his phone. "I'm looking for the message. From when they located the phones. Ah, here it is! I believe it was one o'clock or shortly before that."

"I see. And Zoya's phone was at the same location?"

"Yes."

"So she must have left after that."

"Probably after it stopped snowing," said Nirmala. "Weather report says it snowed till about two in the morning."

"You're probably right," said Alejandro, becoming thoughtful. "But the question is, where is she now? Did you find her?"

"No," said Nirmala, hanging her head. "We have a couple of men stationed at the Rishikesh airport. But no flight to Delhi had her listed as a passenger."

"What?" said Alejandro, standing up so fast that he almost toppled his chair over.

"Please, Mr. Alejandro, have a seat. We are worried about her too," said the Marshal in a reassuring voice. "We'll not let anything untoward happen."

"But how can you be so sure that something untoward hasn't *already* happened? I mean what if they ... I mean the Aifra ... what if they captured her?" asked Alejandro, slamming his hand on the table, his cheeks a shade of burnt sienna.

"You think we didn't consider that already?" Nirmala intervened, placing a hand on his shoulder. "I would've been running around in a frenzy right now if we had any reason to believe that Zoya had been kidnapped."

"Yes, Mr. Alejandro, please be assured that Nirmala and I have been doing all we can, to spot her," Raghav added. "In fact, we know for a fact that she hasn't been kidnapped. Not by the Aifra, anyway. When we didn't find her name on the flights to Delhi or any other major city from Rishikesh, we checked the passenger lists for the trains."

"She's taking the *train* from Rishikesh? Why would she do that when there's a friggin' airport?"

"No, she's booked herself a train ride from Haridwar … to Delhi."

"Oh! How did she get to Harry-whatever?"

"There was a bus from Badrinath. Apparently the first bus to Rishikesh was delayed. But there was another bus around that time headed to Haridwar. She must've hopped on to that one."

"Hmm. Can we send someone to look for her inside the train?"

"That's going to be difficult," the Marshal remarked. "It's a busy train and I don't want to get the rail authorities involved. But you have nothing to worry about. We will have men at the Delhi airport waiting for her. She can't hide from them there. We'll have her back by tomorrow morning at the latest," he assured.

Alejandro plopped into his chair and sighed. He noticed a cup of black coffee waiting for him at his seat. In his agitation he had failed to notice when the server had brought it over. He raised the cup to his lips and took a large sip. "I hope you are right, Marshal Pandey," he said without sounding the least bit confident.

* * *

Alejandro sat in the ample verandah of the Pandey residence with his broken leg straightened over a coffee table and lit a cigarette. It was nearly dawn and he hadn't slept a wink. He stared into space with bloodshot eyes as a white spiral of smoke curled ominously above his lips. In the distance, a curtain of darkness was being lifted from the horizon, lining the contours of his field of vision with a thin streak of vermillion.

Zoya was still missing. Her train had arrived in Delhi two hours late and ever since its arrival, they had checked the passenger lists of every outgoing flight from the New Delhi International Airport but in vain. She wasn't on any of them. The guards who checked the tickets at the door were alerted since last evening. None of them had any record of her arrival either. How could this be? Where could she have gone? India was no safe place for a young girl to be wandering around all by herself. But she was no ordinary girl, was she? She was the legendary Meerabai. Yes, she was. In fact, there she is singing right now. Oh, what a beautiful tune—a homage to her beloved Lord Krishna. Alejandro wished so dearly that he could believe in such things—in God and in miracles. He definitely needed to put his trust in an unseen force right now. Otherwise he'd go crazy.

"Hey, are you alright?" asked a woman's voice from his right.

"Oh, Nirmala, yeah I'm fine," he murmured, without turning to look at her.

"Thank heavens! I though you had passed out or something."

"Really? Why?"

"Well, your phone was ringing but you weren't answering it. So I came running," she said, pointing at the phone that lay next to his plastered leg on the coffee table.

"Shit. Must have dozed off," he said absentmindedly, as he picked up his phone. "Hey, it was from Chris." He noticed the familiar number. "Let me call him back."

"Chris, you called?" asked Alejandro when the call was answered.

"She did? When?"

"Oh, I see."

"How long will it take you?"

"Are you fit to travel?"

"Ha! That's the spirit! Okay, keep us informed."

"Perfect. You'll leave tomorrow?"

"I'll let everyone know. Thanks for calling, buddy!"

When he hung up, Alejandro noticed that Nirmala had settled herself on his chair handle and was staring at him with inquisitive eyes. He smiled at her and breathed a sigh.

"So? What's up? Did he find Amon?" she asked anxiously.

"Uhh what? Oh, Amon … no unfortunately, no. *But* he heard from Zoya!"

"He did? And what did she say?"

"Said she was on her way to Ulan Bator via Hong Kong to join him."

"But that's impossible! We checked all the international flights out of Delhi, even to the remotest locations and her name—"

"Hang on, did you say you checked all the *international* flights?"

"Yeah, I mean, she was going to Siberia …"

"Sure, but there are many ways to get there. She's going through Kolkata, apparently. Must've been the most suitable ticket that was available when she booked it."

"Ouch. That was a stupid oversight. We should've checked the domestic terminal too," said Nirmala, slapping her forehead with the base of her palm.

"Don't beat yourself up about it. We found her in the end. Besides, there are tonnes of domestic flights from Delhi everyday, it would have been really hard to go through all of them."

"Still, I'm really pissed with myself. It was such a dumb mistake. Anyway, what's Zoya going to do when she gets to the Mongolian capital?"

"She called Chris to tell him that she was planning to travel to the village he's at, but he's not going to let her do that. He'll meet at her at the Ulan Bator airport, instead."

"And then?"

"Then I don't know. Zoya has every intention of going back to look for Amon. The ball's in their courts right now. From here, we can hardly control what they choose to do. And neither do I wish to."

"Me neither. But I'm sure Wolfgang would have some thoughts on the matter." Nirmala stifled a laugh.

"You bet! His thoughts won't be worth much though, if those two don't listen."

"Do you think we should go help them? I have a team now."

"Might be complicated. Everyone's going to need a visa in Russia and with the war in progress getting multiple visas … I say forget about it!"

"Wolfgang and Wanda will think of something."

"I sure hope so."

# CHAPTER TWENTY

*Z*oya was baffled to see the vehicle Chris had brought to pick her up from the Ulan Bator airport.

"A van? You brought a *van*? What do we need a van for? We're just going to the hotel."

"Ummm … no, change of plans. We're not staying in Ulan Bator. I'll explain—"

"Miss Zoya, welcome!" exclaimed a mousy haired, young man as he leaped out of the van.

"Who's he?" asked Zoya, under her breath.

The mousy haired man had walked forward and extended his hand to Zoya in greeting before Chris could respond.

"Zoya, meet my friend Nikolai. He's a conservation biologist."

Zoya flicked Nikolai a half smile as she shook his hand and in doing so, she noticed his pale, almost translucent complexion as it contrasted her own ivory black sheen. "Nice to meet you," she said, meekly.

Nikolai put an arm around her back and led her into the van with Chris in tow. Once inside, Zoya realized that this was no ordinary van, but a caravan that doubled as a moving research lab of sorts.

"Wow," she gasped without meaning to. "I mean … this is neat! Never seen anything like it."

"Well, it is our home a lot of the time," Nikolai explained.

There were three others in the van besides themselves including an attractive blonde about the same age as herself. She seemed busy in the lab area. The other two came to sit with them.

"So, is anyone going to explain where we're going?" Zoya asked, once they were on their way.

"Ah yes, to the border," said the redhead next to Nikolai. "I'm Yuri, by the way, and over there is my friend Sasha," he added, pointing to the guy next to him.

"Hi," said Zoya. "You probably already know who I am." She smiled somewhat self-consciously.

"Yes, Chris told us already. You're his colleague at the lab, and very brave too by the look of it." He winked.

Zoya blushed. "I wouldn't …"

"Anyway," Chris cut in, noticing her embarrassment, "as Yuri was saying, we can't fly to Irkutsk as planned. So we're going to cross into Russia on foot."

"How come?" Zoya's eyes widened. "Isn't this going to take way longer?"

"Quite the contrary. If we flew from Ulan Bator to Irkutsk, we'd need to wait months for a visa. We don't have that kind of time. Amon would surely be dead by then even if he'd managed to miraculously survive the fall somehow."

"Is it easier to get a visa at the border?" Zoya asked.

The men exchanged furtive glances. "Urmm … not exactly," said Chris, coughing into his fist.

"We're not going to need any visas where we cross," Nikolai blurted.

"What?" Zoya suddenly stood up.

"Sit," said Chris, pulling her down by her arm. "It's not that bad, trust me. The guys will get us across."

"We did it plenty of times," said Yuri with a smirk.

"But what about Dr. Müller? He's never going to approve of this plan."

"Since when did Dr. Müller's approval matter more to you than your friend's life, Zoya?" asked Chris.

Zoya flinched at this rejoinder as the memory of her risky Iceland expedition in search of her childhood friend Nancy, flitted through her mind. "Alright, alright, you got me there," she said, timidly.

"Plus, if we cross directly at the border we can walk right into the region where we lost him. From Irkutsk, our last campsite is at least half-a-day's drive."

"How long will it take us to get to the border?"

"About twelve hours non-stop. Fourteen to fifteen with breaks. Enough time for us to become best friends," replied Yuri grinning from ear to ear. Through the corner of her eyes, Zoya saw Chris flashing him a dirty look.

Nikolai intervened to ease the tension. "We have more important things on our minds than becoming best friends," he said. "We have a life to save. Zoya, the plan is, we drive until sunset. It's what, six o'clock? So another eleven hours with breaks et cetera. Then we camp for the night. Tomorrow morning, we cross the border, good?"

"You're the boss," said Yuri sarcastically, before Zoya could respond.

Chris and Zoya smiled and nodded.

"But now, you must be hungry. How about breakfast?" Nikolai asked, standing up.

"Actually, I'd like some slee—" Zoya was interrupted by the smell of fresh toast and fried eggs. "Mmm ... what's that?" she asked, turning one-eighty degrees to her left.

"Just some food," said the pretty lady behind her. Somehow, while they were talking, the blonde girl Zoya had seen in the lab earlier, had slipped in to the kitchenette to make breakfast.

"Hana, you did it again!" Nikolai gushed. "Zoya, this is my girlfriend. Always ahead of me at everything, this woman. But I can still make the coffee, right?"

"Go ahead," said Hana, giggling. "Make yourself useful."

Zoya tucked into the warm tasty meal as quickly as she could before finding herself a bunk in the sleeping area and sinking into it for a long nap. When she woke up next, the sky outside had grown dim. She had slept blissfully through lunch and most of the afternoon. Now, a loud growling sound issued from her belly. She yawned and stretched before following the sound of human voices into a section of the van that looked like the kitchen. Apart from a tiny stove and sink, this area held a table meant for four with a couple of extra chairs. It also had large windows on both sides.

Chris and Yuri were there, sipping coffee. "You're awake!" said Chris, noticing her enter.

"Yep," she replied sleepily. "Where are we?"

"In the pantry. Want some coffee?"

"I meant, where are we on the map, but sure I wouldn't mind some coffee."

Chris found a paper cup from a stack on the table and filled it with some coffee from a flask. "Here," he said, handing Zoya the cup. "There's cream and sugar if you need it."

"Thanks." Zoya accepted the cup and sank into a chair.

"We're close to the border," Chris continued, sipping his coffee. "Another hour or so before we park for the night, I think. The guys have a big campfire planned, if it doesn't snow, of course."

"A campfire sounds fun," said Zoya, rubbing her hands together.

"Yep. It's a farewell thing."

"A farewell? For whom?"

"For you and me, of course."

"Why? Where are we going?"

"To look for Amon."

Zoya looked confused. "I thought they were coming with us."

"Only across the border. And then they're going on to their wildlife reserve and we're heading up the mountains." Chris glanced at Yuri through the corner of his eye. The younger man was busy reading a book and didn't look up. Chris lifted a finger to his lips to discourage Zoya from asking any further question. "Want some cookies?" he then asked, rising from his seat.

"Sure."

Chris brought a large tin of cookies from the closet next to the sink and removing the lid extended it in Zoya's direction. Biting into the cookie made Zoya realize how hungry she was.

"Mmm … this is good," she said. "When's dinner?"

"As soon as we get to the border. It's going to be a Siberian-style barbecue, I hear. In fact, let's go and help getting the meats ready," he said, making a gesture with his eyes that hinted at a secret lurking behind them.

Zoya followed him eagerly into the adjacent sleeping area which they needed to cross before arriving at the lab in the front where the freezers for both food and samples were located. This section of the van was empty at the moment, as was expected.

Once in privacy, Chris tugged on Zoya's arm gently, to pull her back. Then lowering his voice, he said, "We have to go search for Amon alone. You understand why, right?"

"Not really," whispered Zoya.

"Let's sit," said Chris, choosing a berth and dropping into it.

Zoya took the lower berth of the tiered beds right across from him.

When they were seated, Chris began to explain. "My fear is that," he said taking a deep breath, "Amon might have been captured."

"CAPTURED? You think so?" Zoya shouted out.

"Shh! Keep your voice low. These guys know nothing about our actual mission. They think we're here to study snow leopards."

"Oh, they don't?"

"No. It's too risky to discuss these things with anyone outside of the Hekameses. But you probably heard … I mean Wolfgang must've told you that we were here looking for the Aifra base?"

"Yes, Alejandro told me. Did you find it then?"

"No, but what if they found us?"

"Oh! What makes you think that?"

"The way Amon disappeared … you know … it was very unusual … he just vanished!"

"Vanished? I thought he fell off a cliff."

"He did, he did …" Chris became thoughtful.

"What is it? What are you thinking?"

"I mean … there were footsteps, signs of his fall and everything … but …" He looked up at Zoya and fell silent.

"No body?"

Chris nodded in agreement. "At first, I thought he toppled over the edge he originally landed on and fell further below, you know. A dread took over me. Surely, he'd be smashed to smithereens if he crashed to the bottom of that steep ravine."

"God!" Zoya gasped.

"But I don't think that happened."

"How can you be so sure?"

"For one, there would've been a second crashing sound. But I could've missed that because of the weather. There was a horrendous storm in progress. The wind was howling. The snow pummelling everything. So I searched with my binoculars …"

"And?"

"And, nothing! I found nothing! He just vanished. Into thin air."

"So what's your theory then? He couldn't have just—"

"Exactly. And that's what got me thinking. Remember the Aifra cave behind the waterfall in Iceland?"

"How can I forget!" said Zoya, as the memory of their last expedition into the dangerous heart of enemy territory came rushing back to her. "You think he fell into a cave like that? An Aifra den?"

Chris shrugged. "Or someone could've dragged him in. It's not the best outcome, but it's still a whole lot better than finding his body frozen into the ground somewhere."

"Hmm. That's true. Did you see any cave nearby, though?"

"That's the strangest part. I did ... but it was empty."

"Oh no!"

"What is it?"

"I had another horrible thought."

"Tell me."

"You said you were chasing snow leopards, right?"

"Correct."

"What if ..."

"No, but it can't be. There was no blood."

"They can kill by jumping on your back and snapping the neck or spine. If the neck snaps under the weight of the animal without its teeth involved, it's possible that blood won't be spilled at all."

"Are you serious? But what about the body?"

"Dragged it off and hid it? They can jump like gymnasts. How many were there? Leopards I mean?"

"Three or four in the vicinity."

"This worries me."

They sat in silence for a couple of minutes, contemplating what might have transpired.

"Well ... no point worrying about it till we get there," Chris said confidently, at long last. "Let's go help with the dinner."

\* \* \*

After dinner, Zoya and the team sat huddled around the campfire, melting chocolate into pots to dip their apples and cookies in. It was Zoya's idea. She considered herself a connoisseur of improvised delicacies, hence this latest experiment in folksy fondue-making. But to her great dismay, this particular culinary adventure was progressing rather hilariously. The bars of chocolate held with tongs were dribbling on to their jeans and dripping down their arms as spurts of flame licked along their delicious edges. Zoya licked her arm and stepped away from the flame when her bar of Cadbury's dark chocolate had completely melted and got collected into a pot. Sitting down on her sleeping bag, slightly away from the flames, yet close enough to bask in their warmth, she sliced an apple into her pot.

The sky was clear and starry this thankfully windless evening. Although she had her winter-jacket on, she could feel the bitter chill of the Mongolian winter nip against her extremities. Without the wind, it was still bearable. On a windy day up in the mountains she couldn't bear to think how bad the weather must get. Like on the day Amon was lost. She hoped that Chris was right. That Amon was alive and warm somewhere, even if in captivity, rather than frozen into the landscape.

A sudden burst of music broke Zoya's train of thoughts. Closer to the fire where Hana and Nikolai sat huddled, it appeared that Yuri had produced a guitar and was strumming it merrily. Suddenly he burst into song. Nikolai waved at Zoya.

"Come, join us!" he shouted.

Zoya made a seat for herself between Nikolai and Chris. Yuri stood in front of them, guitar slung around his chest, swaying on his feet as he sung in a deep operatic voice. He sang in Russian to claps and cheers from his colleagues. Zoya giggled, even though she didn't understand a word. Next to her, Chris too seemed to be enjoying himself.

"He's singing, 'Farewell to the Mountains', it's a popular Russian song. It's about our love for the mountains and how leaving it always breaks one's heart," Nikolai explained, leaning closer to Zoya's ear.

"How relevant, yet ironic," Zoya mused.

Yuri finished the song and walked over with a flourish. "Here, your turn," he said, handing his guitar to Nikolai.

"No, no ... I ... no," Nikolai protested.

"Oh, c'mon," Yuri urged, yanking his friend by the arm.

"Oh alright." Nikolai positioned himself before the crowd and began, "Kalinka, kalinka, kalinka moya! V sadu yagoda malinka, malinka moya," he sang.

"Let's dance," said Yuri, extending his hand to Zoya. As Zoya skipped to her feet, he took her hand and twirled her around with agility. They hopped and skipped and danced around the fire with their audience roaring with applause. When the song was over, Zoya was sweating inside her parka. She hastily removed the jacket and bundled it on the grass, dropping down to sit next to it. Yuri came over to sit beside her.

"That was fun," he said with a broad grin.

"It was!" Zoya agreed. "Thanks for the entertainment. We have a grim task ahead, so anything helps to lighten the mood."

"Not a problem. The mountains are difficult. I know this for a fact."

"Are you from this region, Yuri?"

206

"Yes, I grew up on the other side. Of the border I mean. Siberia—the middle of nowhere." He flicked her a wan smile.

Zoya turned her head in his direction and noticed that his eyes were moist with reminiscence. "I see," she said, clearing her throat. "I spent some time not far from here myself, when I was a child."

"Interesting. Where?"

"Further south, but north of the capital. My father was a doctor in those parts."

"That's quite fascinating. I wouldn't have guessed—"

"Since you're from around here, can I ask you a question?" Zoya interrupted, suddenly remembering something.

"Uh ... of course. Please."

"Have you heard the story of a saint, someone who lived in these mountains and ... brought dead men back to life?"

Yuri scrunched his face and scratched his chin. "The frozen saint, yes I heard about him. It's only a legend of ... how do you call it? The city."

"An urban legend."

"True. But why do you ask? Your friend, he may not be dead. Please ... have hope."

Zoya's stomach lurched as she was reminded of Amon. "Thanks." She gulped. "But no ... it's not that ... it's ... I would like to find his shrine. Do you know where it is?"

"But of course!"

"Could you show me on a map?"

"Yes, in the morning. Now, let's go back to the van with the others. It's getting cold." Yuri stood up and held out his hand for Zoya.

# CHAPTER TWENTY-ONE

O nce the Russian border was crossed without incident, Chris and Zoya stopped at the cave where he and Amon had hidden their additional supplies not so long ago. The cold had preserved much of its contents. They stocked themselves with a week's worth of rations and retraced the trail on which Amon was last seen. Luckily, the weather cooperated this time. Although it was bitterly cold, the clear sunny sky bore the augury of good fortune ahead.

They trekked past the ill-fated ledge where Amon had toppled over, and arrived at a valley between the hills. This is where Amon and Chris had wanted to set-up camp the last time, before their journey was cut tragically short. This area was less than an hour's hike away from the gorge bottom where Amon might have landed if he had fallen all the way to the bottom. It was closer still to the ledge where Chris thought Amon initially landed and the cave which he had then inspected. The idea was to search the area inside out, every nook and cranny, all the caves and trails.

Two days and three nights passed but their search efforts were futile. There was no sign of Amon or the Aifra. Every day, Chris trained his binoculars from the high cliff behind their camp and not a single human being was anywhere to be seen. Not in the day, nor after dark. They hiked to the river bed at the bottom of the gorge and scoured the area several times over. Nothing. Not even human remains. Together they re-visited the cave where Chris had seen footsteps right after the accident. By now those too had disappeared. Buried under a fresh layer of snow. On their third morning at camp, Zoya was lighting a fire outside to make some coffee when Chris joined her.

"Hey, whatchya doing? I want to show you something," he said.

"Oh, just need coffee. What's up?"

"Come take a look. The buzzer's going off the rails this morning."

"The leopard sensor?"

"Yep." Chris ducked into the tent with Zoya close behind.

Once inside the tent, Chris crouched beside the sensor—which was now flashing red and screeching like a painful blister—and indicated for Zoya to sit down next to him. He pulled out a folded piece of paper and flattened it on the floor in front of them. It was a map of the area. From his pocket, he took out a pencil and marked a circle on the map.

"Here. This is roughly where they are," he said.

"*They?*"

"Correct. Looks like at least two. Possibly even three large animals."

"That's strange. For the last couple of days, we've only occasionally seen one. I thought it was its territory. And now there are *three*? Why would there be three?" Zoya became thoughtful.

"I dunno. Maybe they smelled a kill? Or maybe it's training time?"

"Hmmm. Could it be that the cat we thought prowled this area," she said, running her index finger along the circle Chris had just drawn, "just brought back a large kill and now there's competition?"

"Could be. But we haven't seen any large prey in these parts since we got here, have we?"

"What if it's a frozen carcass, from a while ago?"

"Like a fifty-thousand year-old Denisovan corpse, you mean?" Chris chuckled.

"Chris, be serious!" said Zoya punching him in the upper arm. "Oh no!" she then exclaimed, covering her mouth with her hands.

"What? What's wrong?"

"What if you're right …"

"Umm … the Denisovans have been dead for thousands of years. Does it matter?"

"Not Denisovan, you crazy! I meant human. What if it's a *human* corpse?"

Chris winced. "Hmmm. I'm still betting on an Aifra training. This is probably where they bring the leopards once in a while to train them," said Chris definitively, without allowing himself to entertain the possibility that he dreaded the most.

"Well, there's only one way to find out. We'd have a fair view of that area from the summit over there, no?" Zoya asked, pointing towards the east. "The one you usually climb."

"I'd imagine, yeah. Quite a three-sixty-degree view, actually."

"What are we waiting for then? Grab your binoculars. Let's go!" Zoya pulled out a pair of binoculars from her backpack and hurried out.

The climb up to the peak behind wasn't particularly difficult. So, they made it to their vantage point in less than twenty minutes. This hill had a broad table-top summit with a panoramic view of the valley below. Once on top, Chris rushed to his preferred lookout point and adjusted his binoculars while Zoya caught up to him breathlessly.

"Hey, I'm going over there. On top of that boulder," she said, pointing at a huge chunk of rock right behind them. "That way I'll have more elevation."

Chris nodded his approval and focused on the sight in front of him. He knew from memory where to look. He had seen the vision with his headset on. Two to three leopards on the prowl, right in the middle of that clearing over there. His binoculars honed in on the spot behind the cluster of trees that surrounded it. But nothing. He panned across the horizon twice, thrice, four times over. Nothing. Nada. Zilch. Just trees and shady hollows in between.

"Where did they go? I could swear I—"

"WATCH OUT!" he heard Zoya scream.

He pivoted quickly and scanned the surroundings. There it was. Right below the rock where Zoya stood. A massive snow leopard, crouching on its hind-legs, as if preparing for a leap. He searched his pockets for his gun.

"Dang!" He'd forgotten to bring it, in his hurry to get here.

"One more!" screamed Zoya in horror.

She was pointing to the east. Sure enough, there it was, another full grown snow leopard advancing slowly up the cliff. Zoya was trying to climb down the boulder to come to Chris's assistance. Chris raised his hand to stall her descent. He had to think on his feet. Despite the bitter chill in the air around him, beads of sweat were forming on his brow. He wished he had a lighter, like the last time he faced-off with one of these beasts. Today, his fire poi would be of no use.

There was one way out though. But it was risky. And it wouldn't save Zoya. But maybe he could come back for her. He eyed the hanging tree branch again. Less than fifty feet away. The cats were advancing slowly but surely like a river creeping into the sea, heavy with silt but as steady as a gymnast. He had to act quick. He gritted his teeth and started counting down in his mind.

*One. Two. Three.*

"ANOTHER ONE!" came Zoya's frantic screech.

He turned in the direction of her finger and his jaws dropped. The third cat was right there on his left, just below the hanging branch he was planning to use for his escape. Chris was surrounded. His heart raced. The largest leopard was right in front of him now, less than twenty feet away. The cat leaped. Chris instantly shut his eyes from the shock and crouched involuntarily. There was a shrill scream. It wasn't his own. Then a thud. He opened his eyes a wink. Before him a cloaked and hooded man of a tree-like frame was standing with his right arm outstretched. In his left hand he held a staff. Before him a prone and confused leopard was quickly scrambling to its feet. Plucking up his courage, Chris stood up and opened his eyes completely.

A bizarre scene was unfolding in front of him. More hooded men in similar attire were emerging from the woodwork. The second leopard was tossed ten feet into the air by one of them. The third animal was already turning on its tail when a stout, broad shouldered man appearing from below the cliff fired into the air, but the shot sealed the deal. The three leopards ran in various directions and disappeared from view within seconds. Before he could fully process what just happened, Chris realized that Zoya was still on the boulder, screaming deliriously. From joy or from fear, he could not tell.

A shorter portly man started advancing towards Chris. He noticed that this man along with the one who had fired the gun earlier, were the only ones in the troupe not garbed in their cult-like hooded garments.

"Alright, alright boy. C'mon then. A jolly good escape that was, wasn't it?" he asked Chris.

"Dr. Cobb!" exclaimed Chris, moving back a step not sure if he should brace for an attack.

Noticing this, the broad-shouldered man hollered to him from the distance. "It's alright, Chris. Albert is not with the Aifra. These are not the Aifra. Come buddy, you're safe now."

"This … can't be real," Chris muttered, as he hurried in the direction of the muscular man. "Amon! It's true. You *are* alive!" Beamed Chris, as he flung his arms around his friend.

"I told you that you underestimate me," Amon replied laughing. "Now, come. Let's get you to safety. Come Zoya!" He turned around and waved at Zoya.

"I'm not sure I understand what's happening," said Zoya when she had clambered down.

"Neither do I," agreed Chris.

"Don't worry, lad. We'll explain everything. Now, do you have any item to fetch before we head to your new home?" asked Dr. Cobb.

"Err ... umm ... just our tent and bags, I suppose. They're down in the valley that way," said Chris, indicating the direction with his finger.

"Okay, let's go then," said Amon.

When they turned to climb down the slope, Chris noticed that the hooded men had disappeared. "Where did the others go?" he asked, looking around to see if he could spot them anywhere.

"More importantly, *who* are they?" Zoya chimed in.

"Oh, they'll meet us there," said Dr. Cobb. "And we'll tell you all about them soon enough. Don't you worry your little heads about it."

"Yeah, don't worry Chris. Why don't you go on ahead with Zoya and pack your tent? I'll help Dr. Cobb down the hill. He's not going to be able to keep pace with you."

"Alright. We'll meet you down there," said Chris as he made his way to the tent. Zoya waved at them, before trotting down the hill behind Chris.

It took a few minutes to pack up their tent and take what they could carry. Amon also lent a hand with the luggage.

Then they trekked down the edge of the mountain to the ledge where the accident had happened and arrived at the cave, that Chris discovered while searching for Amon.

"Well, *come* on lads, everyone inside. Let's take our positions," Dr. Cobb instructed.

"What positions?" asked Zoya.

"Here, this way," said Amon. "See that nook in the cave wall. We need to stand side by side. Dr. Cobb and I will be on either side and you two stand in the middle."

The four of them walked into a rectangular dent in the cave wall, just about the size of a small closet and aligned themselves in a straight line as instructed. It was a rather snug fit with Dr. Cobb and Amon pushed up against the side walls of the enclosure.

"Ready?" asked Dr. Cobb.

"Yes," Amon replied.

The other two exchanged confused glances. Dr. Cobb placed his palm on the rock surface next to him and the area became suddenly iridescent. Amon copied this movement and immediately the floor beneath their feet began to descend like an elevator.

"Whoa!" exclaimed Zoya, grabbing Chris's arm. "What's happening?"

They descended down the dark rocky shaft at a steady pace as if on an actual elevator. Strangely enough, the interior of this primitive elevator was not as dark as one would expect. The walls seemed to glow with a surreal light, like a peculiar form of bioluminescence. Before anyone could respond to Zoya, the vertical tunnel, they were sliding down, ended abruptly and the elevator floor, which was basically just a slab of rock, floated downwards through an open space—an underground cave.

"Oye!" said Chris. "This is like an amusement park."

Within moments they landed at the bottom of the cave some thirty feet below.

"What *is* this place?" Zoya asked, looking around in every direction.

"Aha! My lovelies, this is Lumania. It has been my home for more than half a year now. This is just the landing area. Follow me, and I will show you around this astounding underground kingdom."

"Lumania? Is that like a lighting company?"

"Hey, that's what I thought too!" Amon roared with laughter. "But it turned out, that this is an ancient, forgotten civilization."

A couple of tall, robed men appeared from a tunnel in front of them. They smiled and bowed and stood on either side of the passage entrance, like a pair of sentries to a fantasy movie-set.

"They don't speak much, these kind Lumanians," said Dr. Cobb, smiling and bobbing his head at them. "But I managed to learn what I needed to, about them. They are telepaths."

"Like us?" asked Chris.

"Not even close. They are far superior to any one of us. Even Wanda."

The company entered the tunnel and the two sentries followed close behind. Zoya turned her head around and eyed them with suspicion.

"Don't you worry, my dear," said Dr. Cobb "They wouldn't hurt a fly, these goofs."

"I don't know about that," said Chris, lowering his voice, "after what they did to those leopards back there."

"Aye! That took a lot of convincing, mind you." Dr. Cobb grinned. "And even then, what they did was not dangerous to the leopards in any way. Just lift and toss aside. Cats are sprightly on their feet. If you toss them, they land without hurt or damage. A lot of fat under their skins and paws."

"Lift and toss aside, you say. From a distance, though? How on earth can they do that?" asked Chris with barely hidden incredulity in his tone.

"That's just it, isn't it? The most fascinating thing about these people. They use sound. Infrasound. Ultrasound. All the available frequencies. Can you believe it?"

"Acoustic levitation," Chris mumbled.

"Precisely! Look at this." Dr. Cobb gestured to the broad passage they were in and Chris noticed that it was not unlike an urban subway station, minus the technology. Except, there was something miraculous about it. The paved floor had been polished and carved out of rock. The walls were laden with creepers, vines and moss, some bearing beautiful white flowers. There was no sign of any electricity anywhere, yet the passage was well lit with a natural, perhaps even biological light. Instead of the familiar odours of sweat, vomit and smoky industrialization that permeate the metropolitan subways, here they could smell wild berries and damp foliage.

"It's beautiful," said Zoya.

"And all of this, mind you, is built with that precise power—acoustic manipulation," Dr. Cobb explained.

"You're kidding!" exclaimed Chris.

"Absolutely not. Ah, here we are—the city. Behold!" Dr. Cobb raised his hands in front of him and flailed them around in a flamboyant gesture of welcome.

They were standing at the entrance to a many-tiered township, hidden completely under the surface of the earth. Every facet of this complex was built with stone—alleys, inclined pathways, staircases, residential quarters on either side, piazzas for gathering. The square they were in right now was lined with flowering plants and creepers. The only thing that was missing from this underground metropolis were its denizens.

"Wow, this is like a Joules Verne novel!" exclaimed Chris.

"A what?" asked Amon.

"You know, like Journey to the Center of the Earth," Chris replied.

Amon shook his head.

"No? Doesn't ring a bell?"

Amon still looked confused, but Dr. Cobb readily jumped into the conversation. "I know exactly what you mean, lad," he said. "What a fine book that was and yes, I must say, the similarities are uncanny. A world underneath our world. What about that, eh?" he slapped Chris affectionately on the shoulder.

"Where are all the people, though?" Zoya whispered.

"In meditation, of course. This is that hour. Actually, they meditate a lot, these ones. Come now, let us go to my humble residence. The one they have graciously offered for my stay. We could grab a spot of breakfast too. What do you say?" He walked over to one of their tall escorts and exchanged some words in a hushed tone. The man nodded and left across the square.

They followed Dr. Cobb to the far end of the square and up a winding staircase made of polished black stone. They didn't have to climb far to reach a landing area where lines of rooms were carved into the cave wall like cabins in a ship. Now that they were closer to the cave wall, the source of illumination in this city became apparent. Glow worms. Small clusters of them at regular intervals clinging to solid surfaces or simply suspended in mid-air, like street lights in a haunted town. But these tiny insects weren't the only organisms lighting up this magical city. The walls, walkways and stairwells were bordered with rows of bioluminescent mushrooms and bacteria. These life forms sprouted next to, and all over the vines and creepers, the shrubs and orchids and the multifarious flora and fauna growing inside this enclave.

"This place … it's a whole ecosystem of its own," mused Zoya, as her eyes wandered around.

Dr. Cobb had heard her. "Indeed it is," he concurred. "Now let me welcome you to my quarters. Please, do step inside." He led everyone into his apartment. It was a single room accommodation. A comfortable bed on the floor made with blankets, pillows and clean white linen could be seen against the wall. A rectangular stone slab at the room's center served as a table with colourful cushions around it for seats. Open stone racks in the walls served as shelves for clothing and other artefacts. There was a straw mat in one corner, possibly for meditation and strange crystals of various colours and shapes decorated the floor next to it.

"Gather around at the table, will you?" said Dr. Cobb, once they were all there. "Breakfast should be on its way."

They stashed their luggage against the wall next to the entrance and sat down. The stone table was large enough for all of them to fit comfortably, leaving room for a couple of others. Shortly after they were seated, one of their escorts entered with a tray of food. Although he was still wearing the same baggy, full-length robe made of a soft brownish fabric, the hood of his garment was now lowered, revealing a long oval face of yellowish complexion and a shiny bald head. He smiled amicably and laid his tray down on the table. It was loaded with all kinds of fruits and cereals, apples, pears, berries, bowls of walnuts and raisins. Behind him a young woman entered with a large jug of milk and a bowl of honey. She was a little shorter but still exceptionally tall for a woman, about five-ten perhaps, and garbed in similar attire. Surprisingly, she was also completely bald, just like her counterpart. Behind her, another man almost indistinguishable from the first, walked in with four sets of brass plates, mugs and cutlery.

"Enjoy," he said, bowing his head and smiling before he left with the others.

"They speak English?" Chris asked Dr. Cobb.

"Certainly. They stay up to speed with the times. C'mon now, let us have breakfast. It's all vegan food. Very healthy."

"Uh, what about the milk?" asked Zoya.

"That's just soy milk, my dear. Animal products do not cross the threshold of the kingdom of Lumania."

"You say kingdom … do they have a king?" asked Chris, before biting into an apple.

"They used to. Not any more of course, since their civilization was washed away by the Great Flood. Their home islands sank beneath the sea thousands of years ago. Those who survived, went to their underground cities. That is where we are right now, in an ancient Lumanian city."

"By the Great Flood, you don't mean the one in the Old Testament, do you?"

"I do not know. And neither do they. Perhaps they are one and the same. Perhaps they are both entirely mythological. Who can say? My guess is that, it refers to a time-period after the last Ice Age, when multiple islands and coasts did end up getting devoured by the seas swelling with meltwater."

"We are not far from such a situation happening again, are we?" asked Zoya, worried.

"What is that, my child?"

"I meant with global warming, the Arctic ice-shelf could melt any day, and entire countries could be lost," she explained.

"Sad, but true. That is what the Elders of Lumania believe as well, and that is why they are determined to stick with their primitive ways."

"Eco-friendly, not primitive, in my opinion," Amon, who had managed to make himself practically invisible for the longest time, suddenly decided to add.

"Yes, yes, you are correct."

"The real question though Dr. Cobb, is how you managed to end up here, in the kingdom of the Lumanians, to begin with?" asked Chris.

"Ah! That's a long story. For now, might it suffice if I said that I was rescued?"

"Rescued? But from whom?"

"The Aifra, of course!"

"Wait, I'm all confused now. Wasn't it your intention to join the Aifra? I mean, when you abandoned us right before our ship sailed for Egypt?" Chris pressed on with his questioning.

"Oh dear me, why *of course* not! I was captured … when … when I tried to rendezvous with my … long lost son." Dr. Cobb hung his head, sorrowfully.

"Sorry to hear that, Professor," said Zoya in a comforting tone. "How did you manage to escape?"

"The Lumanians. The earth parted and they sucked me into their world. Very much the same way you arrived here yourself, this morning."

"And what about the Aifra? And your so—" Zoya was interrupted by the arrival of their Lumanian escort.

"Sir, Madam," he said, "we have prepared your lodging. After your meal, you can follow me." He sat down at the table next to them and smiled affectionately.

"Would you like some fruit?" asked Amon, with an air of hospitality.

"Thank you, kind Sir, but I have eaten already."

Zoya and Chris refrained from asking Dr. Cobb any further question in his presence and ate in silence only making soft munching sounds from time to time as they gobbled down their breakfast. Once they were done eating, their escort rose to take them to their lodging.

"Please, this way," he said.

Chris and Zoya picked up their bags in a hurry and Amon grabbed the tent and some extra supplies. "I'll take these down for you," he offered.

Walking down the corridor, they passed several other rooms similar to Dr. Cobb's—each as spartan as the next. Their design was reminiscent of the ashram in Rishikesh, where Zoya and Alejandro had stayed not long ago, except for the fact that here, the rooms neither had any door nor any wooden structure inside them.

"Wood is forbidden in our land," said the Lumanian. "We do not kill trees."

Zoya blushed. "I figured as much," she mumbled. "You must have read my thoughts."

The Lumanian nodded. "But have no worry. I am not reading your every thought. Only the one's you project. That is our etiquette."

"You lost me," said Zoya.

"You see, there are two types of thoughts. The ones that are completely private. Those are only for ourselves. We call them closed thoughts. And then there are those that we'd like to share with someone but can't. You know what I mean?"

"Kind of … can you give me some examples?"

"Say like right now, you had a question, correct?"

"True."

"But you don't know me well, so you couldn't ask."

"Oh, I see what you mean."

"There could be other such thoughts. Like a question for someone who isn't here. You think you'll ask him, when you see him. Has that happened to you?"

"All the time, yeah."

"These types of thoughts are open thoughts and they have a signal which we can read. Our rules are very strict in this matter. We cannot encroach upon a closed thought without permission, with a few exceptions. But open thoughts, we are allowed to read."

"Fascinating. You say there are exceptions to this rule? Do you mind if I ask what they are?"

"No, I don't mind. There are exceptions for enemies and prisoners but rarely do we have enemies or take prisoners so you have nothing to worry about." He smiled. "We are here. Your room, Madam." He gestured towards the room.

"Thank you! I am Zoya, by the way. And you are?"

"You can call me, Kazhar." He nodded and turned to Chris. "Your room is not far away," he said. "I have arranged for you to be with Amon."

"Oh, that's perfect," said Amon. "I can take him there, myself. Thank you. I will see you soon." He clasped Kazhar's shoulder with his right hand and bowed respectfully. Kazhar returned the gesture and left.

"It's their handshake," Amon explained to a confused Chris when Kazhar had left. "Let's go Chris. Zoya, we'll see you at lunch?"

"I … I mean …" Zoya hesitated.

"Sorry, I forgot to explain," Amon apologized. "There is a lunch area in this district. Every district has one. We can head there together at noon. Is that okay?"

"Ah, okay! That makes sense. Sure."

"We'll come get you then!" said Chris with a wave of his hand as he followed Amon down the corridor.

\* \* \*

Amon's room was slightly larger than Dr. Cobb's. Now it had been upgraded with an extra bed for Chris and additional cushions at the center-table.

They dropped their luggage in a corner and sat down at the table.

"I wish we could close the door to this damn room," Chris complained, as he sat.

"There's no need. You can say what you want. These rooms are sound-proof," Amon assured.

"Haha!"

"I'm not kidding," Amon said, with a straight face.

"Really? No way!"

"Surprising, isn't it? The Lumanians are extremely powerful with manipulating sound. It's almost as if they can touch it. Let me prove it. Stay here," he said and hurried outside.

"Can you hear me?" he screamed from the passage. Chris was shaking his head, and waving his hands around. "What about now?" There was no response. Amon returned to the room and went to sit with Chris. "See?" he asked, slapping his friend in the middle of the back.

"Uncanny! I couldn't hear a single word."

"I told you."

"But how is it possible that with powers like this, these guys haven't taken over the world, yet?"

"Long story. But the gist is that, it's a principle thing. They do not believe in aggression, and that's why they stay hidden. The Elders told Dr. Cobb all this."

"Elders?"

"Yeah, they're the ones in charge of this place, it seems. They are very ancient. According to legend, the Lumanians were vanquished when the world became a violent place, thousands of years ago. When wars were waged between kingdoms and such, the Lumanians refused to fight. So people thought they were routed out. But—"

"They weren't"

"Correct. Their island kingdom sank under the sea but their underground cities sustained by staying hidden. And they have been growing."

"Growing, how?"

"By sheltering people in danger."

"Like you and Dr. Cobb?"

"Yes. But not just any people. Telepaths. Like themselves."

"So, are you saying … that they knew about us … the Hekameses, all along?"

"Yes, and others too. Which would explain the missing Hekameses from the Faiyum scrolls."

"Right. I always wondered why we were so few when the scrolls had predicted so many more."

"They are here. Some of them at least."

"But I still don't understand …"

"What?"

"Why now? Why save us now? If they'd always known about us, and we've been constantly getting into trouble, why didn't they try to save us before?"

"Maybe because we never came to Siberia? I don't know…"

"So what was Dr. Cobb doing in Siberia? Did he tell you?"

"Right, I forgot about that. He wasn't in Siberia. Well, he doesn't know where he was. The Aifra had captured him and taken him to the middle of nowhere, when the Lumanians found him. But I'm pretty sure it wasn't Siberia."

"What makes you so sure?"

"When I accidentally found that cave on the day of my fall and arrived here, the Lumanians were waiting for me."

"Wait, did you say accidentally? So they didn't find you, then? You found them!"

"Ummm … a bit of both actually. I stumbled into the cave to shelter from the storm when they saw me. You know these caves and tunnels they use to communicate with the outside world, they have portals that are transparent on the inside. Meaning the Lumanians can see the outside but not the other way around. So, they saw me, and let me in."

"By opening the portal?"

"Correct."

"And then, what?"

"For a day I was in a daze. Not knowing what happened. They gave me food and this room. We spoke little because I was afraid of them."

"Makes sense."

"And then on the second day, when I became friendly with Kazhar, he told me they were telepaths, just like me. I was surprised that he knew. So he told me that they knew about the Hekameses and others of our kind. Their Elders keep a tally of such people. He said that they had saved another Hekameses in a different city, many months ago, and asked me if I wanted to meet him."

"I see. Different city, eh? Not different country, though."

"No, no, he meant *Lumanian* city, not our cities. Anyway, when I wanted to meet Dr. Cobb, they sent for him. It took a full day for him to travel from where he was, to here. So it must be far."

"That depends, I suppose. Did he tell you how he travelled?"

"Yes. There is only one way to travel inside Lumania. On their trains. They are supersonic."

"Holy shit! But how? How did they build this primitive yet advanced civilization in hiding without ever getting found out?"

Amon shrugged. "Don't know. I guess, whenever someone found Lumania, they came and never left." He laughed heartily at the thought and Chris joined in.

"By the way, before I forget," said Chris when they were done laughing, "does anyone know that you two are here? Wolfgang? Wanda? Alejandro?"

"Nope. My phone is dead and Dr. Cobb had nothing but the clothes on his back when they found him. So ..."

"Okay, we should tell them. Soon. Before my phone dies too. Do phones even work down here?"

"No, but we can go back up a portal near Irkutsk. You'll have coverage there. They use that one all the time to get supplies from the city."

"We should hurry then. My battery won't last long."

"Let's go. Zoya will worry if we're not back before lunch."

# CHAPTER TWENTY-TWO

In the spacious living room of Marshal Pandey's Government bungalow, a few solemn spectators sat in front of the television, watching the news with apprehension written all over their faces.

"'The drones were shot down over international waters which constitutes an act of unprovoked escalation,' said the US Foreign Secretary this morning. He refused to answer any further question about the possibility of a US counter-attack however, stating that at this time deliberations were in progress and all possibilities were open," read the news lady, before moving on to the next story.

"This doesn't sound good at all," said Alejandro as he stood up and started to pace across the plush Persian rug at the center of the room. "What are your thoughts, Marshal Pandey? Do you think the US will launch an attack on Russia?"

The Marshal folded his arms over his chest and frowned. "We'll have to wait and see," he replied after thoughtful consideration.

"Wolfgang just texted me. He wants a conference call this evening. I bet it has something to do with these developments." Alejandro paused to look at his phone which was beeping again. "Oh, there's more, he has news from Zoya and the others. Surprising news, he says."

"What kind of surprising news? Good or bad?" asked Nirmala anxiously.

"He didn't say. I guess we'll find out soon enough."

"Even if there's a war, India will stay out of it. Everyone can hide out here 'til the coast is clear," Marshal Pandey suggested.

"I … don't think it's that simple," said Alejandro.

"Why not? I can arrange for visas if that's what you're concerned about."

"No, it's not that." Alejandro shook his head violently. "We have started this war, it's our problem now. We can't just resign to the sidelines to save ourselves."

"*You* started this war? How? I don't understand …"

One look into the Marshal's eyes and Alejandro was able to pick up a shred of his thoughts. The man had no idea about the episode at the Red Pyramid this spring. Wolfgang must have withheld the story from him since he wasn't an active member of the Hekameses back then. He decided against revealing the details without consulting with the others.

"I meant, by not using our powers to stop it from happening in the first place," Alejandro explained, attempting to control the damage. "The Hekameses are not about self-preservation, you know. As an organization, we exist to jump into the fray and do what is right, to prevent needless bloodshed and destruction. We have been given a rare gift, should we not be using it for the good of mankind? Don't you think that's the right thing to do?"

Originally meant to distract from his initial gaffe, Alejandro had no idea at what point the speech had turned into a passionate exposition and was shocked to find that Xianbin and Haresh were clapping.

"I thought you might say something like that." Pandey sighed. "That's one of the reasons I refused to become an active member of the Hekameses for so long. I am a military man. So I hope you can forgive me for not being a huge proponent of civilians taking law and order into their own hands."

"But you did join us in the end, didn't you?" asked Alejandro, relieved that his tactic had worked.

"I did."

"Why?"

"I guess I started to see the error in my ways and the merit in the argument you just made." Pandey smiled. "I hope you don't think I'm not completely on board now," he added.

"No, of course we don't think that," Nirmala chimed in before Alejandro could respond. "I can attest to the fact that you've gone above and beyond to assist us in the last few months."

"Thank you, Nirmala. What about you, Alejandro? Do you think I can be trusted?"

"I am in a foreign country with a broken leg at the complete mercy of that country's top military official, would I be stupid enough to anger him?" Alejandro chuckled.

"Ha! You don't look like a stupid man to me, my friend. But please do speak your heart, because if my career has taught me anything at all, it's the importance of trust between the members of a team such as ours."

"I was just joking," said Alejandro. "I like to make jokes. Of course, I trust you. You saved my life."

* * *

Amon and Chris came to pick Zoya up for lunch at quarter to twelve and found her chatting with Dr. Cobb.

"Ah! There you are," said Dr. Cobb. "I was here to take Zoya to lunch when she told me that the two of you are meeting here as well. You have made good time. It will take me at least fifteen minutes to walk to the lunch hall and tardiness is frowned upon in Lumania!"

"Yes, let's go. I'll lead the way," said Amon.

"We almost thought we wouldn't make it back in time," said Chris, as they were climbing down the steps from their rooms.

"Make it back? Did Amon give you a little tour of the city this morning?" asked Dr. Cobb.

"No, we didn't have time for that. We were trying to call Wolfgang."

"Ah! That old fool! Did you reach him?"

"Yes, we did. After several attempts. It's not been easy to get through to him these days."

"And why not?"

"I don't know. Maybe he's in some remote location? He didn't tell us where he was …"

"When does her ever." sighed Dr. Cobb. "So what did he say?"

Chris pondered the question for a minute before responding. "Quite a few things, to be honest. Why don't we all meet after lunch to discuss? I want us all to be there."

"Alright. We are almost at our destination. There it is, the lunch room. Do you see it?" Dr. Cobb pointed to a vaulted doorway carved into the rock about ten feet away.

"Yeah, I see it. So everyone can just eat there? For free?" Chris asked, raising his eyebrows quizzically.

"People of this district and guests, yes. But I wouldn't call it free. The concept of society here is very different. Everyone has a purpose."

"Interesting. Sounds like communism to me."

"Ha! You can say that perhaps, although the structure of Lumania did by no means *arise* from communism. They have retained their social structure from time immemorial, much before communism was even born." Dr. Cobb laughed. "And you know what's funny? It works," he added, lowering his voice mysteriously.

"A functioning primitive social structure in the twenty-first century, eh? I'm sure all the researchers of the world would flock to Lumania, if they knew!"

"Primitive? No! I wouldn't call them that. Not at all. Have you seen their trains?"

"Yep, we took one this morning. I didn't mean it like that, of course. I meant—"

"It's alright." Dr. Cobb slapped Chris on the shoulder. "Come, let's find ourselves a seat."

Inside the cavernous hall, Chris noticed that Amon and Zoya had saved them a couple of seats. There were colourful cushions on the floor for the guests to sit with small stone slabs serving as tables. The Lumanians were filing in silently and occupying whatever seat was available. In the front of the room was an elongated table, where the servers were loading plates and bowls with flavourful food items.

"Is it a buffet?" Chris asked Amon, who was seated to his right.

"Yes, but it hasn't started yet. When they finish setting up, the children eat first, and then we will line up with the rest."

"That's a lot of discipline," said Chris. "Must be quite an authoritarian regime."

"No. Not at all, actually. That's the most surprising part. There doesn't seem to be any law enforcement or formal government to compel the people to behave the way they do. Everything is voluntary. Part of their cult-like teaching, and people participate of their own freewill. They can leave if they want to."

"That's hard to believe. Maybe that's how they want outsiders to view them. I'm sure there's more to their story than that."

"Maybe. But I haven't seen it yet. Or even Dr. Cobb, who's been here longer. And now that you're here, you can see for yourself."

"For sure. Speaking of being here, how did you even find us today? That was a close save. I never thought I'd have a leopard jump on me and live to tell the tale one day." Chris laughed. "Thanks, man!"

"No need to thank me. You would have done the same." Amon smiled. "About how I found you … well, a couple of days ago, I had gone up to the cave, where we stored our supplies, hoping to find the walkie-talkie we had left behind. I wanted to let someone know where we were. But when I got there, it was gone. And some other supplies were missing too.

"At first, I thought you had returned to the cave and grabbed them. So I looked for you everywhere. But there was no sign of you anywhere. And then I saw a creature lurking behind the trees—the cheetah."

"Leopard," Chris corrected.

"Ha! Right. For a second I saw its flashing green eyes, before it disappeared into the trees. It didn't attack me. It just left."

"That's not unusual. They don't normally eat humans and don't attack, unless they're threatened or starved."

"Which was great. For me. I was unharmed. What's more, I read its thoughts."

"What? You *know* how to do that?"

"Yes, I'm the only one of us who does. I can pick up the thoughts of animals. But it just works with vertebrates, I think. Wolfgang never told you?"

"No, he didn't. Another one of his secrets." Chris chuckled.

"Anyway, that's how I knew. It was a lady leopard."

"Ha! Lady leopard. That's funny!"

"Why? What do you call it? Woman leopard?"

"Jesus, no! Female leopard."

"Okay, female leopard. She had seen you and another person. She was scared. They were going to surround you

235

and attack in the morning. I knew right away where they were going. The whole gang. I rushed back and alerted everyone. It took a lot of words to get the Lumanians to help. But they value friendship. They didn't want our friends to die. So they joined us and then you know the rest."

"So you knew what time they were planning to attack? The leopards?"

"Didn't know exactly, but I could sense it would be early. Animals thoughts are strange. They don't think like humans. They think sunrise and sunset instead of exact time. I don't know how to explain …"

"No, I get it," said Chris, sympathetically patting his friend on the shoulder. "It's like I can't explain exactly what I see when I'm up on a telephone tower and have visions of people who are nearby."

"Exactly. But I knew. In my gut, I knew the time and place. And that's how we got there to save you."

"That's quite a story and I learned something new about you too!" Chris grinned.

"Look, it's time to line up for lunch," Amon indicated, pointing to the small queue that was forming next to the buffet table.

The vegetarian lunch was unlike anything Chris had ever tasted before. Strange mushrooms in aromatic sauces. Breads made from flour he couldn't recognize. It was like the cuisine of an alien species. Yet, at the same time, the flavours were oddly familiar. The things that grew on earth but mixed and cooked differently, like if you grilled a jackfruit over volcanic lava or fried a zucchini in poppy seed oil. After this antediluvian meal, Dr. Cobb's earlier assertion that the Lumanian civilization was thousands of years old, seemed all the more credible.

They walked back to their rooms in silence. Partly because the atmosphere in this underground nation evoked that kind of tranquility, but mostly due to the fact that they were too full and sleepy to engage in meaningful conversation. Dr. Cobb's accommodation was the first to arrive and they decided to gather there for the Hekameses' meeting.

"Let's keep this brief, because I could sure use a nap," said Chris with a chuckle.

"Me too," Zoya concurred. "But will someone tell me what this is about?"

"Chris and I spoke to Wolfgang this morning," Amon explained. "Just to let him know where we are. And there was a certain thing he wanted from us. So, here we are."

"Yeah, he sounded very worried," said Chris. "Apparently, something grave is about to happen, but he wasn't ready to share more details yet. In the meantime, he wanted us to prepare for it."

"Oh dear Lord," said Dr. Cobb. "How can we prepare for something until we know what it is? Did he tell you how?"

"In fact, he did. He was fascinated to hear about the Lumanians. He thinks that they are our answer," said Chris, animatedly.

"Our answer to what, exactly?" asked Dr. Cobb.

"The crisis we're about to face," said Chris.

"He didn't say it in so many words but we're expecting a massive attack," Amon explained.

"An attack? On whom and where?"

"We don't know," said Chris. "But Wolfgang wants us to ask the Lumanians for their help. Without their assistance, there will be carnage, he thinks."

"Oh my! But that's impossible. Not that I haven't tried. The Elders, they won't budge. Non-violence is their credo, my dear. There is not a soul on earth that could make them break it. As you can see, none have succeeded in thousands of years!"

"But it may not require any violence at all. That's the whole point," said Chris, enthusiastically.

"Like how they saved us from the leopards this morning, remember?" Zoya asked.

"That took a great deal of persuasion, mind you," said Dr. Cobb.

"Yeah, Amon told me. Maybe it'll work again. I mean, we can't just give up without a try. Innocent lives might be at stake!" Chris exclaimed.

"Oh, alright! I'll request a meeting with the Elders. If they agree, it won't be before tomorrow. They only accept meetings in the morning. But before that, I need to know exactly what kind of help, Wolfgang has in mind."

"We can call him again today, if I manage to charge my phone with the battery pack I found in my luggage," Chris quickly volunteered.

"Go ahead, then. Get your phone charged, and we'll call that grouch, this evening."

# CHAPTER TWENTY-THREE

L umania was a peculiar place. Here, the days and nights looked exactly the same, bathed in a bluish mystical iridescence. There was no mechanism for timekeeping. No bells or alarms signalling the hour of day. But life unfolded diurnally in its own spectacular rhythm, almost like that of a living organism, following its biological cycles. It was a wonder to behold. That such a civilization could exist, and be governed by human inhabitants was beyond the expectation of the Hekameses, who arrived here by accident not long ago.

True to this spirit of natural discipline, Kazhar arrived in the wee hours of the morning, to wake Dr. Cobb for their meeting with the Elders. Dr. Cobb was deep in slumber when the nightingale flew into his room and perched itself above his head, singing merrily into the morning, as it pecked on the bird-feed hanging from the ceiling. This was the Lumanian way to awaken the sleeping—a song-bird of choice and its beautiful notes.

Dr. Cobb sat up, rubbed his eyes and walked up to the door to find Kazhar standing there, his back turned to the entrance to allow the guest his privacy.

"Thank you for the wake-up call," Dr. Cobb said, coughing. "I will be right out, and then we can fetch the others. What time is the meeting?"

"The Elders will see you at ten o'clock, Sir, but we must catch the train at seven to get there before the tour," Kazhar replied, his back still turned to the entrance.

"What tour? And oh, for God's sake, do turn around. I am fully clothed over here."

Kazhar turned and bowed reverentially. "I apologize. It's for your own privacy, Sir. It is our custom," he said, blushing.

"Yes, yes, I know, but no need for that with me, my dear. So what of the tour? What is it about?"

"It is a tradition, Sir, for us to offer a tour of the Capital to the respected guests of our Elders. It will be a short tour, about half an hour. But after the meeting, you are free to explore further on your own."

"Your hospitality is commendable and thank you. We look forward to exploring your capital city. I have only been there once since my arrival, and the others have not seen it at all."

"You have been there, Sir?" Kazhar sounded surprised.

"Yes. Why does it surprise you?"

"Forgive me, but I was told that you had not seen the city."

"Why that is true, of course. The Elders wanted to see me. There was a confusion. We met briefly, and I was brought back to my lodgings."

"You are privileged," said Kazhar. "To be summoned by an Elder is considered a great honour in Lumania. You must be very wise."

"I … don't know about that. They thought … mistake … never mind," Dr. Cobb fumbled. "I should get dressed, if we are to catch that train." Dr. Cobb disappeared into the room.

\* \* \*

Zircon, the capital of Lumania was the lifeblood of this kingdom, hosting its treasury and producing the majority of its food crops. From the day Dr. Cobb had landed here, he had been given this information, and since then he had longed to find out exactly how this ancient civilization had continued to sustain itself into the twenty-first century. Today, finally his wish was about to be fulfilled.

As soon as the Hekameses disembarked their train, they were greeted by two smiling Lumanians, a man and woman, dressed in the fashion of the capital—flowing white robes with golden ribbon belts around their waists.

Zircon was breathtakingly majestic and immaculately maintained like a self-sustaining eco-system with each of its elements functioning to support the other. Their Lumanian escorts gave them a walking-tour of the city, diligently pointing out the eating areas, the quarters, the meditation rooms and most importantly the treasury.

The treasury was the most formidable structure in the metropolis—a huge stone hemisphere protruding from the cave wall like an angry blister. It had no doors or windows or even sentries guarding it, just a bulging rotundness resembling the pot-belly of a gigantic stone sculpture.

"How do you get in? To the treasury, I mean," Dr. Cobb asked their male escort. "There aren't any doors."

"There is a tunnel that leads to it. The entrance is sealed and hidden. Only a few can access it," he explained.

"Ah, makes sense," said Chris. "But I still don't understand."

"What do you not understand, Sir?" asked the escort.

"Does your country even do business with the outside world? How does it make money? I don't see any shops or industries—"

"Or currency," Amon interrupted. "What about currency? Do you have one?"

"No, we do not. We don't believe in creating objects of notional worth. Food, shelter, clothing and all basic necessities are supplied to the citizens at regular intervals, determined by the Elders, and everyone is happy."

"That doesn't make any sense. How do you pay for the things you need?"

"We grow most of our food crops. Our garments are woven here. We make flour from grains. We have kitchens in every district. And for everything we need from the outside, we have gold."

"Is that what's stored in the treasury then? Your gold?" asked Zoya.

"Absolutely. You might have heard that we were a very rich kingdom in ancient times. Although we had to go into hiding, and many lives were lost during the Great Flood, we could save much of our gold."

"Gold that is *thousands* of years old. Oh my, that must be worth a fortune!" exclaimed Dr. Cobb.

The Lumanian nodded, humbly. "Some of us also divide their times between Lumania and the outside. They exchange our gold and bring other supplies from various parts of the world."

"I do not see how such a system could work," said Dr. Cobb. "Without proper government, laws or punishment for crimes. How can you trust anyone? How are the resources divided fairly?"

Their lady guide who had been silent throughout this conversation, walked up to Dr. Cobb and smiled. "Kind Sir, let me ask you this then, where is the government or law enforcement in nature outside of man-made civilizations? How do the other animals of the animal kingdom survive? Do they have judges banging their gavels at the offenders? Do they not manage to divide up the planet's resources between them? Then why should humans, the most superior species of them all, be completely incapable of self-governance?"

"Laws are made to instruct the good, and in the hope that there may be no need of them; also, to control the bad, whose hardness of heart will not be hindered from crime," muttered Chris.

"Plato," whispered the guide, grinning with admiration.

"Are you telling me, young lady, that the law of the jungle is to apply to humans?" asked Dr. Cobb.

"Wasn't that how we had lived for millions of years, before the advent of civilization? Did we not survive?"

"But that is total anarchy, my dear. Eat or be eaten. In the wild, there is no equality, no fair distribution of resources, no punishment for wrong-doing. It's about survival of the fittest. How can humans live like that?"

"Isn't that exactly how humans are living this very day? Even with your governments and artificially imposed restrictions and your so-called law enforcement? There are still beggars on the streets and countries full of citizens below the poverty line, while the millionaires are lining their coffers with money stolen from the rest. Where is the equality? Where is the fair distribution? You tell me!"

"I … um …" Dr. Cobb stammered and fell silent.

"She has a point," said Chris, after a moment of silence. "Laws only protect the rich and powerful."

"Exactly," the Lumanian agreed, smiling and nodding at Chris. "Here, we operate on the principle of self-governance. Everyone watches out for everyone else and contributes to the society of their own accord. That's our credo. If you choose to live in Lumania you abide by it. Else you leave."

"What if someone takes advantages of such a benevolent system, though?" asked Zoya.

"That is why we do not admit just anyone. We can see into your minds and hearts. Never forget that. We screen for the right people who are capable of embracing our credo and only open our doors to those who pass the test."

"It's true, your gates are pretty concealed. I wasn't allowed inside the first time I reached your cave." Chris laughed.

"See, you already know." The Lumanian nodded. "If as humans we cannot govern ourselves, cannot act morally, cannot tell right from wrong, then we are no different from the animals we consider less intelligent. Such people cannot live in Lumania."

"It's a good philosophy," said Amon. "Is it time for us to meet the Elders?"

"We have a few more minutes to see the city. Would you like to see our food garden? It's the most beautiful place in this city."

"Yes, of course, we'd love to see it," Zoya said excitedly.

"Alright, this way then."

"Why is it called a food garden?" asked Chris.

"Isn't it obvious?" The woman smiled, but not disrespectfully.

"It's where you grow your food," said Chris, blushing.

"A lot of it, yes. The fruits and vegetables. We get most of our grains from your world."

"Our world?"

"Yes, the world above ground. Now, come."

They followed their Lumanian guides through the winding lanes of Zircon past rows of ferns and bushes, walkways and streams, and arrived at a vaulted gate of foliage that led into a garden.

"After you," said the male guide, as he and his counterpart stood on either side of the door to usher the guests inside.

"Wow, what *is* this place?" exclaimed Zoya, as her eyes focussed on the sight in front of her.

They were standing inside a massive garden, almost a forest of fruit and flower-bearing trees of all varieties extending as far as the eyes could see. There was a soothing earthy smell in the air, like that of rain-soaked soil, overgrown with moss and wild flowers. There was something else about this place. Something that clearly distinguished it from the rest of Lumania. The light in here, was all natural light.

"Are we still underground?" Amon asked their male guide.

"Yes. Why do you ask?"

"Where is the light coming from?"

"Come, let me show you." The guide waved for them to follow.

They passed through the forest of fruit trees and into an area bearing smaller plants and shrubs.

"These are the herbs and vegetables," the guide explained.

The cave walls were visible once again as was its arched ceiling some thirty feet above their heads. Amon looked up at the ceiling. Instead of the polished stone surface he had seen in the rest of Lumania, here his eyes saw a completely different view. The cave ceiling was studded with sword like projections of transparent crystals, that reflected the light inside the cave like a thousand faceted mirror.

"Wow," he murmured.

"Look there!" Zoya pointed right in front of them where, beyond another clump of trees, the bright mid-morning sun filtered through a shimmering glassy surface, drowning the entire forest in a dreamy radiance.

Zoya ran forward past the clump of trees, drawn by this magical light. The others followed close behind. Once the last cluster of trees was cleared, the Hekameses found themselves standing directly in front of a wall-to-wall window of ice, stretching from floor to ceiling, shimmering, bluish and as clear as glass.

"The frozen Lake Baikal," whispered their female guide. "This part has been frozen for centuries."

"This … no it can't be!" Zoya, exclaimed. "It's an underwater cave isn't it?"

"Yes. The ice has sealed the cave entrance. So, during the day, the natural sunlight warms up this garden like a solar cooker. It's all air-tight. The heat doesn't escape and plants can grow. In the evening it cools and the photosynthesis stops. There are air vents in the walls here, just like the rest of Lumania—to recycle the air. Streams of water and ponds form with water seeping from the aquifers. There is one large pond over there." She pointed to the eastern end of the cave. "It's a complete ecosystem. And it grows the food to sustain us."

"Amazing!" said Zoya, walking up to the slab of ice about four feet high and placing her palm on its surface. Inside it, Zoya could see tiny bubbles frozen into place in between colourful crystalline patterns. "There's lake-water below, isn't there?

"Yes, and teeming with life too."

"Wait, but what happens in the summer? When the ice thaws. Doesn't this garden … get flooded—"

"No, never. Not even in the summer. The rest of the lake melts, but the chunk of ice protecting the mouth of this cave remains year-round. Although recently …" She trailed off.

"Recently, what?" asked Zoya.

"In the summers we can see water beyond the icy window of the cave. But the ice protecting the garden is still several feet thick. Recently though, the water has been coming closer and closer and the width of the ice is reducing each year."

"Global warming," Zoya whispered. "Aren't you worried that as the earth gets warmer, one day all the ice will melt in the summer, and the lake will claim your garden?"

The Lumanian's face grew remorseful. "It is not our place to worry about such things. Our Elders bear that responsibility. Let us go now. It's almost time for your meeting with them. You can come visit the garden later, whenever you like."

# CHAPTER TWENTY-FOUR

The Lumanians didn't have watches, clocks, phones, internet or any connectivity through modern technology whatsoever, yet they seemed to know the hours and seconds of the day to a tee. How they achieved this was beyond the understanding of the Hekameses, but when they arrived in front of the cave that housed the Elders, at precisely the appointed hour, not one of them appeared surprised. Their brief stay in Lumania had given them ample reason to believe that maintaining punctuality was a serious business in this mysterious land.

Although it was the seat of the Lumanian Government, the cave of the Elders was as unassuming and commonplace a structure as any with no additional flair in its design or demarcation and nothing royal or regal about it. They entered through a narrow passage lit with the usual bluish bioluminescence, and had walked only a couple of paces, before a strange relaxing sort of music emanated from somewhere, further down the passage.

"What is that music?" asked Chris.

"It is the music of the earth," said their guide.

"Huh?"

"They mean, the natural frequency of the earth, a frequency with which it would vibrate if it were to be struck," explained Dr. Cobb, lowering his voice and leaning his head close to Chris's ear.

"Ha! Does the earth even have a natural frequency?"

"Of course, everything does. It could be a set of frequencies instead of just one, but who is to test for that frequency, eh my boy? The ancient Indians certainly believed in such things. The Om sound. The voice of the universe."

"Oh, I didn't know that. So where is it coming from ... the music ... er ... sound?" Chris looked around him. A few feet ahead, he could see white light issuing from a section of the wall. "Is there a room over there?" he asked, pointing in that direction.

"Yes, indeed there is. Let us take a peek, shall we?" Dr. Cobb hurried towards the light.

There, carved into the cave wall, was a door that led into an auditorium of sorts. The entire space was bathed in a dreamy crystalline halo. Inside, three rows of Lumanians sat meditatively in concentric circles around the room's center. In front of each of them was an oblong crystal, glowing brilliantly in the dark. The combined effect of these individual crystals imparted an ethereal glow to the entire room, that was visible all the way from the passage outside. The men and women sat with their legs crossed, eyes closed and hands on the crystals while a low humming sound filled the room—the sound of Om, the music of the earth.

"They are our Seers," said their guide, noticing Chris and Dr. Cobb huddling at the door.

"Like fortune tellers?" asked Chris.

"Not quite. They are like our police. You were inquiring about law-enforcement, earlier. These are the people in charge of it. They protect Lumania."

"I'm not quite sure I understand," said Dr. Cobb. "Are they armed?"

"Ha!" The Lumanian laughed audibly. "Why does it always have to be about violence? No, they are not armed. They use the seeing crystals to maintain a lookout of our perimeters and watch for attacks and intruders. In fact, that's how we found you."

"So, they're like security!" said Zoya, who had caught up from behind and overheard the conversation.

"Partly. They have other responsibilities too."

"Like what?" Amon asked.

"They can screen people based on their intentions or tell a truth from a lie, for example. That way, we can decide who to admit into Lumania and who to expel," said the guide, as he motioned for them to keep walking.

The Om sound slowly receded in the background and the passage broadened in front of them. A few steps rose up from this area and led right into another room. The Hekameses followed their escorts into this elevated room. It was smaller in size than the one before but similarly glowing with a whitish light. There was only one crystal here. It was larger and placed along the eastern wall with a Seer seated behind it.

Straight ahead, two men and a woman sat in a row on an elevated platform lined with cushions. Their faces were calm and wizened and their backs slightly hunched. Across from them was a similar platform of stone set with cushions. The Lumanians guided their guests into this seating area, before addressing the Elders.

"Wise Ones, we have brought our guests who seek your audience," said the female guide. Both the guides bowed to the Elders by prostrating their upper bodies, and extending their arms along the floor. Then they came to sit among the Hekameses.

The Elders bowed reverentially in acknowledgement. Dr. Cobb too was imitating their gesture and bending forward in greeting. Noticing this, the other Hekameses joined in.

Once the greetings were exchanged, the Elder in the middle spoke. He had a long silver beard and a fluttering moustache to match. The latticework of delicate wrinkles on his forehead bore witness to his years on earth, similar to the rings along the trunk of a tree. "I am Solaris the Elder, and I welcome you to Lumania," he said in a slow rhythmic voice.

"I believe, I've already had the pleasure of making your acquaintance," said Dr. Cobb. "It is an absolute honour to be in your company once again."

Solaris the Elder smiled affectionately. "Speak, now. What is it that you seek?"

"We have come to you in great necessity, oh Wise One," said Dr. Cobb. "You see, we the Hekameses are fighting a lifelong—"

"I know about your fight," Solaris interrupted. "It is unnecessary." He waved his hand dismissively.

There was a low murmur among the Hekameses and they exchanged quick glances

"Unnecessary? But ... you don't ... understand," Dr. Cobb stammered. "We are in great peril. The *world* is in great peril."

"And you can save it?" Solaris asked.

"We must try, mustn't we? We have a gift and so do you. A much greater gift. An extraordinary benediction, in fact. And with your help we—"

"Our help? You seek our help in this?"

"That is what we have come to request, Wise One. We know about your principles of pacifism, but can there really be peace if a deadly force is out to get us, to murder all, to wipe out mankind? We have been hunted all our lives, Respected One. You must know that? What choice do we have, but to fight it? To stand up against the evil? Especially now, when the misguided, war-mongering scoundrels are wrecking apart our world. The human civilization is in great peril. Do you not see, Wise One?"

The Elders stayed silent through this exposition, smiling and nodding pleasantly as they heard him out. In the end, Solaris spoke softly—his voice firm but not unkind.

"This is why we never rescued a Hekameses before. You see?"

"But you *did* rescue us in the end. Why?"

"Because you surrendered your man-made tools of carnage."

"I see ... it was the weapons, you say? I was unarmed when you found me ... but Amon surely had a weapon. Did you not, my friend?" He turned to look at Amon.

"I ... no, actually." Amon fidgeted in his seat.

Chris jolted to attention at this remark. "What? Why, not? I thought we were both armed?" he asked, visibly agitated.

"Ah-h-h ... I figured, the leopards I can communicate with. I could save us from them." Amon paused and sighed. "And the Aifra. Well, our weapons would be nothing if they caught us. If anything, it'd make us more of a target."

"You see now?" Solaris asked with a broad grin across his wizened face. "You see his logic? He is wise among you. Dear Ones, you cannot fight fire with fire. Use your gift and your wisdom."

"But how do we stand and watch and not fight? And we don't necessarily have to take up arms. Only for protection, perhaps. Not for aggression. That is precisely why we need you. With your abilities we could stop the carnage without spilling any blood. Just like how your kind saved my friends from the snow leopards. No harm was done, but lives were saved, weren't they?"

"That is not our philosophy." Solaris shook his head from side to side.

"What is your philosophy then? To run like a coward? To let mankind destroy each other while you hide inside your tunnels and caves?" Dr. Cobb spat.

The Hekameses stiffened in their seats, expecting a severe sort of punishment for Dr. Cobb's sudden display of insolence. Surprisingly, no retribution followed. Instead, the Elder's grin widened.

"Anger is our greatest enemy, Dear One," he said, politely. "Don't punish yourself with it. I know you seek to agitate us with your insults. Lumanians are not agitated thus."

Dr. Cobb took a couple of deep breaths to calm himself. "Tell us then, Wise One, why is it that you don't want to join us in this fray? The world is on a destruction course, as you probably already know, and we might yet save it. But you choose not to participate. How come?"

"Because there is nothing we can do, other than to let the universe take its course."

"Fatalism." Dr. Cobb sighed, as understanding dawned.

"We do think that something can be done, though. We have reason to believe that we are currently living in a Dark Age and that it is about to end with the advent of a new Age of Enlightenment. Ancient wisdom points to this. We also have some first-hand evidence that supports this theory," Amon explained.

"We know about that theory." Solaris nodded. "But it is a single timeline event."

"Huh? I don't understand," said Amon.

"The change of Age, it may happen in one timeline. In the others, the world will perish, possibly."

"I still don't—" Amon started, but Chris stopped him by grabbing his arm.

"I think I get it," said Chris. "It's a time-travel concept. You see, there's an infinite number of possible directions in which the future might play out. Each of them is a potentially valid timeline. If any one tiny parameter changes, the outcome will change and so will our future. You can think that all of these timelines are occurring simultaneously, side by side. In one or more of them the Kali Yuga will end and Dwapara will arrive. In the others it will not."

Solaris smiled gleefully. "He understands," he confirmed.

"How do we know which timeline we are currently in?" asked Zoya.

"There's no way to know," said Chris.

"Wait, but the future hasn't been made yet," said Amon. "So we can make this timeline whichever one we want it to be," he added, excitedly.

"See, he is the wise one. Like I told you," Solaris declared.

"But how do we make this the timeline we prefer ... you know, where the Kali Yuga ends?" Zoya asked.

"Randomness," said Solaris, looking her in the eye.

"I … um …" Zoya searched for words, barely able to hide her confusion.

"He means that we can't control how the timeline plays out. Because of randomness. A random quirk will change its course and outcome," Chris explained.

"Correct," said Solaris, solemnly. "But if an entity were to act against its nature, a low-probability outcome could become possible."

"I don't understand," said Zoya.

Now Dr. Cobb intervened. "What he means is that, the probability of the Kali Yuga ending and Dwapara Yuga being ushered in at this point in time might be low, but this could change if someone or something behaved unexpectedly. Like for example, a tiger decides to become vegetarian or an Aifra soldier goes renegade and joins forces with us or something like that. Do you get the drift?"

"I think so," said Zoya.

"One or several of such aberrations can change the direction of the future considerably," Solaris added.

"What about the Kalki, then? Is that an aberration?"

"What is a Kalki, Dear One?" asked Solaris the Elder, frowning.

"A saviour. One who's supposed to arrive. Speaking of which, oh Wise One, would you happen to know anything at all about the Frozen Saint of Baikal?" Zoya asked.

Solaris recoiled as if he had been scorched. The other Elders murmured and stirred in their seats. "True devilry!" exclaimed the Elder to the right of Solaris, speaking for the first time.

"Why do you ask, Dear One?" Solaris asked. "We do not discuss his name in Lumania."

"Oh, why not? I've heard that he was very powerful."

"Powerful, yes, but evil none the less."

"*Evil*? Are you sure?" Zoya asked, surprised.

Solaris nodded; his face somber. "An ancient twisted soul that one. But he has left these parts. It is better that way."

"But I heard that he had saved many lives. People worship him for that," Zoya protested.

"Bringing people back from the dead, you think that is a healthy trick, Dear One? People are foolish. They worship what they shouldn't."

Zoya hung her head. "I suppose," she whispered. "You said that he left, does that mean he's dead?"

"Dead? No, I fear not. Such wizards do not leave quietly. But he has left the Baikal region, I can assure you of that."

"Is your kingdom mostly in the Baikal region?"

"Lumania is vast beyond your imagination. It stretches across continents," he said with slow deliberation. Gasps were heard all around the room. "But where you are right now, our capital city Zircon, is in the Baikal region."

"Imagine this, Wise One, the evil wizard of Baikal too could be out there as you have just pronounced. Seeking to destroy all that is good and beautiful. Given this, would you not at least re-consider your stance, weighing what is at stake? I pray to you on behalf of all of us to at least give it a thought, for the sake of humanity, if for nothing else," said Dr. Cobb, joining his hands together in supplication.

The Elders fell silent and exchanged some words in whispers. After a moment's silence, the lady among them spoke in the voice of a song-bird.

"We understand your reasoning, Dear Ones. But we are bound by our credo, I am afraid."

"What is a credo that cannot be modified, should the times demand it?" asked Dr. Cobb.

"It is not so simple. Our credo not only forbids us to participate. It restricts us, physically."

"I don't get your meaning, Wise One."

"Let me show you," she said while bending forward to touch the ground in front of her. A square slab of stone set into the floor in between the Elders and the Hekameses, lit up at her touch. It was an inscription, like the stone tablets of yore. "You see this," she said, pointing at the writings.

"This is our credo. It is a set of principles that we are required to follow. Each one of a different import."

"The Ten Commandments of Lumania," Dr. Cobb whispered.

"What is that?"

"I was just making a reference to Christianity. But tell me, Wise One, how do any of these physically restrict you?"

"Not all of them. But the first one."

Dr. Cobb leaned forward to inspect the writing. "What language is this? It's not known to me. What does it say?"

"This writing … I have seen it … but … where?" muttered Chris who was also straining his neck to view the inscription.

"It says, 'Those who can, may not'," Solaris explained in a deep monotone.

"Those who can may not … those who can may not … those who …" Dr. Cobb repeated to himself, his eyes closed. "Is it like the saying, 'fools rush in where angels fear to tread'?"

"I have not heard that one," Solaris confessed. "Our credo has deep meaning on many levels. In this case it means, those who have the power to effect change will not be allowed to do so. It applies to many things, like how the rich can change the world if they wish, but due to social conditioning they are often disinclined or altogether opposed to the notion. That is the figurative meaning. In a literal sense, we the Elders are not allowed to leave Lumania to participate in world-changing events."

"Not allowed? But who is to stop you?" asked Dr. Cobb in surprise.

"Our Mother."

"Where is she? Can we meet her?" asked Dr Cobb. A few chuckles were heard in the background.

"You have already met her. You were born to her. She is the earth."

"So Mother Earth doesn't let you leave Lumania? How?" asked Chris in awe.

"We cannot rise out of our caves. An energy prevents the doors from opening or the lifts from rising when we avail them. We do not know why or how that happens."

"Wait, that can't be right," said Chris. "Just the other day a bunch of Lumanians came to rescue us and the doors opened for them. The elevators worked fine. They were using their acoustic manipulation on everything the doors, the lifts, the lights, and it all worked!"

"You do not understand. This only applies to us, the Elders. Those who *can* may not. We *can*, so we may not. It's a curse of the Mother."

"Ohh … I see," said Dr. Cobb. "So, the belief is that if the Elders rise to the surface, they can turn this age, and that is why it is being prevented, you think?"

"Correct."

"But why would Mother Earth place such a curse?" asked Zoya.

"Do you not understand?"

"Not really …"

"Look at what the humans have done to this planet. They have sinned against the Mother and now they face the Mother's wrath."

"But you, of all people, shouldn't be punished for that. You are reversing much of that evil by living ... er ... so ecologically."

"We are not the ones being punished. All of mankind is."

"You see, my dear," said Dr. Cobb. "If the Elders rise up and intervene, the people above the surface may be saved, but the Earth will not allow this because man has exploited nature for so long."

"Precisely," said Solaris to Dr. Cobb.

"But what if we try to redeem ourselves by protecting nature? From this minute, if we can bring serious change, could we reverse the curse, maybe? I mean, you are already paving the way and that should count for something towards our redemption, no?"

The Elders shook their heads vehemently. "It's too late, I'm afraid," said Solaris. "The above-grounders should have started at least a hundred years ago."

"Oh, I remember!" exclaimed Chris suddenly, digging furiously inside his pockets. All eyes turned to him.

"What is it, Chris?" asked Zoya.

Chris produced a tiny object from his pocket and held it up in his palm. "This! This is where I saw your script," he said, excitedly.

Solaris stood up, abruptly. "Where did you find that, Dear One?" he asked.

Chris held the tiny hourglass between the thumb and index finger of his right hand and peered into it as he spoke. "I ... uh ... on Dr. Cobb's desk ... when I was cleaning his office."

Solaris glared at Dr. Cobb. "But when we summoned you before, you told me, you didn't have it!" he growled.

"I swear, Wise One, I swear … I have never seen this before," Dr. Cobb pleaded.

"You speak the truth," mumbled Solaris. "Unless …" He turned towards the Seer in the room and gestured with his hand.

"No, he is not a Thought Shielder, Wise One. He speaks truth," the Seer confirmed.

Solaris relaxed his expression and sat down on the cushion turning his attention to Chris, this time.

"Do you know what it is, Dear One?" he asked.

"I'm assuming … something that belongs to you?" he asked, tentatively.

"It is a Lumanian artefact, that I can confirm. The Timepiece. It was lost centuries ago. I would like to know how it was found."

"Like I said, found it on Dr. Cobb's desk after he went missing." Chris shrugged.

"Did someone break in to my office? And place it there?" Dr. Cobb thought out loud. "But who would do that and why …"

"Could it be your companion? The one you brought here with you?" asked Solaris, overhearing his mumbling.

All eyes turned to Dr. Cobb. "What companion?" asked Amon in alarm.

"I … well … um"

"Tell us!" Amon barked.

"Peter. My son," said Dr. Cobb in a small voice.

"What? You had found him? He is *here*? Why didn't you tell us? We trusted you!" It was Amon's turn to get agitated.

"He is not here. The companion. We expelled him. Our Seers did not approve of his person," Solaris clarified. "But could it be he, who had The Timepiece and sent it to you?" he asked, turning to Dr. Cobb.

"No, Wise One, it couldn't have been him. At least, I don't think so. He didn't have access to my office, as far as I am aware …"

"I still have many many questions," Amon grumbled. "Albert, we must meet at once in your quarters to get this sorted. You have hidden facts from us!"

"Trust me, Amon I—" Dr. Cobb began when Solaris cleared his throat loudly, and everyone turned to look at him.

"I sense a subtle anxiety in your tribe. May I recommend that you return to your quarters to resolve this dispute expeditiously? Such issues must not be left to fester within a tribe," he advised.

"I think that's a great idea," said Chris. "If you don't mind, then we'd like to take your leave now."

"We do not mind. Our meeting has come to its completion. We have nothing further to add at this time."

"Good," said Chris. "Before we leave, ah … um … you probably want this back," he added, extending the hourglass in Solaris's direction.

"You have found it, and you are one of us now. You can come and go as you like from Lumania, but we will still trust you, because the Seers have accepted you among us.

Hence, I permit you to keep the treasure that you found, but I have one request."

"Very kind of you. What's your request?"

"If ever we want to see it, then you will produce it forthwith."

"Not a problem at all," said Chris. "Oh, one question though, we wondered when we found it, why the sand isn't flowing … it seems to be suspended, the sand," he said, as he strained his eyes to study the stagnant sand inside the device.

"It will flow when the curse is reversed. *If* the curse is reversed."

"Ohhh! It's starting to make sense now," said Chris. He peered thoughtfully into the hourglass one more time before returning it to his pocket. "Thank you for letting me keep it." He bowed respectfully. "Also, thank you for your time today. We should probably get going." He turned to look at the others. Dr. Cobb and Amon were still locked in a staring match.

Zoya bowed to the Elders and stood up. "Let's go, Dr. Cobb," she said, tugging her professor gently by the arm.

# CHAPTER TWENTY-FIVE

When they arrived at their district after meeting the Elders, the Hekameses had to postpone their internal meeting so as not to miss the community meal that afternoon. They arrived together but sat separately at lunch. Chris found a spot next to Kazhar, and Zoya joined the two. Dr. Cobb was at the back of the hall somewhere, chatting merrily with his neighbour, while Amon ate quietly, deep in thought.

"How was your meeting with the Elders?" asked Kazhar, chewing on a puffy, hand-rolled bread.

"Good," said Chris, between mouthfuls of soup. "Could have been better, but still."

"I heard your wish for us to fight with you," Kazhar pressed on.

"We made a request. It was a long shot. But it didn't work. The Elders turned it down."

Kazhar inclined his head and seemed to process Chris's words like a parrot learning to speak. "They don't speak for everyone here," he then said with a smirk.

"Oh?" Chris was startled. "But don't they set the rules around here?"

"In Lumania, it is an open civilization. No one rules anyone. We are guided by our freewill."

Chris's eyes lit up. "So I've heard! It's true then? You really are free to do whatever you please, go anywhere you want?"

"Absolutely. Freewill is part of our credo. Without that there would be no Lumania!"

"Interesting structure. Quite commendable, actually. Aren't you scared that someone could betray you to the outside world?"

"Betray us, how?"

"You know, by giving away your location or your secrets. Facilitating an attack, a raid perhaps."

"That can't happen."

"How can you be so sure?"

"That's why we have Seers. They observe everyone. If they pick up any mischievous thoughts, they'll erase the relevant portion of that person's memory and cast him out. He will forget all about Lumania and never find a way back."

"I see. Are there some Lumanians interested in joining our fight, you think?"

"Maybe."

"What about you? Are *you* interested?"

Kazhar smiled. "Tell me what you need, and I will see if I can help."

"Ha! That was easy!" Chris started laughing. "For starters, I need to find a place to charge my phone."

"Just that? You don't ask for much!"

"That's why I said, 'for starters'." Chris winked.

"I see. We need to go to Irkutsk. I know a place there for you to charge the phones."

"Thanks, my friend. Maybe this afternoon?"

"Just let me know."

"Sure. But tell me, why do you want to help with our fight?"

"I have my reasons. Personal."

"But aren't you supposed to be pacifists or something?"

"We are, and I am. I will not use violence. There will be no need."

"Fair enough," said Chris. He was done eating, and it was almost time for their Hekameses' meeting, so he patted Kazhar on the shoulder and stood up. "Thanks again," he said. "How do I find you this afternoon?"

"We can meet here. In front of the dining hall. What about at two?"

"That works for me!"

\* \* \*

After lunch, Amon was the first to storm in to Dr. Cobb's room, where they had planned to meet. Chris and Zoya followed close behind, to find Dr. Cobb seated at his table drumming its surface with the knuckles of his right hand. Amon was pacing like a caged tiger, arms folded behind his back.

"Do you know how dangerous it is, what you've done?" Amon barked.

"Not as dangerous as you think, Amon," Dr. Cobb protested.

"But he is in the Aifra! Your son. And now he knows where we are! The Lumanians need to be warned, immediately."

"You underestimate the Lumanians, my dear," said Dr. Cobb calmly. "They already know who he is. That's why they expelled him right away."

"Which is even worse. Now he'll go straight to the Aifra with news about Lumania!"

"Highly unlikely," Dr. Cobb objected. "He wouldn't dare go back to the Aifra. He was supposed to bring me back a captive, and he failed. They will slaughter him. Remember what happened to Weilhammer? The Aifra aren't known to be forgiving."

"I would tend to agree," said Chris. "Also, there's something else …"

Everyone turned to look at Chris. "What is it, Chris?" Dr. Cobb asked.

"Well, I just found out from our friend Kazhar that the Lumanians take their own precautions with the people they expel. They probably wiped his memory. He would have no recollection of being here."

"I feared as much," Dr. Cobb mumbled. "He's probably dead, my boy!" His eyes moistened as he spoke.

Zoya reached out and placed her hand on the professor's arm. "I wouldn't jump to conclusions, Professor," she said comfortingly. "It's possible they need him alive. To locate you… and us. After all, he's their only link to the Hekameses."

"I agree," said Chris. "And … it's likely they don't know where he is …" He trailed off, becoming thoughtful.

"What makes you think that?" asked Dr. Cobb, straightening himself in his seat and looking expectantly in Chris's direction.

"Well, I just remembered something … when you were missing … I was in your office one day picking up equipment when a letter came in for you."

"Oh?"

"Yeah, no signature, no return address. Looked like it was dropped off by hand and all it said was 'Where is Peter?'"

Amon, who had stopped pacing and was leaning against a wall with his arms crossed over his chest, let out a loud gasp. "See! They're looking for him. The Aifra!" he said. "They want to interrogate him, for sure."

"Perhaps," said Chris. "But what's strange is that, the letter was on an US Government notepad!"

"Nothing is making sense," said Dr. Cobb with a sigh.

"But if there's an Aifra base nearby, wouldn't Peter have fled there when the Lumanians cast him out?" asked Zoya confused.

"We don't know if there's an Aifra base nearby," Amon said.

"What about all those snow leopards then?"

"I told Kazhar about them when I first arrived here," Amon explained. "I said that we thought it was very unusual for several of them to be hanging out together, and that's why we were here to investigate." Amon paused for breath. "So he told me the story. Apparently, these snow leopards were rescued by the Lumanians. They are aware of these animals and protect them. That's why they all crowd around here."

"Rescued? From whom?" asked Chris.

"Could be the Aifra, but we can't be sure." Amon shrugged. "Kazhar said that they had seen a truck carrying a pair of caged leopards through this area, several years ago, and decided to free them. They didn't know where the truck was headed. Could've been Moscow even. The pair was a couple. Later they had two cubs. Since the Lumanians freed the parents, the whole family has lived near this area. They must feel a sense of protection here."

Zoya sighed. "Great. We're back to square one. Not knowing where the Aifra are—"

"Or where Peter is." Dr. Cobb completed.

"But there is one thing we *do* know," said Chris in a cheerful tone.

"What is that?" asked Amon.

"We might yet be able to get some Lumanian help down the road!"

"Really? But the Elders—" Amon started.

"Yeah, the Elders don't speak for everyone, apparently. Kazhar told me this over lunch," Chris recounted.

"So? What now?" asked Amon.

"We have a call with Wolfgang this evening. Let's see what he has to say."

# CHAPTER TWENTY-SIX

Alejandro's cast came off exactly one month after his arrival at Marshal Pandey's residence, and at once he rushed out of his room, sprinting into the corridor in search of Nirmala. The palatial Pandey mansion was eerily deserted that evening with the entire family out of doors, attending a wedding. Alejandro's voice echoed from room to room as he went about looking for her.

"Sir, I believe Nirmala madam is in the library," said the servant, he almost knocked over in his mad rush down the central staircase.

"There's a library?" asked Alejandro, grabbing the servant by the shoulder to arrest his fall.

"Yes, Sir. In the annex basement, Sir. Over there." He pointed down the main hall towards the east.

"Thanks!" Alejandro exclaimed and hurried in that direction.

The library was in a beautifully wood-panelled little recess that occupied the entire basement of the annex building. It looked like a place that sealed away many secrets. Alejandro tiptoed through the aisles redolent of mildew-streaked teak and mahogany, hoping to catch Nirmala by surprise. He found her in the farthest corner of the room, seated in a cozy little armchair with her feet up on a low table and her nose buried in a moth-eaten old book.

"Found you!" said Alejandro, sneaking up from around a bookshelf.

"Oh my God!" she exclaimed, leaping from her seat. "Ah, it's just you. Hey, your leg …"

"Yep, it's all brand new again." Alejandro smiled. "What are you doing hiding over here by yourself?"

"Not hiding. Reading. I was going to come get you for dinner. I forgot your cast was going to be removed today."

"If they didn't take it off today, I would've killed someone! The clock is ticking, and here we are wasting away like a bunch of cripples," he huffed as he paced around in a circle next to Nirmala's chair.

Nirmala sat up and removed her reading glasses, setting them on the table in front, along with the book she was reading. "Sounds like your mind's been whirring out of control. What are you thinking? Tell me," she said.

Alejandro stopped pacing and sat down on the table in front of her, his face serious. "Just three days left." He sighed. "And we're doing nothing! Can you believe that?"

"You heard what Wolfgang said, the Lumanians aren't helping. Just a couple of them maybe, not more. You were stuck here with your leg broken. Wanda's too old, and all by herself in London. The Novo Hekameses don't have enough training. We have nothing to do but stay out of this and lie low. We are too few!"

Alejandro shook his head from side to side. "That didn't stop us the last time … at the Red Pyramid. And we succeeded, right?"

"But this is different. Armies are involved here. Missiles, fighter planes. It's open war. Just think about the scale. We can't fight this alone!"

"Open war? Hardly. How is it open war, when the Russians don't even know what's about to happen? A bunch of US fighter jets and missiles just going in there in the middle of the night, flattening a city. Just think about the casualties. *The civilians*! And the Russians didn't even *do* anything. It was the Aifra all along!"

Nirmala came over to sit next to Alejandro and leaned her head on his shoulder. "I know how you feel Alejandro. It could be that the Russians were in cahoots with the Aifra. We don't have enough information to judge. But still … civilian casualties … it's just … disgusting."

"The idea of modern war, total war is … so despicable," Alejandro spat. He wrapped his arm around Nirmala's shoulder and sighed deeply.

"Now that you can walk again, could we …" Nirmala sat up, and looked Alejandro directly in the eye. "still go, you think? You, me, Haresh, Mike? We are four, here. If Chris and the others could join, then four more. A couple of Lumanians might be swayed … and then we'll have Zoya too, she's the chosen one, that should count for something, no?" Her voice became more excited with every uttered syllable.

"I … don't think Zoya's the chosen one."

"But what about the Papyrus … her picture there? And … she did summon the Kalki that time!"

Alejandro nodded. "Still. It could've been a coincidence. Or something else. You know I don't believe in any kind of saviour theory."

"I'm not saying that she's like a messiah or something. But the prophecy … what does it mean then? The Faiyum scrolls have been pretty accurate about everything else …"

"Even if the prophecy was true, it probably still won't work."

"Why not?"

Alejandro stood up, his forehead creased and jaw muscles tightened, ideas churning in his brain like a whirlpool. "Nope. Nope. I don't see any route. It's too late."

"It's *not* too late! A direct flight could take us to Moscow in twenty-four hours," Nirmala explained.

"Yeah, but what about the visas? And we have to get there a day early to strategize. It's never going to work. And I can't ask Chris and the gang to risk it on their—"

"Wait!" Nirmala interrupted. "I have an idea. Where's my book?"

"Huh?"

"The one I was just reading."

"Oh, it's right here." Alejandro reached behind him on the library table and picked up the tattered book. "This one, right?"

"Yep. Do you know what it's about?"

Alejandro shrugged. "About the Kalki?" he asked.

"No. It's a research work about lost mythical civilizations and the lore surrounding them. You know, like Atlantis, Lemuria, Lumania?"

"*Lumania*? Someone actually researched about Lumania?"

"Absolutely. And look, let me show you," Nirmala flipped open the book and scanned through it rapidly. "Here, check this out," she said, pointing to a map sprawled across both the open pages. "It's a map of their kingdom. Or at least what the myth said about its boundaries."

Alejandro leaned over the book and examined the map closely, fingering the outline with his index finger as he studied it. "That was really vast. If the myth is true. But why are you showing me this?"

"Can't you tell? You see this shape here? You know what country that is, right?"

"Ummm … India?"

"Exactly!"

"So you think there might be a way to slip into the Lumanian tunnels from where we are?"

"Possibly." Nirmala smirked. "And we wouldn't need visas. Remember, what Chris said about their supersonic trains? They could take us where we need to go in no time."

"Brilliant," Alejandro whispered. "Can you get packed and meet me in the living room in … say half an hour?"

"Make it forty-five minutes. I need to get Haresh and Mike as well."

"Okay. That'll work. I'll call Chris. We have to leave before Pandey returns. I don't want him stopping us," said

Alejandro, before turning on his heel and hurrying out of the room.

* * *

Otto Schmidt was walking towards the bunker where he had planned to meet Alexander Kostas for his evening interview, when the Colonel intercepted him mid-way.

"Otto! Do you smoke?" he asked.

"No, Sir, I don't. Why do you ask?"

"Care to join me on a walk, this evening? We could chat in the fresh air instead of all cooped up in the bunker."

"I don't mind," said Otto. "As long as it doesn't snow."

"Should be alright. The forecast was clear," Alex said, while lighting a cigarette. "Sure you don't want one?" he asked, extending the pack.

"I'm okay, thanks," said Otto, smiling.

It was a beautiful starry night. The ground was covered with the fresh powder from the morning, and moonlight reflected from it with dazzling brilliance. There was a crisp wind blowing, and Otto pulled up the hood of his jacket to protect his face and ears from its biting impact.

"You see that forest over there?" Alex asked, pointing northwest.

Otto nodded. "That's along the border with Belarus, isn't it?"

"Correct. Let's head there. It's been my favourite place to clear my mind. Among the birch trees."

"Are you a nature lover?" Otto asked. They walked briskly to keep warm.

"I am. You?"

"Me too. It's a pity though, how little of it we get to see these days. Living in the cities."

"I agree." Alex sighed. "And we're only making it worse. Gaia will not be pleased."

"What's that?"

They were at the edge of the forest now. Alex dropped his cigarette butt on the ground, and crushed it with the heel of his boot. Then, he reached up to move a tree branch to the side, clearing a path for them to enter the wooded area. "Did I tell you that my family is Greek?" he asked.

"Yes, I believe you did mention that once. I have it in my notes somewhere."

"Then you may be aware that Gaia, the primordial Greek goddess, a personification of our planet earth, bears heavily on our culture …"

"Ah okay, so you mean *that* Gaia. Yes, we are not doing our planet any favour with our reckless industrialization."

"And Gaia will retaliate."

"You mean the goddess?" Otto gazed at Alex with a puzzled look in his eyes.

"I mean the earth—the animals, the plants, the insects, the mountains, the rivers, the rocks and stones." Alex touched a bare tree trunk, and petted it lovingly as if it were an animal. "Have you Sir, heard about something called the Gaia Hypothesis?" he asked absentmindedly, as his eyes roamed around, absorbing every inch of the forest.

"I don't think I have, no."

"It's a theory that suggests life on earth coevolves in harmony with its environment. Animate creatures affect the inanimate elements of nature and vice versa creating a sort of synergy."

"I can believe that. If one destroys that balance, life on earth will no longer be possible."

"Exactly. The entire earth is like a sentient being, an entire living organism on its own," Alex said excitedly, gesturing with his hands. "She's the goddess Gaia. You chop off her hands and her feet will retaliate."

Otto nodded in agreement. "Ancient Indian philosophers also believed that everything, even the rocks and stones and rivers and mountains were in some way sentient."

"Science may not support this theory but—"

"I'm not so sure science doesn't support it," Otto interrupted.

"Oh?"

"I mean, think about it, every quantum of material existence is in some way conscious, is it not?"

"How do you mean?"

"Hmm, how do I explain it …" Otto hesitated. "The way I see it is, matter is made up of molecules, molecules are made of atoms, atoms made of electrons, protons, et cetera, each of which have a primitive form of consciousness. They react on their own to the laws of physics and to chemical processes. They have a sort of memory. To me, that makes them alive."

"Huh! That's a very interesting way to put it, and I guess you understand my point that everything we do to hurt this living environment would bring us one step closer to our doom."

"Yes, I do indeed agree. But I'm curious why we're having this discussion mere hours away from an impending war. Isn't war precisely one of those things that would wreck our planet?"

"Precisely. Yes, precisely is the correct word," Alex muttered. "Would you like to sit down over there?" he asked, pointing to a large rock covered with light snow.

"Sure," said Otto, turning towards the rock.

Alex brushed the snow off the rock surface and cleared a seat for the two of them. "Speaking of war," he said, "I must admit, you are very brave!"

"*Me* Sir?" asked Otto, pointing to himself in surprise.

"Yes, of course!"

"What makes you say that?"

"Because you disregarded my warning to leave the base by today, and decided to stay behind."

"Ah, that! A journalist's job is never without its risks, Colonel. If we didn't shoulder this burden, then the world would never know its true heroes and villains."

"Well said. I applaud your bravery, none the less."

"But the true bravery is yours in this day of great crisis, Sir. I don't know how you do it, but because of it, your name will go down in history and be marked there forever."

"Rubbish!" Alex stood up, suddenly agitated. "This is no bravery! In fact, it's cowardice—a false idealism, do you see?"

"I … er …" Otto flinched, was at a loss for words.

Alex sat down, his head between his hands. "The life of money-making is one undertaken under compulsion, and wealth is evidently not the good we are seeking; for it is merely useful and for the sake of something else," he said. "Do you know that saying?"

"Aristotle, is it?"

"Yes. You are well read."

Otto bowed his head in a mock curtsy. "But you surely don't mean that you're here only to make a living? Army men are patriots. They do it for their country!"

"What if I say, the world is my country and the country not my world?"

"Sounds like a koan." Otto chuckled.

"A what?"

"A philosophical riddle of Zen Buddhism, also called a koan."

Alex dismissed the words with a wave of his hand. "Anyway, enough of philosophy. I need to get something out of the way, before I forget."

"What's that?"

"The reason I asked you out here tonight … here, wait … let me show you." Alex searched inside his pockets and recovering an object the size of a toffee, handed it to Otto.

Otto examined what he had just received. It was small, rectangular and smooth to the touch. "A pen drive?" he asked.

Alex nodded. "It's for you. Consider it your notes from our cancelled interview this evening."

"Can I include it in my book?"

"About that … I have a request. It's very confidential information. Encrypted of course, but still dangerous in the wrong hands."

"Then, why do you trust me with it?"

"It's password protected."

"Oh! And what's the password?"

"It's in my will."

"Your *will?*"

"Yes. So here's the request." Alex turned to face Otto. In the moonlit semi-darkness of this crisp winter evening, his war-hardened features appeared tempered with remorse. "If I die at the end of all this," he said, "I wish for you to hear the information that's on here, and make it public. Include it in your book. Release it to the papers. Do whatever you need to, but *get it out to the public,*" he said, emphasizing on the final phrase. "Do you understand?"

Otto nodded. "And you left the password in your will, is it?"

"I did. My estate trustee will contact you immediately upon my death to hand it over. So, do I have your word?"

"You have a gentleman's promise," said Otto, softly. "But might I ask why you can't release it while you're alive?"

"You can ask, but unfortunately I'm not in a position to respond. You're an intelligent man, Otto. I'm sure you can guess."

"The information is so explosive; it'd be tantamount to a death sentence for you."

Alex smiled a wry smile, but said nothing.

"What if I didn't make it out of this, either?" Otto asked after a moment's silence, while bouncing the memory stick lightly on his palm.

"I don't think that's likely. This base is fairly secure, and I've ordered emergency evacuation for non-essential personnel in the event of—"

Otto raised his hand to stop the Colonel. "I know. I don't doubt your precautions. But say, it were to happen. We can never know …"

"That's true. We can't. So tell me Otto, is there someone that you trust? A colleague? An editor? A deputy? Someone who could execute my last wish in the event of both our deaths?"

Otto became thoughtful. "Possibly, yes."

"Give me a name, and I will have him or her added to my will to act in your absence."

"I can do that," said Otto. "But first, I must send the pen drive out to this person in advance for safe keeping 'til I get back. If something happens to me here, the drive too will be lost."

"I agree. I have a courier going out tomorrow morning with last minute missives from the base. You can send it out with him."

A strong gust of wind found its way to them through the gaps between the trees, and Otto shivered inside his down jacket. "It's getting cold," he said in a small voice.

"Yeah. Let's head back," Alex said, rising from his seat.

# CHAPTER TWENTY-SEVEN

"Moscow," said Kazhar, as the Lumanian train pulled into a large underground station with walls of yellow topaz.

"Magnificent," whispered Dr. Cobb, his eyes wandering about in awe.

The Lumanian name of this city was Topaz as the Hekameses had learned. So the walls lined with this particular gemstone surprised no one. Nevertheless, the wonder was palpable across their faces as they descended from the train at Topaz, deep below the surface of Moscow.

"This way, hurry," Kazhar motioned with his hand, "I've prepared a room for us to strategize in, before we surface."

The Hekameses' team along with Mike and Haresh, followed Kazhar briskly down a winding passageway. The passage was narrow with the tunnel walls on either side hidden completely behind creepers, vines and lichen. It seemed to be a side trajectory leading away from the city's center and towards an enclave along its boundary.

Maybe because it was past midnight, there weren't any others travelling this way. Finding their path clear, Kazhar broke into a jog, and the remaining party picked up their pace behind him to catch up. It didn't take them long to arrive at their destination—a circular chamber surrounded by the cave wall on all sides. A dead end.

"Is this a trap?" Chris exclaimed, turning to Kazhar in surprise.

Kazhar stopped in his track, and frowned at him. "You distrust me?" he asked.

"Of course not, my friend," Chris apologized. "Having been tracked by Aifra all these years, I've trained myself to watch out for their antics and treachery at every turn."

"There's no Aifra here, I assure you. Now, follow me." He walked over to the cave wall on his right and raised his hands in front of his torso, scrunching his face in concentration. In this open circular area, the walls of the cave were bare, devoid of any plant cover. A flat slab of rock directly in front of Kazhar's outstretched arms reacted to his gesture and came apart from the wall. Kazhar pushed this slab to the side and laid it down against the surrounding rock, thus revealing the door to a hidden chamber.

They rushed into the newly revealed room, and the door closed behind them.

"Trapped again." Chris chuckled.

Kazhar simply smiled and said, "It's a conference room for top secret meetings."

Chris looked around. The room was a perfect hexagon with a similarly hexagonal rock slab at its center acting as a table. The perfect alignment between the edges and corners of the table and the walls surrounding it was mind-boggling.

"Impressive," Chris mumbled.

"Please, let's sit," said Kazhar.

As usual, there were colourful cushions on the floor surrounding the center-table and on these the Hekameses arranged themselves in a circle.

"Will there be others joining us?" Dr. Cobb asked Kazhar.

"Yes, two others," Kazhar responded.

"Only two? I thought there were more of you interested," said Chris without managing to keep the disappointment out of his voice.

"I'm sorry. I thought I could convince others. But—"

"Were they scared of the Elders?" Amon asked.

"No, not scared." Kazhar shook his head. "They have been indoctrinated since they were children, in the principles of pacifism and passivity. Those things are hard to get out of the system. The urge to do something is simply not there."

"Even in the face of Armageddon?" asked Dr. Cobb.

"Possibly." Kazhar hung his head.

"Don't worry, we won't tell the Elders that you're a renegade." Zoya chuckled.

"Huh! No need for that. I've already informed them and asked for their guidance."

"You have?"

Kazhar nodded in agreement. "In fact, they wished you good luck, and sent a message."

"A message, you say?" Dr. Cobb sat up. "Well, let's hear it, shall we?"

"Of course. I have it with me right here," said Kazhar, pulling out a fist-sized blue crystal from his cloak pocket and offering it to Dr. Cobb.

Dr. Cobb held the crystal up in front of his face and stared into it intently. "I can not read it. Chris, do you mind—"

"The message must be heard, not read," Kazhar quickly interrupted. "It's a telepathic message, recorded within the vibrations of its container. Please let me release it for you," he added, extending his hand to retrieve the crystal.

Accepting the crystal back from Dr. Cobb, Kazhar placed it at the center of the conference table and held his hands up in front of him, closing his eyes in concentration. The blue stone began to rise smoothly and levitated a few centimeters above the table surface. Then reacting to a slight flick of Kazhar's hands, the message-bearing crystal began to vibrate and the calm baritone of Solaris's voice emerged from it.

"Man is but a taker
Spoiling from his ilk
Hearts of blackened timber
In gossamer threads of silk
Fair weather friends, the sunny birds
Carrion eaters by the night
When bones lay tender stripped by death
The hawks will take their flight
By birth alone, by death alone

Every creature for itself

No struggle in the without

'Fore battles within the Self," he said.

There was a moment of silence with everyone in the room meditating on the words just uttered.

"It's a poem," said Chris finally, looking up at Kazhar. It wasn't a question, so Kazhar simply smiled in response.

"What does it mean?" Zoya asked.

Kazhar shrugged.

"Is he warning us of treachery? A traitor among us?" Amon asked, his eyes darting to Dr. Cobb.

"I don't think so," Kazhar quickly objected, sensing the tension in the room. "The Elders would never expose a traitor this way. They would take care to deliver the message privately. Arousing unnecessary suspicion between members of a tribe is unhealthy, and we in Lumania never operate that way."

"Against your credo, is it?" asked Dr. Cobb with a grin.

"Yes."

"Anyway, whatever the message means, we can't waste any more time dwelling on it, when we have more pressing issues on our hands," Alejandro said, getting impatient. He turned his battle-ready gaze on Chris and spoke with a great deal of urgency in his tone. "Chris, what's the plan? According to Wolfgang, the attack is planned for sometime before dawn, and it's nearly one o'clock. We need to hurry!"

"You're right. We have less than three hours left. I—" Chris was interrupted by a loud grumbling sound from beyond the wall. An opening emerged on one of the sides of the hexagonal room, but not the one from which they had originally entered. Two cloaked Lumanians rushed in and bowed politely.

"They are here, Ishin and Larvo, our two comrades," said Kazhar, greeting the newcomers with a bow. "They had gone to inspect the grounds in advance," he added.

"All clear, Kazhar. Campus is deserted, as expected," said Ishin.

"Good. Is there security?" Kazhar asked.

"Only at the main gates. But we're not going there. We should be okay."

"Perfect. Now, back to the plan. Chris, will you please brief everyone," Kazhar said, turning to Chris.

"Yep, let me get my map." Chris bent over his backpack and unzipped it.

"There's no need for that," Kazhar said. "I have a model. Everyone, please stand back."

A muted murmur emerged from the room, and the Hekameses exchanged bewildered glances. Kazhar stood up and held his arms aloft. The Hekameses too stood up and stepped back a couple of paces. The surface of the conference table started to pivot around its center—as if on a hinge—revealing its underside. What emerged was an intricate three-dimensional model of a tall baroque-style building and its surrounding campus containing gardens, lawns and water-bodies.

"Et voila! The Moscow State University," announced Chris.

"Okay, gather around please." Kazhar motioned with his hands to the standing crowd.

Everyone moved closer, peering over one another's shoulders to get a better look at the structure in front of them. It was made of stone, vividly painted and intricately carved to resolve even the tiniest of details, including the designs on the door panels and the metallic five-pointed star on the main building's fifty-seven-meter-tall spire.

"Alright, what you see in front of you here, is a model of the Moscow State University, located on Sparrow Hill in Moscow. It's the tallest educational institute in the world and used to be the tallest building in Europe up until 1990. From the roof, this structure offers a panoramic view of Moscow city and the Moskva river," said Chris, pointing at the miniature building in front of him.

"Or in other words, a perfect vantage point," Alejandro observed.

"Exactly," Chris agreed. "According to the intelligence Wolfgang received earlier this week, more than a dozen bombers are planning a night time raid over civilian targets at around four o'clock this morning. In all probability, they will have to fly within one-kilometer radius of the university, to reach their destinations. So, from the roof of the main building their flight paths should be well within our lines of sight."

"Wait, that doesn't make any sense," Zoya objected. "I thought you said there's a curfew in place and military patrols in the streets. How are they going to sneak their planes past that?"

"By using Russian bombers, apparently," Chris explained. "Wolfgang says they've planted operatives in the Russian air force to hijack these bombers right before the planned attack."

"Cunning," said Kazhar. "Your friend, this Wolfgang, how does he get this kind of top-secret information?"

"He has his methods, and he shares them with no one," Dr. Cobb responded.

"But it can be trusted?" Kazhar frowned.

"Absolutely. Wolfgang's never let us down before," said Chris. "Otherwise we wouldn't have dragged you into this."

"I believe you," said Kazhar, looking Chris directly in the eye. "Please go on. Explain your strategy."

"Okay, so here's the plan. As you can see, the main building is the tallest. It's thirty-six stories high and flanked by these wing-like, l-shaped structures on either side, which are the dormitory areas and student-housing. The dormitory buildings, all four of them, two on either side forming the arms of the 'l'," said Chris, indicating the buildings in question with both hands, "are only eighteen stories high. But it's clear that they'll provide observation points in all four directions, north, south, east and west."

"So, how do you think we should arrange ourselves?" Alejandro asked, getting straight to the point.

"Yeah, that's what I wanted to discuss. I have some ideas, but I need your inputs."

"Someone needs to get to the top of the main building. And I think it has to be me, since I'll be tripping the engines," said Alejandro.

"Tripping the engines? I don't understand," Kazhar asked, confused.

"Oh right, I forgot to explain that part," Chris admitted apologetically. "You see Kazhar, Alejandro here has the ability to telepathically interact with electronic devices. Or to put it plainly, he can mess up electronics with his mind.

So the idea is for him to use that ability on the planes. He'll shut down their engines remotely."

"But what about the range?" asked Nirmala. "These planes are going to be up in the sky and far. We don't even know how far. Several kilometers even. What if it doesn't work at those distances?"

"Great point, Nirmala," said Chris. "I've thought about that and worked with Albert and Wolfgang to find a solution. We think we might have something that'll help."

"Something? Like a device?" Zoya asked.

"Yep," said Chris, as he dug inside his backpack for the device. "Remember this?" he asked, removing a headset from his bag.

"The puma-hunting headsets?" asked Amon in surprise.

"Correct. We had two of these with us, so we tweaked them a bit."

Alejandro picked up the headset and studied it carefully. It was less like a headset and more like a metallic cage worn as a helmet. "And how does this thing work?" he asked.

"Basically, it will capture the signals you send with your brain, amplify them and transmit them out over these antennas over here," said Chris, touching the little antennas on its surface. "The amplification will significantly increase their range, we think."

"Neat," said Amon. "I'm no engineer, but how on earth did you manage to get from the puma-hunters to these in such a short time?"

"Ah! That wasn't too difficult at all," explained Dr. Cobb. "We already had the mesh of sensors to stimulate the brain of the wearer. Now they will be used instead to capture and filter selective brain signals. As for the antennas, a changeover from receiving to transmitting function did the trick. Add in some power and amplification. Remove the recordings of snow leopard brain patterns and there you have it. Simple enough, eh?"

"Umm … okay. Can we move on, please?" Nirmala asked, rubbing her chin. "We only have two. So who wears the second one? And what will the others do?"

"I have some ability to interact with sensors," said Zoya. "I think I should be the other one to go up on the spire with Alejandro."

"I don't think that'll work," Chris objected. "But don't worry, we'll still have use for your abilities."

"Why wouldn't it work?" asked Zoya.

"Well, we need our top guy for the job—"

"Alejandro," Zoya interrupted.

"Correct. We need him as high up on the building as possible. But the building is thirty-six stories tall, and the elevator only goes to the thirty-second floor where there's an observation deck. Beyond that, one of us will need to climb to the top, free solo, without any harnesses or protection and then secure a top rope to help Alejandro climb up safely. Are you sure you want to be the one to do that, Zoya?"

"I … ah … umm …" Zoya hesitated.

"I thought so." Chris chuckled.

"Only one among us is capable of such a feat, and that is you, my boy," said Dr. Cobb, patting Chris on his shoulder.

"So it looks like me and Chris at the top then, correct?" asked Alejandro.

"Yep," said Chris.

"What about the others?"

"Right. We are very few, so we need to use all our resources to the maximum. Naturally, to help us, we're going to use these." Chris bent over his backpack, and fished out a couple of bracelet-like contraptions.

"They look familiar. Where have I seen them before?" Alejandro wondered out loud.

"Probably on Mike's wrist when he rescued you in Badrinath," Nirmala chimed in. "We've been training the Novo Hekameses with these for a while."

"Ah! It's coming back to me now," said Alejandro as realization dawned.

"They're super-advanced jammers that we've been developing at the lab," Chris explained. "They can pretty much do what you do with your mind, Alejandro. But the range is a bit higher. The best part is that, they work for people without any special mental abilities, or for other Hekameses who can't normally tamper with electronics."

"I see. That's perfect. A multipurpose jammer! But how would the wearer select a function?" Alejandro asked, picking up a device and trying it on.

"I'm not sure I understand," said Chris.

"I mean, with my mind, I kind of select what I want to do by giving the sensor a command. Like if it's a remote, then: 'turn on the TV'. A key-fob, then: 'open the door' et cetera."

"Oh, I see. Well you can do the same here. See the wire dangling from the device? It has sensor tips that you need to attach to points on the wearer's skull and spinal cord. Then you can control the device's functions with the mind. Exactly like how you'd do it," Chris explained.

"That is how we will equip the others, even the Novo Hekameses, to bring down those planes," Dr. Cobb elaborated.

"In fact, both you and I are going to wear them too, for added range," Chris explained to Alejandro.

"The only ones we'll leave out are the Lumanians," said Dr. Cobb.

"And Nirmala," Chris chimed in.

"Why am *I* being left out again?" Nirmala fumed.

"Not left out," said Chris. "You will be in charge of the base station."

"Care to explain?" Nirmala asked.

"Yes, of course. See, we have to spread out. Each of us posted at different points. That way we'll have the widest possible view of the area. But we need someone at a central location, keeping a lookout for everyone and shouting out warnings. So, we're going to set up an amateur radio station at the observation deck on the thirty-second floor. The person stationed there will communicate warnings and sightings via two-way radio to the others. I'm hoping that you'll take on this role since you've been training the Novo Hekameses for some time now, and that makes you best qualified for a team-coordinator type role."

"Hmmm. Okay, makes sense," Nirmala agreed. "What about the Lumanians? Why are we leaving them out?"

"We have no use for such devices," Kazhar said. "We can displace and ground the planes with sound waves."

Chris nodded. "Exactly," he said. "They can move anything with sound. We have seen it with our own eyes. Should be a piece of cake for them to tumble a bomber or two."

"Cake? What is cake?" asked Ishin the Lumanian, who had been paying close attention the whole time.

"It's a type of … it's just a … figure of speech. A way of saying it will be easy for you to do this," said Chris, fumbling for words.

"Alright lads, as Wanda would have said, time is of the essence. Have you decided on all our positions, yet?" Dr. Cobb asked.

"Chris and I are climbing to the top floor of the main building. Nirmala sets up a base station on the thirty-second floor, slightly below us. That leaves eight more of us to deploy … how about two on each side-building … the …err … dormitory wings?" Alejandro asked.

"That's a great strategy. That way we'll have lookout posts for all four cardinal directions."

"So who goes where?" Zoya asked, leaning forward attentively.

"It doesn't really matter," said Chris. "As long as we form the right pairs. Each pair can take one of the four side wings."

"I think one person in the pair should be a lookout, scanning the area with binoculars while the other uses the wristband to trip engines," said Alejandro.

"That's a great idea," said Chris. "Zoya, who do you want as your lookout?"

"I recommend, Haresh," said Nirmala.

"Okay, Zoya and Haresh. How about Amon and Xianbin?" Chris asked. They both nodded.

"We need our maximum strength on the two wings that face the city. So the Lumanians need to be placed there," said Alejandro, rubbing his chin. "Dr. Cobb do you want to pair up with Ishin and take charge on one of them?"

"That'll do," said Dr. Cobb.

"Ishin?" asked Chris. Ishin nodded in agreement.

"That leaves me with Larvo on the last wing," said Kazhar. "I'm okay with that."

"Good," said Chris. "You guys will need to be in the most strategic location. I'm told, the bombers will arrive from over the Moskva river. So, this building over here, should have the best coverage of that area," Chris said, pointing to one of the dormitory buildings.

"This other building over here is second best, in my opinion. Dr. Cobb and Ishin could take that one," Alejandro chimed in.

"Does everyone agree?" Chris asked, looking around the room. Everyone seemed to be nodding. "Very well, then. Each pair will get one hand-held radio to receive cues and warnings from Nirmala. Any other questions?"

"Yeah, I mean … how do we even get inside the university with the curfew and patrols in place?" Zoya asked.

"Ah! Great point," said Chris. "Kazhar's going to address that. He's been taking care of those arrangements."

Everyone turned to look at Kazhar.

Kazhar cleared his throat. "Believe it or not, we are already there," he said, grinning. "This nexus we're in, it's under the university grounds. The six faces of the hexagon are connected to tunnels, each leading to a different point inside the campus, the garden, the lake, the main building. That one over there, leads to a location just outside the main campus gates," he added, pointing behind him. "The university was shut down last week amid tensions of war, and the dormitories have been evacuated. Ishin and Larvo were just up there, and they confirm the site is clear. Only one security guard outside the main gate. We are going nowhere near the main gate. Past that gate are the lawns as you can see in the model. At the center of the lawn is a decorative pool and our tunnel will take us under the pool and straight into the lobby of the main building. From there, we can access the dormitories using the connecting corridors."

"What about locks on the doors to the side wings and roof et cetera?" asked Alejandro. "Are they electronic? We could breach—"

"The building is very old-fashioned, unfortunately. The locks are all manual. But we have been entering this campus after dark, for years. We know how to get in," Kazhar said

"They remove the window panels and put them back in when they leave," Chris clarified.

"Looks like we have everything figured out then," said Zoya. "So, what are we waiting for? Let's go."

"Yes, we should get going," Chris agreed. "But first, let's get in gear. We want the operation to be as neat as possible. Get in and get out without getting caught. Makes sense?"

"Yep," said Zoya.

"Perfect. Alejandro, come with me. I'll show you how to fasten the headset. Albert, could you please hand out the bracelets? They're in my backpack. Everyone, start getting into pairs. Binoculars and walkie-talkies are with Amon. I'll carry the base-station equipment." Chris rushed to his backpack, as he shouted out instructions.

# CHAPTER TWENTY-EIGHT

"C'mon buddy, you can do it! One last ledge," shouted Chris as Alejandro clambered up the spire of the Moscow State University, while attached to a top rope and harness. "I gotchya. You're not gonna fall. Just one more step."

"My left leg." Groaned Alejandro as he lifted his right foot onto a window sill and tried to haul himself up. "Can't … put … pressure …"

"It's probably still weak from the fracture," said Chris. "Try leaning on your right, and grab on to the climbing rope. Yeah … that's it."

Nirmala was on the lower deck looking up anxiously. "You can do it, Alejandro! You're almost there," she shouted.

There was a tumbling sound. The climbing rope stiffened, tensing inside Chris's grip, as Alejandro skid off the ledge and caught the window sill just in time to prevent a fall down four stories. He was now dangling by his right arm and the climbing rope. Chris's memory harked back to the incident with Amon in the Sayan mountains.

*No, not this time!* he told himself.

"Hold on!" he screamed, as he lunged forward on the roof, and extended his arm down to Alejandro. "C'mon, grab it!" he commanded.

"I ... can't," Alejandro said, as he struggled to reach out with his left hand.

"Yes, you can. Just a little further." Chris leaned half his body over the ledge and stretched his arm as much as he could. A chilly gust of wind swept over them sending a shiver down Chris's spine. He braced himself against the wind and threw his right leg over the low roof wall, straddling it as he doubled over and reached for Alejandro. Alejandro hoisted himself up with ferocious determination and grabbed his extended hand. Chris pulled back with all his body weight and landed with a thud on the roof, with Alejandro crashing over him.

Hmph ... we made it." Chris panted.

Alejandro got up quickly and grabbed his radio. "This is Alejandro. We're at the top. What do you see? Over," he broadcasted.

"Amon here. Nothing yet. Over."

"Haresh and Zoya. Only patrol vehicles in this direction. Over."

"Albert speaking. All clear for now," said Dr. Cobb. "You have to say, 'over'," came Ishin's muffled voice.

"Uhh ... over," huffed Albert.

"Nirmala at base station. Nothing in any direction. But hold your positions. Over and out."

\* \* \*

The hours trudged on in deathly torpor. Every minute felt like an hour and every hour an eternity. The wait, the constant vigilance, the fluttering of anxiety, was starting to bear heavily on everyone. A birdsong here, a dog bark there and all heads turned at once, binoculars trained. But no sign of an attack. No bomber crafts, helicopters or boats. It was already half past four. Thirty minutes past the expected hour of assault. Unspoken questions about the sanity of Wolfgang's judgement, were taking shape in all their minds.

Alejandro checked the time and turned to Chris. "Do you think it was a false tip?" he asked.

"Could be," said Chris glumly. "The Lumanians may never trust us again."

"Hey, look at the bright side," said Alejandro. "It's better this way. If we failed today, many lives would have been lost."

"True. But I don't think we've seen the end of this. Maybe someone deliberately planted a false tip with the wrong date and—" Chris was interrupted mid-sentence as their portable radios buzzed to life after a long silence.

"Amon here. Attention all. I see something. Northwestern sky. About ten kilometers out. Over."

"Haresh here. We see it too. Looks like drones. Shit! Explosion! They're carrying missiles!" He panicked.

Chris immediately grabbed their binoculars and trained them in the indicated direction. "I can see them, look over there," he said to Alejandro, pointing towards the horizon. "Can you get them?"

"They're too far. I'm trying," said Alejandro. "Nah. Too far."

"Chris here. They're out of our range. Over," Chris screamed over his radio.

The radio buzzed again. "Albert here. Ishin is trying. But they are too far out. Kazhar, please report. Over."

"Kazhar here. We can't see them. Blocked by buildings. Over."

"Where do you think they're headed? The city's in the opposite direction?" Chris asked Alejandro.

"I don't know. Is there a waterbody that way?"

"The river's right here—"

"No. Larger?"

"I … umm … the Baltic Sea?"

"Bingo! Oil tankers. They're after an economic target."

"Could be," said Chris. "Wait, what's happening?"

"What?" asked Alejandro.

"They're turning around. Towards the ice … the river I mean … river ice!"

The radio crackled. "Nirmala here. Something strange is happening. The drones have turned and are crash landing into the ice. Over."

"Amon here. Yes, we see it too. Why would they do that? Over."

"Haresh here. Maybe the Russian patrol has downed them. Over."

"Amon here. Nope. Nothing's being fired. We don't see or hear firing."

"Technical failure?" Alejandro asked Chris, flashing him a quizzical look.

THE CURSE OF GAIA

"Can't be. They're all going down at once. Just crashing on ice."

"Strange! Why do you think one of them fired missiles in the beginning? If they're going to the Baltic—"

"*That* could've been a technical issue."

Muffled sounds emerged from the radio. "Nirmala here. Looks like it's over. All drones down."

A siren went off.

"Amon here. Finally, the Russians are in the game. They've sounded the alarms. Let's get out of … WATCH OUT! Yak-130 jets, due north. Over."

Alejandro looked up in horror. A fleet of about twenty Russian Mitten bombers was swerving like a convocation of eagles in the northern sky, heading straight towards the city as predicted.

"Could the drones have been—" Alejandro started.

"A distraction. Possibly. Quick! Get in position," said Chris.

The radio buzzed. "Nirmala here. All teams assume position. Fleet heading right in our direction. Estimated time, two minutes. Over."

"Okay, I have the range," Alejandro screamed, as he aimed his wrist at the first jet in the formation. "Engaging engines." The plane did an abrupt dive and a peculiar angular manoeuvre.

"It's working," Chris yelled over the din of battle. "He's trying to get back his balance. Probably lost an engine."

To his right Alejandro noticed Kazhar with his arms raised above his head. The second jet started spinning in the sky and took a tumble towards its left. Zoya was aiming for the same jet and going after its engines. Ishin and Larvo were picking up jets and throwing them out of the sky. Xianbin was performing all kinds of acrobatics to aim for the engines of the jets being bombarded by the Lumanian sound waves. Nirmala was furiously shouting commands over the radio.

"Amon, nine o'clock."

"Zoya, Haresh watch out!"

"Alejandro, behind you!"

"Dr. Cobb, Ishin, duck!"

"Kazhar downed the second bomber. Two more to go."

In about fifteen minutes, ten of their crafts were affected and the others were already turning on their tails.

"Russian patrol cars on the scene. Over," Nirmala shouted.

"I think we have victory. Over."

"Patrol cars heading to downed planes. Wait, no! Some of them are enemy vehicles. Fire is being exchanged," Nirmala updated.

Chris peered through his binoculars in the direction of the ground forces. "Strange," he said.

"How's that?" asked Alejandro.

"Some of the American attack vehicles on the ground are sputtering to a stop."

"Hit by Russian patrols, you think?"

"No, look." He handed the binoculars to Alejandro.

"You're right. That does look suspicious. No patrol cars near that one," said Alejandro, pointing to the east, "but it's stalling. Curious."

"Nirmala here. Patrol car coming towards us. Everyone, hide! I repeat, patrol car on its way. Please, duck. I'll keep watch from inside the observation deck. Over."

A couple of minutes of silence. Then the radio buzzed again.

"Nirmala here. Someone from the patrol car is waving a white flag at us. I'll check it out. Over," she said softly.

Another minute passed.

"Nirmala here. It's Wanda! Wanda Faraday! How exciting! She's with the Novo Hekameses. She's waving at us. Someone, please fetch them. Over."

"Kazhar here. I'm on my way. Over."

Alejandro and Chris, who were crouching behind the roof wall, stood up straight and exchanged a startled look. "What the hell is happening?" Alejandro asked.

Chris, who was staring through his binoculars, chuckled in response. "It's Wanda alright," he said.

"We should probably start climbing back down. We have to clear out of here before the patrols turn this way," said Alejandro.

"Yep, good point," said Chris. "Chris here. We're coming down to the thirty-second floor. Getting ready to evacuate. Over," he shouted over the radio, wiping beads of perspiration from his brow.

"I go first, right?" asked Alejandro.

"Yeah, this is just a rappel down. Should be no big deal. Just hang on to the rope and balance with your feet against the wall."

In about five minutes, Chris and Alejandro were back down on Nirmala's level. "Kazhar's already back in the tunnel with Wanda and company," Nirmala announced, once they had landed. "They should be with us any minute now. We should start packing."

"Good idea," said Alejandro, as he crouched over to pack the equipment.

An electronic buzz startled him. Someone was speaking on the radio again.

"Holy shit! Ballistic missiles! Ten … no … fifteen of them. Straight south. God help us!" Amon's voice boomed through the speaker.

Alejandro looked at the others, horror etched over their faces. Then he focused on the southern sky. There they were. More than a dozen ballistic missiles capable of flattening a city—maybe even two—zooming over the horizon at terrible speed. Straight towards Moscow city.

"CAN YOU GET THEM, ALEJANDRO?" Zoya screamed over her speaker.

"I … ahhh … too far," Alejandro got into position, his face as white as death. He raised his wrists at the monsters. Chris was right beside him copying his moves. Nothing budged.

"Nirmala here. Ishin and Larvo, please do something! This is beyond our scope. Ishin and Larvo, do you copy? Over."

"Ishin here. We're trying. They're several tonnes. And we are only two. Kazhar isn't back! Over."

The missiles raged through the sky streaking it with their comet tails of destruction, brilliant to the eye, fierce to the ear. But not one of them, neither Hekameses, nor Lumanians could alter their course."

Alejandro could feel the warm wet drops of sorrow gushing down his cheeks now, burning where they touched. His heart racing, cheeks throbbing with blood. And then he heard something strange. A song. A chant. A choir. *What is it? Is this heaven? Are we dead?*

"Look," said Nirmala grabbing his upper-arm. She was pointing to the dormitory building on which Zoya was positioned. She was singing. Softly at first, but now with growing cadence. Like the music of heaven or was it a lark, a nightingale perhaps?

"Songs of Meera," Nirmala said softly. Alejandro noticed that she too was crying. "It's exactly like the last time. She goes into a trance. Probably can't help herself."

Haresh had joined her in song. He was singing with abandon. His voice resonating in the darkness.

"He probably recognizes the words," Nirmala whispered. "He used to visit the temple of Meerabai with me sometimes."

Suddenly Alejandro was jolted back into reality by a solid smack on his shoulder. It was Chris. There was awe in his eyes. "The southern sky! I can't believe it!" He gasped.

All eyes turned towards the south. A twister was rising there, a whirlpool of white smoke. It was swallowing the missiles and tossing them high into the atmosphere, probably into outer-space, and beyond that, into oblivion. For a second, Alejandro thought he saw a white light emerge from the twister's belly, shaped like a horse—a horse and its rider galloping away into the farthest reaches of the universe. Below was the street, empty except for the reflected light from the aerial warfare and street lights fading slowly with the approaching dawn. The missiles were cast up into deep space, like a geyser spouting pressurized steam. At that very instant, a lone figure galloped down the empty street below the sky, silver hair billowing in the wind, saffron robes flying about her.

"The Kalki!" exclaimed Chris. Zoya's chanting had stopped, and an eerie silence fell over them.

\* \* \*

Otto rushed into the Colonel's office in panic.

*Why the urgent summons?* he wondered, his heart racing.

"Alex, you called?" he asked.

Alex was standing with his back to the door, arms crossed behind his back. An unnatural pose for a military man, diligently trained to expect a Trojan Horse.

"Yes, please close the door," said Alex, pivoting on his heels.

Otto did as he was told and walked over to the Colonel's desk to stand awkwardly next to a chair. Alex placed his arms firmly on his desk and leaned forward, still standing. The action drew attention to his firm biceps and Otto flinched slightly.

"I know who you are," said the Colonel in a flat voice.

"Sir, I—" Otto began.

Alex raised his palm to interrupt him. "Wolfgang Müller, is it?"

Wolfgang cleared his throat. "Yes, I am," he said, realizing there was no longer any point hiding his identity from this man who had grown to become a friend.

"Engineer, scientist, ex-diplomat, leader of a covert army of mutants. A man of many, talents, aren't you?"

"All true. It seems that you have my background nailed."

"I'm not surprised," said Alex with a twisted smile. "Thank you," he then said, softly.

"I'm sorry?"

"No, *I* am sorry. For having been so dense for so long. So self-centred. I'm a changed man now. I did the right thing. So thank—"

There was a loud bang and the door flew open. Three burly military men with assault rifles emerged through them.

"Put your hands on your heads and don't move!" said the tallest of them, as he signalled to his companions through the corner of his eyes.

The other two soldiers hurried up to Wolfgang and Alex and twisted their arms behind them before locking them with handcuffs.

"Move, let's go," said the man behind Wolfgang with a kick to the small of his back.

Within a minute the soldiers had left with their captives and Colonel Alex's office stood abandoned, its silence howling into the night.

\* \* \*

Zoya and Haresh were received at the observation deck to roaring applause from the rest. Amid the laughs and cheers, a voice of reason sounded, Alejandro's.

"Guys, we have to get out of here," he said. "Before the Russian patrols get here. We can celebrate once we get to Lumania."

The cheering stopped. "You're right. Let's pack," said Chris as he started shoving equipment into his backpack. Amon came over to help.

"What a night, my God!" he exclaimed.

"I know I almost—"

There was a loud shriek. "Military helicopter, duck!" said Zoya.

"It's probably just a Russian patrol," Chris said, looking up.

"It's FIRING! It's seen us! Everyone inside!" Alejandro roared.

"Friendly fire, shit," said Chris, as he and Amon dived for cover inside the thirty-second floor.

"Ahhhhh!" A scream rented the predawn sky.

"Noooo! Nirmala! She took a hit," Alejandro wailed. "Quick, someone help me carry her inside."

Chris hurried over to the observation deck. Nirmala and Alejandro were the only two outside. Together he and Alejandro lifted Nirmala's prone form and carried her into the room. Her head was lolling to the side but her eyes were still half-open. They laid her on the floor. Blood was gushing onto her t-shirt front from a bullet shaped hole right under her collar bone. Alejandro cradled her head on his lap and rocked back and forth, his chest undulating with spasmodic sobs.

Chris observed the scene play out as if through a haze. Like he was hungover or drug-addled or walking through a dream. His immediate reaction was to think of something practical. A way to arrest the blood loss. He unbuttoned his shirt and ripped off a large section from the bottom. Then he rushed to Nirmala's side.

310

"Hang on. I'm going to stop the bleeding," he said, lifting her gently off Alejandro's lap. His hand brushed against a tiny piece of metal dangling over Nirmala's collar, a locket. He extended his hand to move it aside, when he noticed something unusual. The object was glowing with a strange pale light. Chris stared at it, transfixed. Involuntarily, his hand was pressing the locket into Nirmala's collar, right over the wound, as if trying to cork the bottle that was spouting her blood.

"What are you doing? Are you crazy?" he heard Alejandro say. But the words came, as if from a very great distance. A faint whisper from beyond the ether.

And then, the bleeding stopped. Just like that. Chris lifted the locket slightly, carefully, so as not to hurt it. Nirmala's wound had healed. She was stirring slowly and looking up, a flicker of a smile across her lips.

"It's the locket of Heka," someone said to Chris. Chris looked up at the speaker. It was Wanda Faraday. She had arrived.

"What?" Chris asked, incredulous.

"Nirmala was wearing the locket of Heka. It has healed her wound," she said, wiping the tears from her eyes with the back of her hand. "It's very ancient magic," she added. "We are truly blessed today. But now, we must leave before we get caught."

Alejandro helped Nirmala to her feet and she threw her arm around his shoulder, smiling.

"It truly was a blessed day," said Alejandro, as they walked towards the elevator to make their way back to the Lumanian tunnels.

# MESSAGE FROM THE AUTHOR

Thank you for taking the time to read this book. I hope you enjoyed it as much I enjoyed writing it. If you liked it then please take a moment to leave a review for the book on Amazon (www.amazon.com) and/or Goodreads (www.goodreads.com). Your valuable opinion can make all the difference.

# OTHER BOOKS BY THE AUTHOR

Colour Me Confounded
Thought Warriors: The Coming of Kalki

# PRAISE FOR COLOUR ME CONFOUNDED

"Written in simple and lucid language with economic use of words, she puts forward the life of modern women as it is, minus the embellishments or the jargons of feminism and alternative living."—*The Statesman (Kolkata, December 9, 2018)*

"I applaud Poulomi Sanyal for crafting a work that captures the subtle complexities of women's lives. I look forward to reading more of this author's future works." —*J.G. MacLeod (Author)*

"Excellent work and incredible writing by Poulomi Sanyal!" — *Steven Nedeau (Author)*

# ABOUT THE AUTHOR

 Poulomi Sanyal has been writing poetry since she was ten years old, and she even created her own literary magazine when she was twelve. Sanyal was born in India but has lived all over the world, including Hong Kong and, more recently, Canada. She is fluent in English, Bengali, and Hindi, and she also speaks conversational French.

Sanyal received her master's degree from McGill University in Montreal and has spent the past ten years working in engineering in Toronto. In her free time, she enjoys writing, painting, acting, and traveling.